T0279382

Praise for *An Improbable Season*

"I adored every page. It was a *Little Women* meets *Pride and Prejudice* romance that charmed and entertained me thoroughly."

—Kasie West, author of *Sunkissed*

"If you're looking for your next *Bridgerton*-esque fix, it's all too probable you'll find *An Improbable Season* as utterly charming as I did."

—Jennieke Cohen, author of *My Fine Fellow*
and *Dangerous Alliance*

"The trio's friendships with one another shine throughout the story; their fights and loving interactions are true highlights. The heroes, for their parts, are kind and thoughtful, making them matches worthy of cheering on. Outings to Regency hot spots and balls are entertaining and include historical details for readers to enjoy. Regency fans will enjoy this comfortingly familiar feeling story of endearing young women chasing happy endings through a maze of societal rules."

—*Kirkus Reviews*

"*An Improbable Season*, which contains just enough twists and turns to keep the familiar beats and tropes exciting, will delight fans of Regency novels. Eves pens compelling romantic moments, but the real strength of this novel is the depiction of the strong love the young women have for each other." —*Booklist*

AN UNLIKELY PROPOSITION

ROSALYN EVES

FARRAR STRAUS GIROUX
NEW YORK

Content warning: This story contains one incident of attempted sexual assault.

Farrar Straus Giroux Books for Young Readers
An imprint of Macmillan Publishing Group, LLC
120 Broadway, New York, NY 10271 • fiercereads.com

Our books may be purchased in bulk for promotional, educational, or business use.
Please contact your local bookseller or the Macmillan Corporate and Premium Sales
Department at (800) 221-7945 ext. 5442 or by email at
MacmillanSpecialMarkets@macmillan.com.

Library of Congress Cataloging-in-Publication Data
Names: Eves, Rosalyn, author. | Eves, Rosalyn. Improbable season.
Title: An unlikely proposition / Rosalyn Eves.
Description: First edition. | New York : Farrar Straus Giroux, 2024. | Series: Unexpected
seasons ; 2 | Audience: Ages 12–18. | Audience: Grades 10–12. | Summary: As another
Season begins in 1818 London, recently widowed seventeen-year-old Eleanor and her
hired companion Thalia navigate both new and old relationships.
Identifiers: LCCN 2023024544 | ISBN 9780374390273 (hardcover)
Subjects: CYAC: Interpersonal relations—Fiction. | Friendship—Fiction. | London
(England)—History—19th century—Fiction. | Great Britain—History—1789–1820—
Fiction. | LCGFT: Novels of manners. | Romance fiction. | Novels.
Classification: LCC PZ7.1.E963 Un 2024 | DDC [Fic]—dc23
LC record available at https://lccn.loc.gov/2023024544

First edition, 2024
Book design by Meg Sayre
Printed in the United States of America

ISBN 978-0-374-39027-3

1   3   5   7   9   10   8   6   4   2

To Trisha and Nellie,
who love a good romance

AN
UNLIKELY
PROPOSITION

CHAPTER ONE

Eleanor

Fortune is like a widow won,
and truckles to the bold alone.

—William Somerville

London, April 1818

"What is the point of having money and independence," Eleanor Lockhart asked, "if one must still be proper? I did *not* come to London to be staid and boring. One might do as much at home in Wiltshire." Eleanor tugged the green ribbons of her new bonnet into a bow beneath her chin.

Miss Fanny Blakesley dithered before the front door to the fine town house Eleanor had rented for the Season, as though she might physically prevent the younger woman from leaving the building. "To go walking by yourself, and you so young? You'll appear a sad romp."

Eleanor picked up a pair of gloves from the table beside the door and slid them on. "I am seventeen and a half," Eleanor said with dignity. "I may be young, but I have been married *and* widowed, so by anyone's reckoning I am not a child, nor should I be treated as one. And I shan't appear a sad romp at all, Miss Blakesley, because

I feel quite elated. I shall smile at everyone I meet." As if to prove her point, she smiled at her companion.

"Oh, Eleanor!" Miss Blakesley backed herself against the door, shaking her head so iron-gray ringlets trembled about her cheeks.

Eleanor's merry expression faded. She had hoped that hiring an older woman as her companion would give her countenance to do as she pleased. Perhaps she should have sought a younger companion after all. "If you please, Miss Blakesley, I mean to go out alone. I shall be quite safe and keep to public thoroughfares. I do not pay you a handsome salary to thwart me, and if you persist in resisting me, I shall call the butler to remove you."

Miss Blakesley moved hastily away from the door. "Only, do but tell me where you mean to go. Else I shall be so worried."

Eleanor sighed. "I mean to walk to Green Park, perhaps as far as St. James's Park. I have a hankering for fresh milk."

"Isn't that rather far?" Miss Blakesley asked. "Pray, do not exhaust yourself. And consider how it must look, to drink your milk in the open air like any commoner. Oh, and do stay away from St. James's Street. No lady should venture there without a gentleman to accompany her."

"I shall not exhaust myself, and I rather think people have better things to do than observe me drinking milk, should I get so far. Do not fret yourself so—I shall be back in an hour, perhaps two, and then you may accompany me. I must get the clasp on Mama's necklace fixed."

Miss Blakesley brightened a trifle. "Of course. Your dear mama!" She grasped her hands at her bosom, conveniently forgetting that she had no real knowledge of Eleanor's mama. Nor, indeed, had Eleanor herself. "Might I suggest a fine jeweler I know of on Poland Street?"

"You may suggest whomever you like—after I return."

Eleanor pulled her shawl more tightly about her shoulders, opened the front door, and stepped firmly down the stairs into a blustery April day. Not until the door shut behind her did Eleanor's stiff shoulders ease.

Miss Blakesley was a decent woman, and the impoverished cousin of Eleanor's deceased husband, Albert, besides. It was not her fault that she was a bore—at least, not entirely her fault. Surely she could temper what nature had given her with just a bit of exertion. But Eleanor knew what it was like to be poor and desperate, and she could not find it in her to turn the woman away.

A brisk wind chased down Curzon Street, blowing Eleanor's brown curls into her eyes. She tucked the hair back beneath her bonnet and strode on. The chill wind might have daunted a soul made of less stern stuff, but not Eleanor. It felt good to be out of doors, alive, and in London.

She admired the tulips bobbing along her route and nodded to a gentleman and a lady who looked vaguely familiar. While the gentleman returned her nod rather stiffly, the lady pretended not to see her. Perhaps they had not yet met, after all.

Or perhaps Miss Blakesley was right, and it was truly not done for a woman—even a widow—to walk alone.

Well, Eleanor did not care. She was finally in London, free of the stifling walls of Lockhart Hall, free of the small town where people were kind enough, but where she would always be known as the little nobody who had snagged the rich Mr. Albert Lockhart. She knew people had looked askance at her when she married a man old enough to be her father (whoever *that* had been), but Albert had wanted a wife and heir, and she had needed a home, rather desperately. At least Albert had been kind.

She sighed. Albert had always meant to bring her to London, to show her the museums and the gardens and the society parties. But then he had contracted putrid throat less than a month after their marriage and died shortly after. She had mourned a full year for a marriage that had not lasted nearly so long. Poor Albert.

She shook herself. She would not be maudlin, not now, not ever.

Eleanor passed by a small church. Miss Blakesley had pointed it out on their arrival as the site of many clandestine marriages in the eighteenth century, including that of one of the famous Gunning sisters. Eleanor had some fellow feeling for Miss Gunning, as an impoverished young woman catapulted beyond her station by her marriage to a duke, though once widowed, Miss Gunning had rapidly married another duke, and Eleanor did not mean to marry again.

She understood how fortunate she was to have her own money and her independence—she would not jeopardize that.

Making her way down Half Moon Street and alongside the railings lining Piccadilly, Eleanor at last reached the gate into Green Park and slipped in. It was blessedly quiet beneath the canopy of trees fringing the meadows—too early still for the fashionable crowds who gathered of an evening. Eleanor followed a narrow pathway, spying a late daffodil waving like a yellow flag at the world.

She intended to trace the path south and east until she reached

St. James's Park, but she had not gone far before she found herself accosted by a tall, well-dressed gentleman.

"Eleanor," the man said, and everything inside her seemed to curdle.

"Mr. Lockhart," she said, refusing the familiarity her husband's nephew seemed determined to force upon her.

He frowned down on her. "What are you doing abroad, alone?"

Eleanor didn't dignify his question with an answer. "How did you find me?"

"I called upon you at home," he said. "I have procured vouchers to Almack's for you and Miss Blakesley."

"To the marriage mart? How . . . kind." But was it kind? George Lockhart had considerable motivation to see her married again, given the conditions of her husband's will. Eleanor did not know what to make of her husband's nephew, who had been polite to her the few times they had visited, even if he was a rather indolent man, and disinclined to bestir himself for others. He was handsome, if one liked men with tallow-colored hair and long noses, but she suspected he disliked her, though she had no reason for her belief other than the flat look she sometimes caught in his eyes when he was watching her.

"As you are new to town and have no one to advise you how to get on, I took it upon myself to call on Countess Lieven. I am sure you will wish to be comfortably established in society sooner rather than later, and I can escort you myself Wednesday next."

"Thank you," Eleanor said, "but I do not believe Miss Blakesley or I need you as an escort."

Was it only her imagination, or did his brows twitch at that?

7

"As you wish, though I think you may soon discover that it is more comfortable to have a male companion at such events."

Eleanor began walking again, hoping that Mr. Lockhart, having accomplished his errand, would leave her in peace. He made her feel like a child, though he was not more than half a dozen years older than she.

Instead, he fell in step beside her. "May I accompany you?"

No, you may not, she thought crossly. But she didn't say that. She might not like Mr. Lockhart, but he was the closest thing she had to family, and she could not bring herself to burn *all* her bridges. That did not mean she had to entertain him, however.

They walked in silence toward St. James's Park. As they crossed into the park, Mr. Lockhart said, "Your country upbringing is showing. No London-bred lady would indulge in so hearty a walk. Shall I escort you home? My carriage is just outside Green Park."

Eleanor stiffened her back and her resolve. "If the walk is too much for you, by all means, return to your carriage. I shall go on."

"I assure you, my advice is kindly meant. You have not been much in society, having married my uncle direct from school. I would not see you barred from society before you have begun your conquest." His blue eyes glinted at her, his thin lips pressed together. Was that a warning?

Eleanor tamped down a flare of anger at his presumption. She would not give Mr. Lockhart the satisfaction of seeing her react.

They walked on, coming eventually to a round, rosy woman with several cows clustered around her.

Mr. Lockhart sighed. "What are you up to now, Eleanor?"

Eleanor looked at him innocently. "Did not Miss Blakesley tell you? I mean to try the milk in the park. You must try it too—please, it shall be my treat." Eleanor had had the foresight to bring a small pewter cup with her from the kitchens. Fetching it from her reticule, along with a coin for the milkmaid, Eleanor approached the woman.

Mr. Lockhart's lips tightened in irritation. For a moment, she thought he would refuse her, but then his eyes went to the woman watching them and he forced a smile.

The milk was warm and frothy and considerably better than that which was delivered to the house, which Eleanor suspected was watered down.

In any case, it was worth all the displeasure of Mr. Lockhart's company to see him choke down the liquid in a cup the milkmaid offered—a drink, he would tell her in an undertone on the way back to his carriage, that only children and fragile young maidens partook of.

Eleanor ignored the jab at her spurious fragility, and reassured Mr. Lockhart that no one seeing him drinking the milk would assume he was either a child or a maid.

"Of course not," he said. "But they might think us both witless."

"Surely not," Eleanor said, smiling sweetly at Mr. Lockhart as he helped her into the carriage. "That would require them to suppose you had wit to begin with."

Mr. Lockhart's hand tightened around hers, and the strength in his fingers sent a sudden chill shooting through Eleanor. Had she said too much? For a moment, he looked as though he would like to strangle her. But he only released her hand and leaped lightly into the carriage, picking up his whip before remarking, "*She hath more hair than wit, and more faults than hairs.*"

Eleanor recognized the line from Shakespeare's *Two Gentlemen of Verona*. She had been taught something at school, after all, before the sudden cessation of funds from her unknown father had forced her out. Was Mr. Lockhart trying to return her insult?

She folded her hands in her lap as the carriage jolted forward. *Do not engage*, she told herself. But Eleanor had always favored valor more than discretion, and she could not pass up a good sally. "You forgot the last part."

Mr. Lockhart gritted his teeth. "And what is that?"

"*She hath more hair than wit, and more faults than hair, and more wealth than faults*," Eleanor said. "I should rather be accounted witless than penniless, wouldn't you?"

Whereupon Mr. Lockhart, whose expected fortune had gone to Eleanor on his uncle's marriage, growled something unintelligible and did not speak to Eleanor again until depositing her on her doorstep—and then, it was only to wish her a rather curt "Good day."

The jeweler's shop Miss Blakesley directed their coachman to that afternoon was a neat little building tucked between two teahouses. The mullioned windows let in abundant light that gleamed off clean counters and sparkled off jewelry nestled on black velvet displays. Eleanor, rather to her own surprise, approved.

The middle-aged proprietor, Mr. Jones, looked up from a conversation with a customer as they entered. Smiling widely at them, he said, "Good afternoon. We're a bit shorthanded today: our regular shopgirl is out sick. But I'll have my son show you anything you want." He turned and shouted behind him, "Owen!"

A young man with the same heavy eyebrows as his father emerged from a door down a narrow hallway tucked to one side of the room. He was tall and thickly built, and he looked rather harassed, frowning at the company until a significant look from his father made him blink and clear his expression. He made his way toward Eleanor and Miss Blakesley.

"Oh, Eleanor, do but look at this cunning brooch!" Miss Blakesley said, inspecting a miniature silver peacock with a tail of sapphires and emeralds. It was quite lovely, though a bit florid for Eleanor's tastes.

The young Mr. Jones studied Eleanor. His eyes were dark and warm, and when they met hers, something inside her pinged, as though with recognition, though she was sure she had never met the man before. "Are you in the market for such a brooch? Gold would suit your coloring better, I think."

"And your account books too, I imagine," Eleanor said, more tartly than she intended, discomposed by her own reaction to this stranger. She did not, as a rule, find most men particularly attractive (not Albert, goodness knows, though she had liked him well enough). But there was something about the strong planes of this young man's face that she found appealing.

Mr. Jones tipped his head to one side. "True enough. But those jewels add considerable value. A more humble gemstone in a simpler design would offset the cost." He turned to another display and plucked up a pair of earrings—small spikes of golden-brown topazes set like a sunburst. "These, for instance."

"Oh—" Eleanor found she could not speak, her throat clogged with sudden emotion.

Miss Blakesley peered at the earrings. "Those are quite pretty, though I prefer a good ruby myself."

Mr. Jones bent nearer to Eleanor in some concern. "I beg your pardon. Have I said something to upset you? I am not normally allowed near the front: My father says I frighten the customers."

"No." Eleanor forced herself to smile. "Are you the craftsman?"

His eyes widened in alarm. "Lord, no. My father makes some, and some he purchases. I prefer working with accounts. Numbers, you see, don't require any particular artistry."

"Well, the earrings are lovely," Eleanor said, taking herself firmly in hand. "I am afraid I am not shopping for something new today." She opened her reticule and carefully removed the scrap of silk she had wrapped her mother's pendant in. She unfolded the silk, laying bare the delicate filigree cross set with topaz stones.

The exact golden brown of the earrings the young man had shown her.

Mr. Jones's gaze flicked from the necklace in her hand to the earrings in his own, then looked a question at her. To her annoyance, Eleanor found herself flushing. "It is my mother's. The clasp has broken, you see." She pressed her lips together before she could tell this frank stranger that the necklace was all she had of her mother, aside from a hazy memory of a halo of gold hair and a pretty smile, though she sometimes wondered if she only imagined she remembered.

"It *was* her mother's," Miss Blakesley corrected, and Eleanor wanted to kick her.

"Was?" Owen asked.

"She passed away when I was small," Eleanor said, trying to keep her voice light.

"I am very sorry to hear that," Owen said. "I lost my own mother some ten years ago and still miss her. We shall take the best of care of her necklace, I promise you." He set the earrings back on their velvet display. "Let me take down your information. We shall notify you when the clasp is finished."

In a matter of minutes, this business was completed, and Eleanor was heading toward the exit when the door opened, and a familiar gentleman stepped in. The young man, his brown hair groomed and pomaded within an inch of its life, was dazzling. He wore a delicate peach-and-silver waistcoat and a perfectly fitted blue superfine coat; the gloss on his white-topped boots rivaled even the shining counter-tops.

Eleanor stopped in dismay.

"Mrs. Lockhart—Eleanor," the young man said, bowing deeply. "What a pleasant surprise."

Miss Blakesley tittered. When Eleanor glanced at her, she saw that her companion's cheeks were flushed, but the woman did not seem entirely surprised. Eleanor's eyes narrowed.

"Please do not call me Eleanor, Mr. Smythe-Hampton," Eleanor said. "I have not given you leave to use my Christian name."

"My deepest apologies, Mrs. Lockhart," Mr. Smythe-Hampton said. "Please take my negligence as a compliment. Only one so charming could make me forget myself."

"Well then, good day to you, sir," Eleanor said, edging around him. Miss Blakesley clamped on to her arm, and Eleanor found she could not move unless she dragged the older woman from the shop.

13

"This is such a delightful coincidence," Mr. Smythe-Hampton continued, as though he had not heard her. "I had just come in search of some pretty trifle for a lady of my acquaintance, who is growing rather dear to me."

Good heavens, had the man just winked at her?

"I was hoping that you might be persuaded to help me select the perfect item."

"Really, sir, I am not sure it's my judgment you need," Eleanor said, trying to move again. She suspected she might have bruises from Miss Blakesley's grip. "And I truly should be going."

"No one better suited than yourself," he said.

As they had only had three conversations, all centered on Mr. Smythe-Hampton's own travails with his wardrobe, Eleanor was not certain how he could gauge this. Then the full import of his words sank in. Eleanor stopped trying to pull Miss Blakesley along and looked Mr. Smythe-Hampton directly in the eye.

"Let us understand one another. Are you suggesting that this trinket you mean to purchase is for me?"

He smirked at her.

"You can have no reason to purchase such gifts for me. I beg you will not do so."

He raised an eyebrow at her. "Ah, your modest protestations reflect well on your character, but I assure you, it is quite the mode for a gentleman to bestow such a gift on a lady whose good impression he seeks."

"Indeed," said Mr. Jones, coming to join them. "Any number of gentlemen buy them for their mistresses."

Eleanor looked at the younger Mr. Jones in shock, while

Mr. Smythe-Hampton garbled something incoherent. She caught a smile, quickly suppressed, on Mr. Jones's face, and realized he was baiting Mr. Smythe-Hampton. He might lose his father a customer that way, but Eleanor would not regret it if only the man would go away.

Mr. Smythe-Hampton turned to Eleanor. "I have no such improper intentions, I swear to you. Only the most honorable." He reached out as though to take her hand, and Eleanor, who had no desire to be proposed to in a jewelry store (or anywhere, really), put both hands behind her back.

Clearly, nothing but plain speaking would serve here. Or perhaps . . . Smiling shyly up at Mr. Smythe-Hampton, Eleanor said, "Oh, do you mean to propose to me? Well, I own it would be *such* a relief to have my future settled. I suppose you are very rich?"

Beside her, Mr. Jones abruptly became very occupied in adjusting the contents of a display.

Eyes bugging slightly, Mr. Smythe-Hampton said, "I—but you are so wealthy, surely it doesn't signify whether I am or not?"

A fortune hunter then. Had Mr. Lockhart set him on her? It would be just like him.

"Oh, but don't you know? My late husband set a rather unfortunate condition to his will: I am to have the majority of his estate, but only until I marry, at which point the estate reverts to his nephew, and I am to have a small jointure, enough to cover pin money. Dear Albert did not want me to marry someone who only wanted my money. But you must love me, to wish to marry me despite all?"

Mr. Smythe-Hampton's face was white beneath the brim of his

hat. "I said nothing about marriage. I am afraid you must have misunderstood me. Good day, Mrs. Lockhart." He wheeled about and exited the store so swiftly, he tripped over the threshold.

As the door swung shut behind him, a small bell rang in the store. The laugh Eleanor had been holding in finally escaped.

"Neatly routed," Mr. Jones murmured, and pleasure washed through Eleanor.

"That was not very kind of you," Miss Blakesley said.

"Oh, perhaps not, but no more than he deserved," Eleanor said. "Come, we've taken up enough of Mr. Jones's time." She turned to the young clerk. "I do appreciate your help, but we must be going."

She tucked her arm through Miss Blakesley's and tugged her, finally, into the street where their carriage waited. A handful of raindrops plopped onto their heads, and Miss Blakesley shrieked.

Eleanor allowed her companion to precede her into the carriage—from her cries, one might assume she was afraid of melting—and then settled herself beside Miss Blakesley. When they were moving, Eleanor spoke again.

"You did not seem surprised to see Mr. Smythe-Hampton."

Miss Blakesley said, "Such a nice boy. I am sorry you did not like him."

"How did he know where to find us?"

Miss Blakesley looked out the carriage window and fiddled with a handkerchief. "Whatever could you mean?"

"You told him where I meant to be, did you not?"

Miss Blakesley was silent for a long moment, her only movement the handkerchief twisting between her fingers. "Do not be angry, dear Eleanor. I always had a weakness for romance."

"If I marry," Eleanor said, "I would no longer have need of a companion. Do you care so little for your position?"

"Oh, but surely your husband would—"

"I have no idea what my hypothetical husband would do," Eleanor said. "I will have no control of my finances or my staff, once I marry."

"Oh, but Mr. Lockhart promised—" Miss Blakesley fell silent, one gloved hand going to her mouth as though she'd said more than she meant.

"Mr. Lockhart promised to secure your position if you helped him?" Eleanor hazarded.

Miss Blakesley did not respond, which Eleanor took as confirmation. She steeled herself. "You have reported on my movements to him for some time, have you not? And I think this is not the first suitor you have tipped off."

"Slang, Eleanor!" How Miss Blakesley could contrive to look offended when it was she who had misbehaved, Eleanor could not fathom. "The *ton* will think you belong to a lower class if you speak so."

"Then perhaps it is good I am not a true lady, so we may speak frankly. Miss Blakesley, I told you this morning that I would not brook interference from my companion, and so I shan't."

"Oh, but you cannot dismiss me! Please, Eleanor, where would I go?"

To Mr. Lockhart, Eleanor wanted to say, but she knew too well the terrifying feeling of an uncertain financial future to wish that on Miss Blakesley, no matter how irritating the woman was. She took a slow breath. "For the love Albert bore you, I will continue to pay you a stipend, but you cannot stay with me. I will write to hire a new companion at once, and when she arrives, you may go wherever you like so long as it is not here."

"Oh, but Eleanor—"

Eleanor turned to look out the window as Miss Blakesley poured out a litany of grievances mingled with tears. Really, perhaps this was for the best. Eleanor meant to enjoy herself in London, and it was rather hard to do so when her every move was criticized or strategized against. A young companion, that's what she needed. Enough to satisfy the gossips but not enough to hobble her.

And she really ought to do something to put off all the suitors who saw her only as a naive, rich young widow, ripe for the taking.

CHAPTER TWO

Thalia

The window opens on the moor,
Where April's sweetness rides the breeze.
The flowered hedges all adore
Lamentably do make me sneeze.
I must confess: It's quite a bore.

—Thalia Aubrey

Oxfordshire, April 1818

Thalia Aubrey dug through the papers on her small desk in her father's study with increasing desperation. Her newest poetry manuscript had been just *here* earlier that morning. She was certain of it. When her search turned up nothing, she abandoned it with an oath her mother would not approve of and left the study.

She followed the hallway down to the room shared by her two youngest siblings, Urania and Edward. There was no sign of either child, but there was a stray quill and an overturned inkpot, its contents slowly seeping into a haphazard pile of pages. With increasing dread, Thalia picked her way through the mess to rescue the first of the papers. It was, indeed, her manuscript: some fifty poems that she had copied out in her fairest hand to send to a London publisher.

Now those same poems bore everywhere the mark of a seven-year-old boy: a thumbprint here, a spatter of ink there, and across her favorite poem, the skull of some frightful monster—it looked rather like a long bird's beak, with teeth.

Gritting her own teeth, Thalia gathered up all the abused sheets, returned them to her desk, and then fetched a rag and some water from the kitchen to clean up the ink.

Had Shakespeare ever been subject to the indignity of cleaning a child's mess? She rather suspected not: His wife would have cared for such things. Or his sister. Or his mother.

As she carried the ink-stained rags back to the kitchen, Edward came barreling down the hall, nearly bowling her down in his rush. He popped into his room, and then popped back out almost immediately. "Thalia! What have you done with my drawings?"

"Your drawings?" she echoed. "Those were *my* poems."

He shrugged. "Papa won't let me disturb his papers and I needed something to draw on." He brightened. "Did you see my monster?"

"Yes. Whatever was that?"

"A giant fish monster. Charis told me about it. They found it near Lyme Regis. Imagine going fishing and catching something like that!"

Thalia shuddered. "I'd rather not."

"It's a pretty good drawing, right?"

"Yes, very clever, but you really should not deface my work."

He wrinkled his nose. "They're only poems." Then, apparently bored by the conversation, he ran back down the hall and disappeared in the direction of the kitchen.

Thalia sighed. What she needed was a room of her own with

a lock on the door. Better yet, a room in London where she could mingle with other poets and aspiring writers, where she could seek out publishers in person. Almost a year after her disastrous London Season, she was beginning to feel a returning interest in the intellectual world her former suitor, James Darby, had so nearly ruined for her. He had seduced her with poetry and sparkling salon debates, convinced her to run away with him, and only at the last moment revealed that he had no real love for her. Thalia had no wish to return to London for the marriage mart, but she longed for the society of congenial minds.

But Aunt Harmonia had no interest in opening their London house while Charis was abroad in India with her husband. Thalia's own mama could neither afford to rent a house nor spare the time to escort Thalia, and both she and Aunt Harmonia had decided it was not worth the expense of a Season if Thalia did not mean to seriously seek a husband—and perhaps it was best to let some of last year's whispered gossip about Thalia and Mr. Darby die down. Next year, Aunt Harmonia promised.

Thalia did not want to wait until next year.

She drifted back into her father's office and plucked up a newspaper from his desk. Perhaps there would be an advertisement that would suit her (though the past three weeks of searching had so far turned up nothing).

But luck—perhaps as recompense for abandoning her poems to Edward—was with her.

Tucked away in a small corner, Thalia read: *A widowed lady, recently emerged from mourning, seeks as a companion an honest, intelligent, biddable young lady to accompany her on errands and to select social gatherings. Interested parties may apply to no. 10 Curzon St., London.*

Thalia read it again. She was certainly honest, intelligent, and young, and she could be biddable if it meant a chance to return to London. Accompanying an older woman about town sounded rather soothing, in contrast to the chaos of looking after her younger siblings at home. And surely she would have days or half days off, when she might pursue errands or attend the occasional intellectual salon. It would, of course, depend on the temperament of her employer, but Thalia was willing to risk it.

She settled down at her desk, pushed aside the spoiled papers, and began to write.

Thalia was hovering on the front lawn three days later, waiting for her father to return from town with the post, when a rider cantered up to the house.

"Adam!" Thalia said, throwing her arms around the lanky young man after he dismounted. Growing up, Adam had been her particular friend, but their London Season had changed all that. Adam was now engaged to marry Thalia's sister Kalli, though as a clergyman it might be some years yet before he could support a wife. By law, he could not be ordained and given a living until he was twenty-four, some three years away. In the meantime, he studied with Thalia's father and wrote the occasional sermon for him.

"How fares your work?" Thalia asked.

"The research goes on apace—if you are asking about my sermon,

I think it did not put so many people to sleep this week, so we are making progress." Adam smiled a bit ruefully, tipping his head so that sunlight flashed against his spectacles.

Kalli emerged from the house in time to hear this last and shook her head at him. "Adam is being modest. You heard Papa read his sermon, about our duty to all our brothers and sisters, not just the ones we happen to like." She stood on tiptoes and gave Adam a kiss.

"Ah," Thalia said. "Well, you may have Edward with my blessing."

Kalli laughed, having already heard about Edward's drawing.

Thalia caught sight of her father, returning on foot to the house. She abandoned Kalli and Adam and raced toward him.

His eyes crinkled as he smiled at her. "I've been gone but two hours, Thalia, though I'm flattered you missed me so."

Thalia halted and bit her lip, trying to restrain her eagerness. "I am expecting a letter."

Appearing more amused than anything, Mr. Aubrey retrieved a pair of letters from his coat pocket. "Well, let's see. There is one here from Charis—prepaid, luckily, as we'd never afford the cost from India."

Kalli, coming up beside Thalia, snatched the letter from Charis. Thalia did not fight her for it. The arrival of a fat new letter from their cousin had never been disappointing before, but Thalia was hoping for something else. Kalli broke the seal on Charis's letter. "Oh, for goodness' sake. She's crossed her lines again. One almost needs a private course of study to make out what she's saying. Here, I think there's something about a caste—or perhaps a castle?—on the Tapti River. No, I'm quite sure it must be a castle, as she says something about ramparts. And insects. A full half page devoted to some sort of beetle." She looked up, grinning. "It's reassuring to know some things about Charis will never change, no matter how widely traveled she is."

Thalia watched her father. Perhaps that second letter had nothing to do with her.

Her father relented, holding out the other letter, where Thalia's name was written in an unfamiliar script. "Was this, perhaps, why you rushed me so anxiously?"

Thalia took the envelope, studying the return address. Curzon Street. Her hand tightened on the letter.

"Are you all right, Thalia?" Adam asked, studying her over Kalli's head. "Not bad news from London, I hope."

"Oh, is it another rejection?" Kalli asked, clearly trying to be sympathetic. But the truth was, these days Thalia received more rejections than not. It was becoming tediously commonplace.

Indeed, it might be a rejection, though not of Thalia's poetry.

Mrs. Aubrey came out then to urge them all inside out of the sun, fussing over Adam, who pretended to brush it away but wouldn't stop smiling. As soon as they were indoors, Thalia excused herself to the room she shared with Kalli.

Fingers trembling a little, Thalia broke the seal and scanned the letter. It was blessedly short, in a schoolgirl's careful, neat hand.

My dear Miss Aubrey,
I have read through your letter and your impressive
credentials and found everything to be most satisfactory.

If you are amenable to this salary——, please reply with
your acceptance. I look forward to your (hopeful)
arrival in London at your earliest convenience.

Sincerely,

Mrs. Lockhart

Thalia read the letter through a second time. She'd done it. She'd secured a position in London—in the heart of Mayfair, no less. She was going back.

Her family's reaction, however, when Thalia carried the letter back to the sitting room, was not quite what she'd anticipated.

"To London?" her mama echoed. "But we know nothing of this woman. And cannot you write as well at home as in a stranger's house?"

"It's not just the writing, Mama, it's the inspiration," Thalia said. "So many clever people are in London, talking about the newest ideas in poetry. I miss all that here."

"But a companion, Thalia?" her father asked. "I do not think you will have the time to write that you think you will. Or the freedom to engage in society."

"I do not engage in society here," Thalia pointed out. "Whatever scraps of freedom I have in London will afford more engagement than I have buried in the country."

"How long have you felt like this?" Kalli asked.

"Some months now—I have been actively searching for a position for several weeks."

"I didn't know," Kalli said, a flicker of hurt on her face.

"Because I didn't tell you. You have been consumed with your own affairs." Thalia glanced from Kalli to Adam, and both blushed.

Adam curled his arm around Kalli and said, "I think you should follow your heart, Thalia."

Thalia's mama sighed. "I've never been good at denying you children something you wanted, and you're hardly of an age where I can demand you stay home. But, Thalia—are you sure?" Her mama set her hand upon her stomach, a protective gesture that Thalia recognized, but had not seen for several years. Not since—

"Mama?" Thalia asked. "Are you—is there a reason you want me to stay?"

Mrs. Aubrey exchanged a look with her husband. "We didn't want to say until we were sure. I thought I was well past such things, but it seems there will be another Aubrey come midsummer."

"A baby?" Kalli asked in surprise.

Edward and Urania came barreling through the room in time to hear this last.

"Whose baby?" Urania asked suspiciously, coming to a halt in front of Kalli.

"Not mine," Kalli said, blushing again. "Mama's."

"Hooray!" Edward said. "Another brother!"

"No," Urania said. "It might be a girl."

"Maybe it will be *two* babies," Edward said.

"Let us pray not," his mama said, shooing her two youngest children away. They tromped out of the room, still arguing about the possibilities of their future sibling. Mrs. Aubrey turned back to Thalia. "I don't want to influence your decision, but you ought to know."

"If you want me to stay, I will," Thalia said, feeling rather noble and selfless as she made the offer.

But her mama only laughed. "As though I haven't given birth to six children without your aid! Though I admit you were a help when Edward and Urania were small. You are always welcome here, of course, and I shall be sad to see you go, but you must make this decision for yourself."

Her mother, father, Kalli, and Adam looked at Thalia expectantly. Thalia hated it when her mother was reasonable like this. Outright opposition, she could face with a clear conscience. This kind concern, on the other hand, made her feel rather beastly, especially leaving her mama when she was expecting. But—

"I want to go," Thalia said. "Surely I can come home to see the baby when he—or she—is born."

"Paid companions do not always have such freedom," Mr. Aubrey said.

"If Mrs. Lockhart is such a gorgon as to refuse to let me visit my mother and new sibling," Thalia said, "I shall resign on the spot and come home anyway."

"I'll miss you," Kalli said, and Thalia felt her eyes prickle.

"I'll miss you too—" Thalia began.

"Only please do not fall in love with another scoundrel and attempt to run away," Kalli said, her lips curling up into a grin.

Thalia's tender feeling vanished. Drawing on all the dignity she could muster, she said, "I am going to London to find a publisher, not a lover."

"Methinks the lady doth protest too much," her father said.

"You might do both," Kalli said. "I am sure there must be eligible young publishers."

"Or not so young," Adam added.

Thalia grumbled as she stood and walked from the room, the gentle laughter of her family following her out.

Riding into London on the public stagecoach four days later, Thalia found the city both louder and smellier than she remembered. But her relief softened both sensations: Until she reached the city, she had been half afraid that something would happen to call her home. Having arrived without incident, she felt as though her life was beginning afresh. This time would be different. *She* would be different: braver, bolder, and more rational. No romantic diversions, no distractions. Just her work, as a companion and as a writer.

A footman and driver were waiting for her with a hand-printed sign at the London hotel where the stagecoach stopped. It took only a few moments to direct the transfer of her trunk from one coach to another, and then the footman handed her up into the open carriage and climbed up beside the driver.

"What is Mrs. Lockhart like?" Thalia asked. "Is she a good employer?"

The footman glanced over his shoulder. "Not my place to say, Miss Aubrey. Any case, you'll find out soon enough."

Thalia fell silent, watching the streets of London pass alongside the carriage. They reached the wealthy neighborhoods of Mayfair, and the carriage pulled up behind number 10, Curzon Street, just as dusk was settling. The windows gleamed with light. Thalia exhaled. She was here. She had made it. Now to meet her new mistress and then—hopefully—retire early.

The footman led Eleanor through the tradesmen's entrance and to a drawing room on the second floor, where a young brunette sat on a rather ornate green-and-yellow chaise longue, flicking through the pages of a book. She was pretty, with a faint dusting of freckles, but her mouth was turned down in a sulky expression.

"Miss Aubrey," the footman said, bowing Thalia into the room.

At once, the sulky expression lifted, and the young woman tossed her book to the side and sprang to her feet. "Miss Aubrey! I'm so glad you've come. I'm Mrs. Lockhart, but you may call me Eleanor."

Thalia, a trifle dazed, took the hands Mrs. Lockhart—Eleanor—extended to her. The young woman was half a head shorter, but her gaze was bright and direct. This was no aging female in need of assistance.

Eleanor's lips turned up in amusement. "I fancy I am not quite what you expected."

"Your advertisement said you were a widow—" Thalia said.

"And so I am, of more than a year's standing."

"I am sorry for your loss," Thalia said. She wanted to ask Eleanor her age, but did not think Mama would approve, and managed to keep her mouth shut.

"Thank you." Eleanor sighed. "Poor Albert's sickness came on him rather suddenly, not long after we were married."

"Oh." Thalia was not certain how she ought to respond. "Was he very young?"

Eleanor shook her head. "Nearly fifty—not young, but not old either." She caught Thalia's eye. "I know what you're thinking—that I must be some kind of horrid fortune hunter, to have married a man so much older than I am. It was not like that, I assure you."

Thalia could imagine several other scenarios to account for the marriage of a very young woman to a much older man, most of them unpleasant. But whatever motives had driven Eleanor's choices, they were none of Thalia's business. "I am sure you must have had good reasons for your choice." Thalia ventured a small smile. "Only consider your good taste in hiring me."

To Thalia's relief, the tension between them dissolved, and Eleanor laughed. "Yes, I have exquisite taste! Now tell me, are you very tired? I had hoped to go to a play tonight and would like you to join me, but if you are too fatigued, I shall ask my tiresome nephew to accompany me."

"Your . . . nephew?" Thalia asked. Surely any nephew to this young woman was likely to be a child himself.

"My husband's nephew, George Lockhart. You shall meet him soon enough."

"I shall look forward to it," Thalia said.

"I suggest you don't. He's rather an ass." Eleanor whipped her hands across her lips. "I do beg your pardon. Not that it isn't true, but I shouldn't subject you to such language."

"So long as you pay my wages, you may say whatever you like," Thalia said.

Eleanor tucked her hand into Thalia's arm. "Oh, I knew I was right to hire you! We shall be merry as grigs. So you will come tonight?"

Thalia did not remember saying anything of the sort, but she found herself being whisked away to a bedroom on the same floor as Eleanor's, with Eleanor directing the maid to see that Thalia was well turned out.

So much for a quiet night at home.

In just under an hour, Eleanor and Thalia were stepping into the box Eleanor had rented for the season at the Theatre Royal at Drury Lane. The whole of the lavish, gold-accented theater interior was lit by gas lamps, a novelty Thalia had never seen before, as the lamps had been adopted after her brief Season the year prior. From Eleanor's wide-eyed expression, she had not seen such a thing before either.

They had scarcely settled in their seats when a pair entered the box, and Eleanor sprang up again with a joyful exclamation. "Anne!" She embraced a young woman with red-gold curls.

Thalia recognized the lady, whom she had met a handful of times during her Season, as Miss Salisbury. But it was the young man standing behind her, a dimpled smile on his face, that made Thalia's insides squeeze with a curious mix of embarrassment and pleasure. She stood.

"Mr. Salisbury!" The last time she had seen Mr. Salisbury had been just after Charis's wedding. The time before that, he had rescued Thalia from her disastrous elopement with James. He had done her a great favor, but Thalia still squirmed thinking of that day, of her heartbreak and humiliation.

Did he think of that as he looked at her?

Eleanor ignored Mr. Salisbury and tugged Miss Salisbury into an open seat beside her, animatedly discussing something.

Henry Salisbury came to stand beside Thalia. His smile deepened. "Hullo, Miss Aubrey. I didn't know you were to be here."

"I didn't know myself," Thalia said. "I've only just come to London, as a companion to Mrs. Lockhart."

His eyebrows rose a fraction. "As a companion? But you're scarce older than Eleanor."

Eleanor, he called Mrs. Lockhart. Thalia put her shoulders back. "As she is a widow and I am no ramshackle miss in my first Season, I think we shall deal well enough with one another."

"Yes, provided she does not drag you into her larks," he said.

"Is she prone to them?" Thalia asked. "How well do you know Mrs. Lockhart?"

"She and my sister were thick as thieves at some private school in Wiltshire. Anne could scarcely contain herself when she found Eleanor was in London."

"And you think I shall be out of my depth, as her chaperone?"

Mr. Salisbury held up his hands. "Pax, Miss Aubrey. I didn't mean to insult you by observing you are both young. I am sure you are capable of anything you set your mind to. Is your family in town with you?" He looked about the box, as though he might discover Kalli or Charis hidden in a corner.

"No," Thalia said, remembering that Mr. Salisbury had proposed once to Kalli and been turned down. "Kalli is still in Oxfordshire with her betrothed, and Charis is abroad in India with her husband."

They spoke for a moment about their respective families, and somehow, when the play started, Thalia found herself still beside Mr. Salisbury. The play did not offer much of a distraction from her thoughts, though it was the kind of dramatic fare Kalli would have enjoyed. The romantic lead was played by the great Edmund

Kean. *The Bride of Abydos*, based on a poem by Lord Byron, featured pirates and a clandestine love affair set amid a Turkish harem.

Thalia found herself wondering if Lord Byron had visited a Turkish harem during his time in Turkey, and how accurate this staged version was. She wondered too about the scandalous rumors circling Byron and his half sister, and if those rumors had fueled the love affair between the daughter of the pasha and the pasha's supposed son (though, of course, as the son was *not* the pasha's real son, the play was not so scandalous as the life it imitated).

The poem was a tragedy; the play was not. Thalia did not find this an improvement.

"Well?" Mr. Salisbury asked, in the break before the comedy that was to follow. "Did you enjoy the play?"

"Mr. Kean is a fine actor, but I do not think this role shows his talents to advantage."

Mr. Salisbury laughed. "How very politic of you. Mr. Kean plays more powerfully to the tragedies: Shylock, Lear."

"The young woman who played against him was a rather fine actress. Do you know who she is?" The dark-haired girl had spoken her lines with spirit and passion, elevating what might have been funny in a lesser actress to something almost moving.

"Miss Sophia Montgomery? She's becoming very popular, just now. Half the young men of the *ton* are in love with her."

"Are you?"

Mr. Salisbury hunched one shoulder in a pretense of bashfulness. "Miss Aubrey, you should not ask me such things."

Mortified, Thalia said, "I'm sorry. I didn't mean—"

With a laugh, Mr. Salisbury straightened. "It's all right. I was funning you. Miss Montgomery may be lovely, but I've no interest in competing for her hand. Too much work."

There was a stir in the pit, a knot of young men pushing against one another and shouting. Thalia stood and pressed toward the front of the box for a better look. "Goodness, I hope no one is hurt."

"Likely a quarrel over Miss Montgomery. It has happened before," Mr. Salisbury said, joining her.

A young blond man stumbled back, drawing her eye. He twisted as he fell, giving her a glimpse of his face.

Ice prickled down Thalia's spine. That face—she knew it almost as well as she knew her own.

What was Frederick doing in London? He was supposed to be finishing his last term at Oxford.

"Miss Aubrey? Are you all right? You've gone pale."

"It's nothing," Thalia said, turning to smile reassuringly at him. Her lips felt stiff. When she glanced back down into the pit, her brother was gone.

CHAPTER THREE

Eleanor

To live is not to breathe; it is to act; it is to make use of our organs, our senses, our faculties, of all the parts of ourselves which give us the sentiment of our existence. The man who has lived the most is not he who has counted the most years but he who has most felt life.

— Jean-Jacques Rousseau

Eleanor snuck a glance down the row at her new companion, sitting on the other side of Henry. The young woman had a nice profile, though her chin was perhaps a bit too strong. Thalia seemed intent on the stage, her eyebrows drawn together. Henry watched Thalia rather than the play, and a slight smile tugged at his lips. Eleanor noted his attention thoughtfully.

"What do you think of our Mr. Kean?" Anne's whisper pulled Eleanor's attention back to her old school friend. Of all the delights in London, this had been the most delightful—to find Anne largely unchanged and, most important, still fond of the relative nobody she had befriended at school.

"I think he is very passionate," Eleanor said. In truth, she found him a bit *too* passionate to be believable, but she could tell from Anne's slight blush that her friend did not share her objection.

"And handsome too, is he not?"

"Hmm," Eleanor said, but Anne did not seem to need any encouragement to gush about his performance. The famed actor was not tall, but trim and mobile, with piercing eyes under dark hair. A different dark-haired man flashed into Eleanor's mind—the tall, broad-shouldered young man from the jeweler's shop. She pressed her lips together in vexation. Young Mr. Jones might be attractive, but she had no intention of thinking of him.

Eleanor enjoyed the comedy that followed Mr. Kean's performance more than the play itself. It felt good to laugh, particularly in friendly company where no one would look down on her for indulging in it. Anne had been laughing too: Her cheeks were still pink, her eyes bright. *This*—this was what Eleanor had dreamed of all those long, dark months after Albert had passed away. The sparkle and excitement of London, the thrill and sweetness of friendships.

Following the curtain's descent, Anne and Henry took their leave, after promising faithfully to call on Eleanor the next day. Eleanor and Thalia descended the long staircase at the front of the theater amid a glittering throng. Her companion seemed distracted though, craning her head this way and that.

"Are you looking for someone?" Eleanor asked.

Thalia flushed. "I beg your pardon. I thought I saw my brother earlier, and I had no notion he was in London."

"Elder brother?" Eleanor asked, though Thalia could scarcely have a younger brother at large on his own—the girl claimed to be nineteen, but had she not sworn she had a Season behind her, Eleanor would have thought her a debutante.

"Yes, older. Not quite two years separate us."

"Shall I help you search?"

Thalia smiled. "He looks rather like me, but I don't suppose we will find him in this crowd. I'll write Papa in the morning and see if he knows anything. That is, if you do not have pressing business for me?"

"I plan to be a most lenient employer," Eleanor said, "though I do have something I hope you can help me with. But enough, we can discuss it tomorrow."

They reached the road full of waiting carriages and hackney drivers without sighting Thalia's fair-haired brother. A brisk wind whistled up the street, and Eleanor pulled her wrap more closely about her. The evening air was heavy with the scent of rain.

"Eleanor!"

Eleanor closed her eyes for a fraction of a second, weighing the advantages of pretending not to hear her husband's nephew against the difficulties he might cause later. She opened her eyes and forced herself to smile. "Mr. Lockhart. How . . . unexpected to see you. Were you at the play just now?"

"Yes. I had a notion you'd be here. I meant to call on you during the break, but was held up with other business." George Lockhart turned toward Thalia, his brows raising in polite question.

How did he always manage to make Eleanor feel uncouth? She should have begun with the introduction. "Mr. Lockhart, may I present my new companion, Miss Aubrey. Miss Aubrey, George Lockhart, my late husband's nephew."

A muscle pulsed in the corner of his jaw. Eleanor braced herself against his anger, but he said only, "I heard you had let Miss Blakesley go. No doubt you believe yourself justified in doing so." He bowed his head slightly. "I am pleased to meet you, Miss Aubrey. You have a familiar look to you. Have we met before?"

Thalia curtsied. "I do not believe so, Mr. Lockhart, but perhaps we crossed paths last year? My sister and I were here with our cousins, the Elphinstones, for the Season."

"Sir John Elphinstone?" Mr. Lockhart asked, his stiffness softening some. George always had been a snob.

Thalia nodded. "My uncle."

"A good man. You do not stay with him? I presume he is in town for Parliament."

Trying to keep her voice light, Eleanor said, "I *presume* that is Miss Aubrey's business, not yours." To Thalia, she said, "You needn't answer that."

As Mr. Lockhart's eyes narrowed, Thalia said, "I don't mind. It's a natural question. My uncle has come to London alone and has taken rooms at the Albany, where, as it's a bachelor's establishment, I should be most in the way. This arrangement suits me much better."

Mr. Lockhart looked as if he would like to ask additional questions, but at that moment Eleanor spotted her coachman some six or so carriages down the street. "I beg your pardon, Mr. Lockhart, but it is late, and Miss Aubrey has just come to London today, and I have already kept her from her bed an inexcusably long time."

"Indeed, you have," Mr. Lockhart agreed. "Let me walk you to your carriage."

Without waiting for Eleanor's assent, he extended his elbows for both ladies. Eleanor took his left arm, feeling as though she were touching a snake. Probably a snake was less poisonous.

Once at the carriage, Mr. Lockhart helped Thalia in. He turned back to Eleanor, ostensibly to assist her, but he blocked her ascent with his body. He was so close, Eleanor could feel the warmth radiating from him. Shivering, she took a step back.

His hand shot out, his fingers encircling her wrist like a clamp. "Why did you dismiss Miss Blakesley?"

Eleanor struggled to shake his fingers loose, but they only tightened. Not wanting to cause a scene, she stopped fighting.

"Answer my question."

"I do not like spies in my household. Why do you take such an interest in my affairs?"

"As you are my young, inexperienced relative on the town for the first time, it's only natural that I should take an interest, don't you think?"

"No," Eleanor said flatly. He released her at last, and she stepped away from him. Her wrist hurt, but she refused to give him the satisfaction of knowing as much.

"No?" he echoed, laughing a bit. "Well, perhaps you are right. Let us say then that I take a keen interest in your good fortune."

Eleanor knew, from things Albert had let slip, that George Lockhart had borrowed against his expectations for several years and had been most displeased to find himself supplanted by Eleanor in his uncle's will.

Mr. Lockhart continued, "An unmarried young woman needs protection."

Was that a threat? George Lockhart's handsome face had not changed expression. Anyone hearing his words would take them only as the concerns of a near relation. But he was no blood relation of hers, and his words made her pulse lurch.

"You could always marry me, you know. That would solve both of our problems nicely."

Cold flooded through Eleanor. "Say rather, *your* problem. I should rather die in poverty and squalor than marry you."

Eleanor pushed past him to climb into the carriage. Shaking, she took her seat opposite Thalia. Mr. Lockhart shut the door behind her—no doubt appearing the perfect gentleman to anyone who happened to be watching.

Eleanor leaned back against the carriage seats. She released a long, slow breath, and rubbed her wrist where Mr. Lockhart had grabbed it.

Thalia frowned at her. "Are you all right?"

Eleanor reminded herself that Thalia could not have heard from inside the carriage what Mr. Lockhart said to her. She was unharmed, only shaken, but this young woman did not need to know that. Eleanor Williams Lockhart had always relied upon herself, and this time would be no different. "I'm fine. Mr. Lockhart was only being asinine, as is his wont. I believe I warned you of such."

Thalia smiled, as Eleanor had meant her to. "You did."

Eleanor forced herself upright and infused her voice with cheer she did not feel. "Now, let us speak of plans for tomorrow . . ."

Eleanor was up earlier than she liked, unable to sleep. Mr. Lockhart's words—both the threat and the horrifying proposal—rattled around her brain. She had to do something to be rid of him before he spoiled the whole Season. The beginnings of a plot coalesced in her head, but it would take more planning before she could act.

At length, Eleanor threw a dressing gown over her nightdress, lit a candle, and padded down the stairs and into the small room beside the drawing room that served as a study. She had taken the house furnished, and the volumes on the bookshelves showed a sad air of neglect. Eleanor ignored them. Instead, she made her way to the trunk in one corner. A key rested in the lock. Alfred had always slept with that key in his pocket, afraid that someone might try to steal his life's work. Eleanor, more afraid of losing the key than the contents, kept the key with the trunk.

She set the candle in a candlestick on the desk behind her, turned the key, and lifted the lid.

Untidy piles of paper met her eyes, most of them bearing Albert's jumbled scratching. She could see him now, bent over his desk of a morning, sunlight falling on his balding head, his slight paunch hid beneath the surface of the desk. If she did not feel the weight of these papers so keenly, she might have smiled at the memory.

Instead, Eleanor sighed. Albert had asked only two things of her, when he lifted her from penury and endowed her with his worldly goods. She had already failed at the first, the birth of a child and heir. She did not blame herself too harshly for that, as Albert had fallen ill so soon after their marriage and they had never—she cut off that reflection.

There remained only this, a single request tucked into his will: *To my wife, Eleanor, I bequeath my papers, that she might publish my life's work and present it to the world.*

Eleanor knew Albert had been fond of her, but he had been

passionate about his work. An amateur mathematician, interested in data about people, like average heights and life expectancies and class habits, Alfred had tried many times to help Eleanor share his passion, but his explanations had slid through her mind like water—not that she had tried very hard to understand them. She had assumed, at first, that there would be time later for her to understand. And then, when it was clear there would not be time, he was too weak to explain again.

What had Albert been thinking? He might have bequeathed these papers to one of his many correspondents, who might know what to do with them. Eleanor had no notion. She had come to London to enjoy herself, not to feel like an ignorant schoolgirl. She had so far managed to pretend that the papers did not exist, but on this gray morning, she found she could not pretend any longer.

Thalia discovered her still kneeling by the trunk some hours later, the morning light making the papers increasingly visible, if not clear.

"What are you doing?" Thalia asked.

"Trying to make sense of my late husband's work," Eleanor said. "I don't suppose you have a head for mathematics?"

"No, sadly." Thalia knelt beside her, watching as she shifted papers from one pile to another. "Have you eaten?"

Eleanor's stomach gurgled. "No." She stood, dusting her hands on her thighs. "This will keep until later." When she figured out what to do with it.

After a light luncheon of cold meat and fruit, Eleanor and Thalia were discussing plans to go out shopping when Anne and Henry

Salisbury showed up. Eleanor rushed to hug her friend after the footman announced her, but she did not miss the slight flush on Thalia's cheeks as Henry entered. She frowned. It would not do at all to have her companion form a *tendre* for Henry, likable as the young man was—not if her plan to deal with Mr. Lockhart were to work. She needed to act soon.

Eleanor drew everyone into a small group, herself and Anne on a chaise longue, with Henry and Thalia in a pair of chairs facing them. Soon Henry had them all laughing over an unfortunate incident with his tailor, who had misunderstood his request.

"When I showed up for a fitting, the tailor had outfitted me in the most lurid, dandified getup imaginable, complete with padded shoulders, nipped-in waist, and a waistcoat so bright it could be seen half the length of the street," he said.

"Surely you set him straight," Thalia said.

Anne smiled. "Not Henry! He's got no backbone for confrontation."

Henry rubbed at the side of his nose. "To be sure, my tailor expressed some surprise at my order, but he seemed so pleased at how he had carried it off that I felt I had no choice but to purchase it. My valet burst into tears at the sight and told me I must burn it at once or he would leave my service."

Eleanor found herself giggling too. "How very like you, Henry. To make a great inconvenience for yourself only to spare someone else's feelings. You do know that your tailor, like any artist, must be used to criticism."

"All the more reason why he needn't endure mine. Dash it, I like the fellow! He's quite clever with his needle, and good-humored besides."

"Did you burn the suit then?" Thalia asked.

Henry sighed gustily. "I meant to, but then I thought of how it must make my tailor feel, to hear of it—his artwork, destroyed! So I buried the suit at the back of my closet and promised my valet I would never wear it."

Anne shook her head. "Henry, you mustn't let everyone impose upon you so."

"It's only an imposition if I let it be," Henry said.

"I think it's charming," Eleanor said. "Imagine the world we might have if everyone was as kind as Henry."

"Stop," Henry said, his cheeks turning pink. "You're putting me to the blush."

"Oh," said Eleanor, smiling wickedly. "I'm afraid I have not yet begun to do so."

Henry turned to Thalia and mouthed, *Help me.* Thalia laughed.

Feeling pleased with her merry little quartet, Eleanor turned to Anne. "Come, walk about the room with me."

Anne nodded absently and threaded her arm through Eleanor's. She did not say much, letting Eleanor chatter as they began to circulate about the room.

Once they were out of earshot of the others, Eleanor stopped. "You needn't dissemble with me, Anne. I can see how it pains you to smile today. Something is wrong."

Anne traced one finger across a nearby windowpane. "It's nothing. A trifling megrim, Mama says. I must exert myself more."

Eleanor did not think much of Anne's mama, who had always been more concerned for her own pleasure than her children's well-being.

She had banished her sensitive daughter to a boarding school because her own "nerves were too fragile."

"Humbug," Eleanor said frankly. "One's emotions are not fully biddable—one cannot always be calm on demand, or happy. But if you are feeling blue-spirited, will you let me cheer you up? I have ever so many plans for enjoying London."

Anne pressed a gentle kiss on Eleanor's cheek. "Dear Eleanor—you've always been like a sister to me. Only Henry and my sister, Amelia, have a nearer claim on my heart."

Eleanor squeezed Anne's hand in return. "And you are all the family I never had. Come, let us return to the others. I have something I must speak to Henry about."

CHAPTER FOUR

Thalia

Let me not to the flowering of true friends
Serve as barrier. Friendship cannot grow
Choked by shallow starts and self-serving ends,
Or flourish untended by affection.

—Thalia Aubrey, "Meditation on Sonnet 116"

Thalia watched her employer circle the room with Anne Salisbury. Eleanor Lockhart had proven to be many things that Thalia had not expected: young, energetic, forthright, with a streak of toughness in her. She had not previously seen the gentleness with which Eleanor approached her old friend. She tucked the observation away and turned back to Mr. Salisbury.

"I beg your pardon—you were saying something, and I was not attending."

"Alas, a common occurrence in my life," Mr. Salisbury said. But the dancing light in his eyes belied his mournful expression.

"I do not believe that for a moment. A man like you, with manners, address, and a comfortable position in society? I daresay you are quite popular."

"Oh, yes. With middle-aged hostesses. With the young ladies, it is quite another matter."

"Nonsense!" Thalia said.

"Perhaps only the Aubrey sisters? You're devilishly hard to please. First Kalli would not have me, and now I cannot even keep your attention though I am right in front of you."

Thalia flushed and changed the subject. "I was thinking of Mrs. Lockhart and your sister. I have not seen her so tender with anyone else."

"Hmm," Henry said, his eyes following the two girls about the room. "Eleanor has had a hard life. Try not to judge her."

"My father taught me that I should not judge anyone," Thalia said.

"But you make an exception for fribbles? No, don't frown at me. I've seen you in society before—you cannot abide a fool."

"But I do *try*," Thalia said. How did Mr. Salisbury manage to see so much of her? Even James had not fully seen her, and she'd wanted to marry him. Not particularly liking this conversation, she changed the subject again. At this rate, she would be out of conversational topics before the quarter hour was up. "Tell me, Mr. Salisbury, have you any hobbies?"

"Besides looking ornamental? I am a most useful friend to have in society. Practiced in all the social niceties, able to advise one in any matter of delicacy, and so forth."

"Surely you do more than look ornamental. Do you read? Study science?"

"I do occasionally study the science at Gentleman Jackson's pugilism academy—not precisely what you meant? And I have been known to read the occasional journal. Read most of your poems, haven't I?"

"Have you?" He'd mentioned reading one before, but she'd thought that was a fluke.

Henry grinned at her. "Surprised, are you? I'm not illiterate, and a true ornament to society can converse upon all topics. How goes the *ars poetriae*? Working on anything new?"

"I am trying to. I am currently recopying several poems after my youngest brother desecrated them. Though they are not as good as I had supposed."

"Perhaps you are too hard on yourself?"

"No, the sorry truth is that I am not yet the writer I aspire to be."

"I suppose that is the challenge of all artists, isn't it—to work until your craft can encompass your vision? It's why I've never attempted anything truly artistic. That gap is daunting. I'd far rather be known for my wondrous vision than prove to the world that my skills cannot reach it."

"Yes," Thalia said, rather surprised at his insight. "Though I'd rather reach across that gap and fail than not."

"Was that aimed at me?" Mr. Salisbury asked, smiling. But before Thalia could reassure him that it was not, Anne was settling back on the chaise longue and Eleanor was standing before them.

"Henry? Might I borrow you for a moment? I have something I must discuss with you," Eleanor said.

With only a glancing look at Thalia, Mr. Salisbury nodded and followed Eleanor from the room. Thalia supposed Eleanor meant to show him the trunk in her study with her husband's papers. Perhaps Mr. Salisbury, with all his connections, would know someone who might help.

She waited for Anne to say something. As Eleanor's paid

companion, it was not really Thalia's place to initiate the conversation, though she and Anne had been introduced last Season.

But Anne did not say anything, only stood and returned to the window. After several long minutes, when Eleanor and Henry did not come back, Thalia gave up on propriety and joined her.

"Mrs. Lockhart says you are old friends, that you knew one another at school. Was it a pleasant place?"

Anne pressed her lips together. For a moment, Thalia thought she would refuse to answer. Then, reluctantly, "No."

"I imagine you must find London more to your liking than school."

Anne shrugged. "It's well enough."

Thalia eyed Anne. Why was the young woman being so cool with her? She had known Anne a little during her own Season— Anne's mother was friendly with Aunt Harmonia. Anne had been closer to Kalli, however. Truth be told, *most* people had been closer to Kalli. Or Charis. Thalia had been so caught up in James, she had not bothered with anything so trivial as friends—or even acquaintances.

Was Anne putting her off because of her demotion in status to that of a companion? Thalia would not have pegged her for a snob. Maybe she was distant on Mr. Salisbury's behalf, feeling the affront of Kalli's refusal of his proposal? Thalia did not know how else to account for the young woman's near-rudeness.

Thalia dropped her attempt at conversation and returned to her seat. She began composing a poem in her head.

She had just settled on a satisfying opening stanza when the door opened, and Henry and Eleanor returned. Eleanor looked a trifle flushed. Mr. Salisbury, in contrast, was rather pale. His gaze went first to Thalia, but when she met his look, she could not quite decipher what she saw there. He seemed agitated about something, but she must have been misreading him—one of the most delightful things about Mr. Salisbury was his restful nature. He was seldom worked up about anything.

Eleanor nudged Mr. Salisbury, and he cleared his throat. "Eleanor and I have something to tell you—"

But whatever it was he meant to say was lost. The door behind them burst open, and a blond young man tumbled into the room, landing on his knees before Thalia.

"Good heavens! Frederick! What on earth are you doing here?" Thalia scarcely registered the lovely dark-haired woman who followed her brother into the room. Her brother was in the grips of some powerful passion: His blue eyes flashed, and a lurid bruise decorated one cheekbone. *Had* he been part of that fight in the pit she'd seen the night before?

Freddy looked up. "Thalia! You've got to help us."

CHAPTER FIVE

Eleanor

> But still he would be her husband. Without thinking highly either of men or of matrimony, marriage had always been her object; it was the only honorable provision for well-educated young women of small fortune, and however uncertain of giving happiness, must be their pleasantest preservative from want.
>
> — *Pride and Prejudice*, by the author of *Sense and Sensibility* (Jane Austen)

Less than fifteen minutes before a vaguely familiar blond boy burst into her drawing room, Eleanor had led Henry to her small study. Piles of paper decorated every spare surface, but she ignored them. They were not pertinent to the conversation she meant to have.

Henry had studied the narrow space, glancing from the piles to the window and back to Eleanor. "And why have you brought me here? Do you mean to seduce me?"

Eleanor had fought back a blush. She would not be embarrassed before Henry, whom she had known these past five years and more. "Something like that."

Henry's mouth fell open. "You cannot be serious."

Eleanor had laughed, taking some pleasure in his obvious discomfiture. Henry grinned back at her, his posture relaxing. Then Eleanor said, "But I do have a proposition for you," and his shoulders tensed again.

"Hear me out, please, before you say anything," she continued. "I believe you've met my husband's nephew, George Lockhart? He is bent on making my life a living hell. He wishes me married, so that my late husband's property will revert from me to him. He has sent every kind of dandy and fortune hunter after me—heaven knows why they accept. Lies? Bribes? He has set spies in my household. He has even offered for me himself. I do not think he will desist until he believes I am to be wed."

Henry had frowned. "But surely no well-bred gentleman would harass a lady so."

"Do you doubt me?" Eleanor had asked, something fierce boiling up inside her.

His frown deepened. "No, of course not. If you say it is so, it must be. Only say what you require from me, and I shall do it. Shall I challenge this dastard to a duel?"

"Please don't talk nonsense right now," Eleanor said. She turned away from Henry, tidying the papers on her desk. "I require no duels. But I do require some kind of protection. I have been thinking and thinking, and it seems to me that the best course of action is to acquire a fiancé. If Mr. Lockhart believes I am to be married, he will stop his assault long enough for me to come up with some other plan."

She looked back up at Henry. His eyes widened a fraction, and he clasped his hands behind his back. "A fiancé—meaning me?"

Thank goodness Henry was not stupid. She rushed on. "Only a sham fiancé, you know. I would not be so cruel as to hold you to our supposed engagement. But for six months, perhaps a year, until I can find some other solution. Then I shall cry off."

Henry murmured, "I do not like the number of spurned proposals I am collecting."

"I beg your pardon?" Eleanor asked.

"Nothing of consequence. So this is all you require of me? A sham engagement, to be terminated at some point of your choosing?"

"Yes, if you're agreeable? And perhaps you shall need to escort me places, to make it seem believable."

There was a funny look on his face, as though he were chewing on something distasteful.

"If you dislike it, you have only to say no," Eleanor said in a rush. "I won't allude to it again."

"I don't *dis*like it, precisely. But—are you certain? There may be some scandal attached to your crying off."

"Oh, pooh," Eleanor said. "As an unmarried woman? Perhaps. As a wealthy widow, it shall only be counted eccentric." She thought, suddenly, of the way Thalia had blushed when he came in, how he had watched Thalia at the opera. Best clear that up at once. "There is not someone else, is there? Shall I be putting a spoke in the wheels of some grand romance of yours?"

"No," Henry said. "There's no one else."

"Then you'll do it? You'll help me?"

"I should be delighted to help you. Eleanor Lockhart, will you do me the honor of being my false fiancée? There—now no one can claim that *you* asked *me*."

"But I did ask you."

"Not in so many words. And now I've asked you, you can set the blame at my feet."

"Very well then, I accept your offer. To be duly terminated at some point in the future."

Henry had held out his hand, and Eleanor had taken it, feeling a rush of gratitude and affection that Henry had made a potentially awkward proposal so much easier than it might have been.

They made their way back to the drawing room. Henry had just begun announcing their engagement when a young man and woman burst into the room. The boy knocked into Eleanor in his rush to Thalia, throwing her off balance. Henry caught her.

His arms were warm and firm around her, and for a tiny fraction of time, something flickered inside her, something she had thought long dead and buried. But Eleanor did not as a rule let people close to her—no one besides Anne had so much as hugged her since Albert had died.

She untangled herself from Henry and stepped away. "Thank you, I'm fine."

The earlier rush of gratitude evaporated. Eleanor was no longer sure how she felt, other than unsettled, uncertain, and unmoored—all the feelings she had determined she would never feel again after agreeing to marry Albert. In any case, it was done. She was engaged—in appearance, if not in truth—and Mr. Lockhart would hopefully leave her in peace for the Season.

Henry looked as though he wanted to say something, but let his extended hand drop. Eleanor turned back to her uninvited guests, wondering how they had eluded her butler.

She recognized the young woman standing just inside her drawing room, her expression torn between amusement and vexation.

Miss Sophia Montgomery, the actress who had caused such a stir on the stage the previous night.

The blond boy was still on his knees in front of Thalia, who stared at him wide-eyed. Eleanor looked from the boy to Thalia and back again. There was something similar in the cast of their features, the delicate bridge of their noses—and hadn't the young man called Thalia by name?

Thalia sighed. "Eleanor, please meet my brother Frederick Aubrey. Freddy, Eleanor." She continued with the introductions as the young man stood up, smiling rather sheepishly around the room.

"I do apologize for barging in on you like this, but I couldn't think where else to come. Sophia—Miss Montgomery—was in the devil of a fix, and I determined I must help her."

Miss Montgomery crossed her arms and pursed her shapely mouth. "You told me you knew someone who could help me. I had no notion—if I'd known he meant to burst into the drawing room of a lady of quality without so much as a by-your-leave, I should never have agreed." She turned dark, appealing eyes on Eleanor. "My most abject apologies, Mrs.—"

"Eleanor," Eleanor said automatically. "Please, call me Eleanor." The girl's anxious expression plucked at something deep inside Eleanor. "And please stay. I'll ring for tea and some of my cook's delightful cake. I think a bit of sugar will do us good."

She settled her new guests into comfortable chairs, bade Henry to take a seat near his sister and Thalia on the chaise longue, and issued directions to a maid. Then she sat down herself. "Now," she said. "Why don't you tell us what this is all about?"

Frederick Aubrey drew a deep breath. "It was entirely the fault of that dastard—beg pardon, ma'am. That man. He won't stop pestering Miss Montgomery. Appears at most shows and rehearsals. He was waiting for her after today's rehearsal with a blooming big bouquet of roses."

"Surely it's not uncommon for admirers to show up with flowers?" Anne asked.

Indeed, from the expression on Mr. Aubrey's face, Eleanor suspected that *he* had also shown up with flowers—and perhaps been overshadowed.

"It's not the flowers. It's what the man wants," Mr. Aubrey said, managing to look both self-conscious and indignant.

"Most admirers with flowers want rather more than my thanks," Miss Montgomery said frankly. "He wishes to set me up as his mistress, but I have no intention of becoming such."

"*I* don't wish for more than thanks. Your mere presence is all that I dream of," Mr. Aubrey said, gazing at the actress soulfully. Eleanor eyed him. Had Thalia said this was her *older* brother? He was acting like a schoolboy in the throes of his first infatuation.

Miss Montgomery, on the other hand, was decidedly *not* infatuated. She patted Freddy's hand. "Yes, I know."

Eleanor fought back a smile. That pat was closer to what one might give a favored child—or an elderly relative in their dotage. Poor Mr. Aubrey.

"But surely," Anne said, "if you only tell the man no, he will leave you alone?"

A grimace flickered across Miss Montgomery's face. "Men of your class may accept a refusal from a lady with reasonable grace.

But I am not a lady and those rules do not apply to me. If I say no, it is seen as a tease or a challenge, something to be overcome with time and gifts."

"He's a damned blighter!" Mr. Aubrey said. "In any case, he was most pressing today, and I thought it best to get Sophia—that is, Miss Montgomery—out of his reach. We hoped Thalia might have some advice. My father wrote that she'd be here."

Thalia blinked at her brother. "Some advice? What made you suppose that I knew the first thing about discouraging a man who wants a mistress?"

Henry choked—though when Eleanor glanced at him in concern, his red face suggested he was fighting laughter rather than pain.

"Oh," Freddy said. "Er." Clearly, that aspect had not occurred to him.

Tea arrived then, a blessed interruption. Eleanor poured the tea with a steady hand and passed around the cups and saucers, along with thick slices of a fragrant spice cake.

"I don't expect you to help me," Miss Montgomery said. "I am capable of caring for myself. I will own, however, today's encounter was a trifle unpleasant, or I would not have let Frederick prevail upon me to come here."

"I don't imagine Freddy gave you much choice," Thalia said. "He's rather fond of knight-errantry."

Henry said, "You might try other means of discouraging the man. Most men lose their ardor pretty quickly when they've been embarrassed."

Miss Montgomery had been lifting a bite of cake to her mouth, but she stilled, then carefully replaced her fork. "I do not think this gentleman would take well to humiliation."

"You might let me protect you," Mr. Aubrey said. "Be my wife. He can scarce pressure you if we are married."

Wife? Eleanor blinked in surprise. Across the room, Thalia dropped her face into her hands.

Miss Montgomery turned a fond look on Mr. Aubrey. "That is kind of you, Frederick, but I cannot accept such an offer and you know it. In any case, I'm afraid not all actors or nobility consider marriage bonds an impediment to such arrangements."

"I do not know it," Frederick Aubrey said. "I care for you, very much. You inspire me to be a better man. Your very presence awakens my inner muse."

Miss Montgomery merely shook her head. "Please believe me when I say it is impossible, though I do thank you for your kindness."

"On that note—" Henry cleared his throat and stood, looking at Eleanor.

Wife, Eleanor thought, her stomach dropping. Perhaps she ought to have thought this through more thoroughly. Heat stole across her cheeks.

"This is not precisely how Eleanor and I had envisioned making this announcement, but as we are all friends here, I should like to tell you that Eleanor has made me the happiest man alive by agreeing to marry me."

CHAPTER SIX

Thalia

A man about town is admired, they say,
For his wit and his dress, for his social cachet.
His luster is only enhanced by a mistress,
Particularly one who's expensive and pretty —
But let a young woman attempt for the same,
And all it will do is redound to her shame.
Reader, I ask you — is this justice?

—Thalia Aubrey

Marry.

Henry—that is, Mr. Salisbury—and Eleanor.

Thalia felt as if someone had landed her a facer. She could not seem to catch her breath, and her chest hurt as though she'd been struck. Eleanor had said she did not mean to marry again, and she seemed to view Henry—Mr. Salisbury—with the affection of a sister, not a lover.

And Henry?

Never mind. Thalia was a fool. Of course Henry would like Eleanor, who was petite and pretty and daring.

So he had offered, and Eleanor had said yes. Thalia might speculate on her motives—affection, a desire for the security of Henry's position—but in truth, it was her employer's business, not hers.

Anne sprang up from her seat to hug first Eleanor, then Henry. "Oh, I am so pleased! Since Amelia has become Lady Salisbury and has a child besides, I have been in sore need of another sister."

"Congratulations," Thalia said, smiling through stiff lips. "When do you mean to marry?" How long before she would need to find other employment?

"Oh, we are in no hurry," Eleanor said airily. "I daresay it shall be a longish engagement, as such things go."

Thalia released a soft sigh. That was a relief, at least. She should not have to leave London at once. She wished she did not feel as though a gray pall had settled over her. Doubtless it was only the surprise of it all.

And Freddy's appearance. Which, possibly, ought to have concerned Thalia more than her employer's sudden engagement. Thalia studied Freddy, who was whispering something to Miss Montgomery. His whole face softened as he whispered, and Thalia groaned inwardly. She had seen Freddy in the throes of calf-love many times growing up, and every time it had ended in weeks of moping and discomfort for his family.

Thalia would have to ask Freddy privately what he was doing in London when he was supposed to be studying at Oxford. He had said something about Sophia being his muse—surely he did not mean to take up writing again? Thalia ought to be more worried about the fact that Freddy had publicly proposed a most ineligible match, but Miss Montgomery seemed a girl of sense, and in any case, Thalia considered Freddy's inability to support a wife a bigger barrier to marriage than Miss Montgomery's occupation.

Henry was speaking again, pulling Thalia from her muddled

reflections. "Yes, no hurry about the wedding, so long as it comes out right in the end."

He was watching Thalia, a slight frown drawing his eyebrows together. Thalia found she could not bear the weight of his regard and looked down, studying her fingers. There was an ink smudge on her right ring finger, from her writing earlier.

As a point of fact, she had a poem she could be working on now— that stanza she had only just begun when Eleanor and Henry came back into the room. It suddenly called to her rather desperately. She could settle things up with Freddy later, as soon as she found where he was staying. She rose from her seat and crossed the floor to her brother.

But before she could say anything to Freddy, the door opened again.

The footman announced, "Mr. Owen Jones."

Thalia had never seen this tall, broad young man before. He looked rather irate, his heavy eyebrows lowered over his eyes. But his effect on the company was electrifying. Miss Montgomery gasped, and Eleanor's pale cheeks flooded with color.

Was this the man who had threatened Miss Montgomery at the theater? But no—he could not be. Freddy was regarding him with a curious, benign expression.

Then who was he?

CHAPTER SEVEN

Eleanor

I know that two and two make four, and should be glad to prove it too, if I could —
though, I must say, if by any sort of process I could convert 2 and 2 into 5, it would
give me much greater pleasure.

—George Gordon, Lord Byron

Heat scalded through Eleanor, followed by a roaring in her ears. And
for what? A jewelry salesman she had seen but once in her life. The
younger Mr. Jones had not been present when she returned for her
repaired clasp, and though she had wondered about him, she had
not asked after him. What was he doing in her drawing room?

Miss Montgomery gasped. "Owen, how did you find me here?"

Was it possible Mr. Jones was the man who was pursuing Miss
Montgomery so insistently? Eleanor's stomach fell with a brutal
lurch. No, impossible. She remembered how he had teased her own
insistent suitor about mistresses, and besides, Miss Montgomery had
clearly implied it was a member of the *ton*. Mr. Owen, the jeweler's
son, was not a gentleman.

Nor was he someone who deserved so much time in her thoughts.
Rather irritably, Eleanor stood and asked, "May I help you?"

The young man lifted one hand, as if to beg for patience, while he sucked in air. His face was red, as though he had just run the streets to her house.

Eleanor plucked up an extra teacup, filled it with the now luke-warm liquid, and handed it to her unexpected guest, who downed it with a murmured thanks.

"Sophia," Mr. Jones said, when he'd caught his breath, "are you all right? I stopped by the theater to bring you home, and they said you'd gone off with some gentleman, that there had been a fight."

"To *bring you home*?" Frederick Aubrey echoed, also rising. "Sophia, who is this man? What claim does he have on you?"

Miss Montgomery tugged Mr. Aubrey back into his seat. "Don't be ridiculous, Frederick. This is my brother, Owen Jones. Owen, this is Frederick Aubrey, his sister Thalia, our hostess, Eleanor . . ." She paused, dismayed. "And I'm afraid I've forgotten the rest of the names. I am sorry!"

Eleanor stepped smoothly into the breach and introduced Anne and Henry. Anne seemed a trifle bewildered by the new faces, but Henry looked distinctly amused. She could only pray he would not say something reprehensible. "Montgomery" must be a stage name—it was certainly more distinctive than Jones.

Following the introductions, Miss Montgomery turned back to her brother. "Owen, truly, I'm fine. There was some unpleasantness with an admirer. Mr. Aubrey insisted I come with him for my safety, and it seemed easier to humor him than not. I own, it was a trifle disagreeable, but I would have handled it if I had to. How did you know to come here?"

"I followed as quickly as I could, but I'm not as fast on foot as a carriage and I had to ask after you a few times. It's as well that your Mr. Aubrey chose a hansom cab with a distinctive horse." Mr. Jones approached Freddy and extended his hand, which Freddy took and shook. "Thank you for looking after her."

"Your sister is something rare. A precious pearl more brilliant than any other gem in the ocean!" Mr. Aubrey said, with fervor if not strict accuracy.

"Are there other gems found in the ocean?" Henry asked—thankfully, he kept his voice low, and Freddy did not appear to hear him.

"Er, yes, I suppose so," Mr. Jones said. Now that his initial urgency was fading, he looked rather uncomfortable. He tugged at his neckcloth. "We should be going."

Eleanor was never entirely sure afterward what possessed her to speak. "Oh, do stay and rest a moment. I can ring for fresh tea, and I daresay you'd enjoy some cake."

Mr. Jones lifted one eyebrow at her. "You daresay?" He rubbed his broad stomach, almost unconsciously. "And why is that?"

Flustered, Eleanor said, "I didn't mean anything precisely, only most people seem to like cake."

"Owen," Miss Montgomery said, "don't embarrass your hostess. She was trying to be polite."

Mr. Jones grinned at Eleanor and some traitorous part of her fluttered weakly. "You would be quite right, ma'am. I do indeed enjoy cake, as my size no doubt attests. Thank you. I should be glad to stay for a moment, if I am not inconveniencing you."

Eleanor turned to gesture Mr. Jones into a seat, but hesitated: They were all full, save her own former seat. Henry came to her rescue by rising and tugging Anne up beside him. "Mr. Jones, please have my seat. We've already stayed longer than we intended. Eleanor, will we see you at Almack's tomorrow night?"

"No—we haven't received vouchers yet." And likely would not, for all Mr. Lockhart's promises. "But we will be at the Dollands' cotillion tonight."

"Save me a dance?" Henry squeezed Eleanor's hand briefly as he passed her.

Anne stopped to hug her. "Eleanor, I must congratulate you again. I am so happy for you and Henry!" She pressed a kiss on Eleanor's cheek before slipping away to join Henry at the door.

Mr. Jones paused just before the chair Henry had vacated. "Are congratulations in order?"

Eleanor found it strangely hard to speak. "Yes, thank you. I have just become engaged to Mr. Salisbury."

"Ah. My most sincere congratulations to you," Mr. Jones said, taking his seat. Try as she might, Eleanor could not read anything from his neutral tone.

Eleanor surveyed her guests: Thalia had slipped into easy conversation with Miss Montgomery about her newest play, with Mr. Aubrey adding occasional asides. Eleanor walked to the door recently vacated by the Salisbury siblings, to call a maid to bring fresh tea.

Eleanor returned to her seat, which perforce put her beside Mr. Jones. He was silent, watching Eleanor with a wary expression. She struggled to find something to say. It was not, precisely, that she thought a tradesman beneath her notice—she had grown up in a community surrounded by them, and for all she knew, the unknown father who paid her bills at school might have been a tradesman. It was more that this particular man drew her notice more than she liked.

Mr. Jones spoke first. His gaze dropped briefly to her cross and then returned to her face. "I see that your necklace has been repaired satisfactorily."

"Yes, thank you."

"I would assume no less. My father, whatever his other faults, is an exceptional jeweler."

"And what is it that you do, Mr. Jones? I know we met at your father's shop, but I did not see you there when I returned for my necklace."

Mr. Jones made a wry face. "I am pressed into work as a shop clerk when my father is short of hands, but typically I keep his books for him while trying to finish my studies."

"Oh? Where do you study? Oxford? Cambridge?"

A faintly pained expression flickered across his face. "Neither, I'm afraid. I study on my own."

Eleanor felt herself blushing again. "I'm sorry, I shouldn't have assumed—"

"It's all right. Not everyone can be born to wealth."

Mr. Jones's voice was without rancor, but Eleanor found herself bristling anyway. "And you think I was?"

He gestured vaguely to the room around them, the rich draperies and carved ceilings, the touches of gold. "I merely follow the story the evidence suggests."

"Then you would be wrong. I was not born to wealth. I—" Eleanor hesitated, then finished defiantly: "I married into it." She remembered, too late, that she had just announced her betrothal to Henry. She must sound like a bigamist. "I'm widowed."

"My apologies, madam. And condolences." He sighed. "This is the devil of polite conversation: so many pitfalls one might stumble into unthinkingly. I try to avoid it when I can."

Eleanor could not help smiling at his chagrin. "You could not have known my situation. And I would not for the world make you uncomfortable. You needn't converse if you'd rather not."

"I don't mind talking with you," he said. "Even if I do occasionally put my foot in it."

"Well then, will you tell me what it is you study on your own?"

"Are you asking to be polite or because you want to know?"

"Is it impossible that I should do both?"

"I study mathematics. I should like to work for the Stock Exchange or an insurance company eventually."

Her eyes grew wide. "Mathematics? As in life tables and mortality rates and things like that?"

Mr. Jones smiled. "Yes. Things like that. Have I bored you completely?"

Eleanor shook her head. "Not at all. I should say, rather, that you've shown up like an answer to prayer."

One dark eyebrow lifted. "Clearly, there is a first time for everything."

"Yes—that is, will you let me show you something?"

At his nod, Eleanor led Mr. Jones from the drawing room to her study. It was the second time that day she had stood in the room alone with a man. Oddly, while that earlier conversation had touched on a more intimate subject, this one *felt* more intimate. Perhaps it was only that Mr. Jones was a bigger man than Henry and filled more of the space?

Mr. Jones looked around the room with open curiosity. He bent nearer to a pile of papers on the desk, then lifted the top page up, studying it. "What is this? These are mathematical notations of a very high level, but I have not seen them before. Unpublished?"

She nodded. "My late husband's work. He charged me in his will to see it published, but I have not the first idea how to do so. I have sorted some by date, and his correspondence by respondent, but the notations might as well be Greek."

A faint smile flickered across his face. "Some of them are."

"Would you—" Eleanor hesitated. "I need someone who understands the work to help me. Would you be willing to do so? I would compensate you for your time, of course."

His brow knit. "Are you certain? You know nothing of my abilities—I might tarnish your husband's reputation as soon as make it."

"Perhaps a trial then? You may write up a portion of the work, and I will send it to one of my husband's old correspondents for corroboration?"

"Why not simply ask them?"

A fair question—and one that Eleanor had wrestled with herself. "I've not met any of his correspondents to speak to. And they would likely demand I send all Albert's papers to them—once out of my possession, how could I have any say in what happened to the articles? Here, you may help me understand what you're about, and we can decide together what must be done with the work."

Mr. Jones thrust out his hand. "I'm willing to try it if you are— what little I've seen looks fascinating. And it will shock my father no end if I make an honest living from my studies."

Eleanor took his hand. Her fingers were dwarfed in his, but she rather liked the sensation. After a too-long moment, her thoughts caught up with her emotions, and she released his hand quickly. "Excellent. Will you come by Friday, and we can agree on a contract?"

"I shall be delighted."

Agitated voices floated down to them from the drawing room, interrupting them. Eleanor cast a quick glance at Mr. Jones before lifting her skirts and darting toward the noise. She reached the ruckus just in time to see Frederick Aubrey pull back his arm and then plant a facer on a tall, tallow-haired man.

CHAPTER EIGHT

Thalia

Hear me —
You see,
I cannot love you, John,
Or wake with you at dawn.
I cannot wear your wedding ring
And listen to nightingales sing.
I'd be untrue
To swear to you.
Your kisses do not burn,
Or make my heart unlearn
The way it beats
When him it meets.

—Thalia Aubrey (attempt at an Old English hexaduad form)

The most pressing thing, Thalia decided, was to keep Freddy from mauling Eleanor's nephew again. She stood up from the chaise longue and started forward. "Freddy!"

Mr. Jones beat her to Freddy, flying into the room with Eleanor a step behind him and catching Freddy in a firm grip just as he lunged forward a second time.

George Lockhart dabbed a handkerchief to his split lip and looked sourly at Thalia's brother.

"Do you always keep such low company, Eleanor?" he asked.

Eleanor flinched.

"You're a damned blaggard," Freddy said to Mr. Lockhart, straining to pull away from Mr. Jones.

Mr. Lockhart ignored him. "Eleanor, who are these people?" On the surface, his voice was calm, but Thalia heard the anger edging his tone.

Eleanor's face was pale as she answered, though Thalia could not tell if she was furious or fearful. "This is Frederick Aubrey. His sister Thalia is my companion, as you must remember. Miss Montgomery, you appear to know. The young man restraining Mr. Aubrey is *her* brother, Owen Jones." She took a deep breath, as though steeling herself. "Everyone, Mr. Lockhart is my late husband's nephew."

Behind Thalia on the chaise longue, Miss Montgomery sucked in a gasp.

An almost comical look of surprise wiped away Freddy's fury, and he stopped struggling. "He's your *nephew*?"

"Late husband's," Eleanor corrected.

"Then I'm very sorry for you," Freddy said. "Did you know *this* is the man we spoke of—the one who was pressing Miss Montgomery to accept his insulting offer?"

Thalia shut her eyes briefly. Well, this was a fine muddle. She couldn't decide if she was more upset with Mr. Lockhart for harassing Miss Montgomery, or with Freddy, for being an actual ass.

Surprise—or resentment?—must have made Mr. Jones slacken his hold, because Freddy lunged forward again. Mr. Lockhart sidestepped him neatly. When Freddy turned as if to try again, Eleanor inserted herself between them.

"Enough, if you please. I will not have a brawl in my drawing room."

While Freddy seethed, Mr. Jones took his sister's hand. "Thank you for the tea and cake, Mrs. Lockhart. We must be going." He paused for a moment, his gaze sweeping the room and landing everywhere but on Eleanor. "I'm afraid I cannot take you up on your kind offer, after all. If what Mr. Aubrey says is true, then I won't allow myself or my sister near a house where Mr. Lockhart is welcome."

With a clipped nod, he swept from the room, his sister tucked protectively under his arm.

Eleanor seemed to wilt. Thalia hesitated for a moment, torn between going to Eleanor or Freddy, but opted to twine her arm through Freddy's, in case he decided to hit Mr. Lockhart again, now that Mr. Jones was gone.

"Kind offer?" Mr. Lockhart asked.

"It was nothing," Eleanor said.

"I've a kindness of my own to offer then, which I hope is *not* nothing. I've brought you vouchers to Almack's, as promised." He held up two squares of paper with elegant calligraphy. Eleanor made no move to take them.

Thalia leaned toward Freddy. "Next time you decide to start a fight, please do it somewhere outside of Eleanor's drawing room."

"But that man—"

"That man deserved a trouncing, yes. But Eleanor didn't deserve the humiliation."

Freddy started to respond, but Thalia held up a finger. Mr. Lockhart and Eleanor were whispering furiously and, from the way Eleanor slowly retreated before him, it appeared as though she might need some support. Thalia pushed Freddy gently toward a chair. "Do sit down for a moment."

"I did not invite them here," Eleanor was saying. "They simply showed up, but I could not turn them away. Miss Montgomery was distressed."

Mr. Lockhart waved a hand. "That business was between her and me. She"—he cast a quick, dismissive glance at Freddy sitting in the chair—"*they* had no right to involve you in it."

"Had you not behaved despicably, they would not have done so. Surely some of the blame lies with you."

Thalia came to a halt beside Eleanor, and Eleanor grasped her hand. This close, Thalia could feel her employer trembling.

"Such middle-class morals," Mr. Lockhart said. "You'll find the *ton*'s acceptance hard to come by if you mean to sit in judgment of every man who mounts a mistress."

Eleanor's wince was almost imperceptible, but Thalia caught it.

"Surely it's more agreeable if the mistress is also willing?" Thalia asked, trying to draw Mr. Lockhart's attention from Eleanor. Freddy, still seated but visibly fidgeting, laughed louder than the comment warranted.

His lips tightened. "You talk very freely for a companion."

"And you talk very rudely for a gentleman," Thalia said. "I suppose that makes us even."

Eleanor's grip on her hand tightened. "Mr. Lockhart, there are two things I must tell you."

Mr. Lockhart cocked his head, listening.

"First, I am engaged to be married. To Mr. Henry Salisbury."

Mr. Lockhart's brows rose in pleased surprise. "But this is excel—"

Eleanor interrupted. "Second, I must ask that you never come here again. For the love I bore my husband, I have tolerated you. But you come to my home only to lecture me, abuse my guests, and bully me. I won't have it anymore."

"Brava," Thalia murmured, and Eleanor smiled faintly.

"Will you also bar Mr. Aubrey from your home, for abusing your guests?"

Eyes fierce, Eleanor said, "I do not believe I owe you an answer to that."

Mr. Lockhart stood frozen for a moment, his own eyes like ice shards. In one swift movement, he tore the prized Almack's vouchers into two pieces, then four, and let the fragments flutter to the rug. "When you have calmed and come to your senses, you will no doubt feel that you have overreacted. It does not *do* to burn your bridges. My olive branch is extended whenever you choose to receive it."

With that, he bowed his head and walked swiftly from the room.

"Do you think he could have used any more clichéd metaphors?" Thalia asked, hoping the question might diffuse the heavy mood in the room.

Eleanor released Thalia's hand with a small laugh. But then she knuckled a tear away from one cheek. "I hate that man. I hate that he makes me feel so small, as though the problem here is me and not him!"

"You were right to send him packing," Freddy said.

Eleanor started. "Oh, Mr. Aubrey. I'd nearly forgotten you were here. Will you both excuse me? I'm afraid I've got a headache starting."

"Do you need anything?" Thalia asked.

"No, only some rest. Do, please, carry on without me." Eleanor slipped from the room.

Thalia frowned at the door after it had shut, feeling certain that Eleanor was not telling the whole truth. But she was a paid employee, not Eleanor's friend, though she was beginning to care for her employer like one.

She turned back to find Freddy tucking into some of the leftover cake with gusto. It was one of the many minor stings of his life that he did not lose his appetite during times of emotional trauma like a real romantic. Freddy caught her eye and flushed, then shoved another bite of cake into his mouth almost defiantly.

Thalia settled beside him, watching him for a moment. When he had cleared the plate of crumbs, she asked, "Why aren't you at Oxford, Freddy?"

His flush darkened. "Why do you want to know? So you can tell Papa on me?"

"I'm no snitch. But I suspect you might be in trouble."

He shook his head. "No trouble. Only the classes are pointless. We study the work of dead men, and the lectures seem designed to make everything as lifeless as possible. There's no true feeling in it, no real artistry. And why should I study from dead men when the forefront of literature is here in London?"

Thalia pressed her lips closed over a boil of emotions. Though she shared a similar feeling about the opportunity to learn from living writers, it galled her that Freddy should so blithely squander an opportunity she would have sold her soul for. Well, perhaps not her soul. That would horrify both her parents. But she would have given a great deal to study at Oxford. More to the point—

"You know Papa has sacrificed to fund your study at Oxford. Have you told him how you feel?"

Freddy waved a hand in the air. "He wouldn't understand. And I'll take care of things. Heavens, Thalia, you're my little sister—you don't have to nag me so."

Thalia breathed through her nose. "Well then, we won't speak of Oxford. What have you been up to in London? How did you come to meet Miss Montgomery?"

Freddy brightened. "I came down to London with a friend of mine to see a show. Must have been inspired, because I saw Miss Montgomery, and that was that. Her beauty, her grace, her passion—I went back to my hotel that night and wrote a poem to her. I tell you, Thalia, I've found my muse, and she could not be more perfect."

"You know she is a person too," Thalia said, with some dryness. "Be careful you do not set her so high on a pedestal that you are both hurt if she falls."

Freddy laughed. "There is no worry of that! Everything she does is perfection. She could not disappoint me if she tried."

Thalia gave up her gentle warning. Freddy would not hear what he did not want to hear.

"By the by," Freddy said, "I've been invited to a salon this Friday evening. Heard that there will be several writers present. Would you like to come with me? I know you've had a bit of a dabble with writing here and there."

A dabble. Thalia clenched her fists. *I have published poems where you only talk of publishing them.* Then she shook herself and unbent her fingers. She was being ungenerous. Freddy was trying to invite her to be part of his life.

"I should be delighted to come," she said, "provided Mrs. Lockhart does not need me."

Thalia did not see Eleanor until they met at dinner that night, just before the cotillion. Eleanor seemed distracted, but Thalia did manage to ask about attending the literary salon Freddy had proposed for Friday.

"I'm sure you would be welcome to come with us," Thalia said.

"We shall see. If nothing else presents itself, I may come. I've never been to a salon."

The two young women readied themselves for the evening separately, Eleanor with the help of her maid, Thalia mostly on her own, though Eleanor's maid peeked in just as Thalia was finishing. She wore a rather simple ivory dress with a single flounce along the hem, and she had pulled her hair up in a knot.

The maid surveyed Thalia's hair critically, teased two curls free to frame her face, and then sent her off to join Eleanor.

The Dollands' cotillion was in full swing when they arrived. After greeting the hosts near the door of the ballroom, Eleanor glanced around the room. A brief flash of fear tightened the muscles surrounding Eleanor's eyes, but as Thalia watched, Eleanor planted a bright smile on her face and said, "There's Anne and Henry!"

Thalia followed Eleanor through the crowd to where the Salisbury siblings were chatting with their mother, a pretty woman in a rather daringly cut silver-and-blue gown.

"Oh, Eleanor," Mrs. Salisbury said, "it is lovely to see you again, child. Anne and Henry have been telling me all about your engagement. I own that it is not quite what I expected, but I am sure it will be . . . delightful. You will be able to chaperone Anne, if she does not take, which will be such a relief to me."

Eleanor pressed her lips together and made no comment. Anne, beside her, grimaced and slid her arm through Eleanor's in a gesture of solidarity that made Thalia like the girl better than she had during their stiff conversation in Eleanor's drawing room.

"Well I, for one, am in no rush to see Anne married off," Henry said cheerfully. "She will have a house with me so long as she likes— I'd much prefer that to having her marry a cursed fool. She can afford to be choosy, and any man would be lucky to have her."

Both Anne and Eleanor smiled at this, though Mrs. Salisbury merely wafted a fan before her face. "Yes, yes. Of course. Only I do worry so. It's a mother's right, is it not?" She smiled appealingly at Thalia, who did not know what to say. Or rather, she *did* have a few things she wanted to say, but thought better of voicing them. A mother's worry she understood, but the way Mrs. Salisbury managed to put down both Eleanor and Anne with her faux thoughtfulness set Thalia's teeth on edge.

"And my dear Miss Aubrey, how is your aunt? She wrote to me some weeks ago, but I am afraid I simply have not had the time to write back."

Thalia was beginning to suspect that Mrs. Salisbury was the type of woman who did not have time for anything that did not bring her immediate pleasure. "She is quite well. She is home in Oxfordshire and enjoying her gardens immensely."

"And her daughter, who married the gentleman with the Indian mother? I know Lady Elphinstone must have been quite relieved to have her daughter married well. Such an odd child."

"My cousin is quite happy," Thalia said, her words sharpening. "Those of us who love Charis do not find her odd, but charming."

"Oh, yes," Mrs. Salisbury said vaguely. She turned back to Eleanor. "And what of your family? I have been asking Henry to tell me more about where your family is from, but he does not seem to know much. The dear boy is not always the most attentive."

Thalia wondered how much commotion she would create if she stabbed Mrs. Salisbury with one of her hairpins.

"I do not know much about my family, ma'am," Eleanor said. "As you may remember, my mother died when I was young, and I do not know who my father is."

"Oh! Well, I suppose it is good that you will bring money into this marriage, if you do not mean to bring a name."

Eleanor said nothing. Her face was pale but calm, scrubbed free of any emotion.

Henry held out his hand. "Eleanor, would you dance with me? A new set is about to start."

Thalia dropped her fingers from her hairpin.

But Eleanor did not take Henry's hand. Instead, she watched his mother for a moment, then shook her head. "I'm sorry. The air in here is rather close, is it not? I think I shall take a turn about the garden."

"I'll come with you," Henry offered.

Eleanor shook her head again. "No need. I would not wish to keep you from the dancing. Why don't you dance with Thalia?" Before either of them could answer, she slipped away through the crowd.

After biting her lip, then casting a furtive glance at her mother, Anne followed.

Henry looked at Thalia. "Well, are you willing to risk a dance?"

"Henry is a most beautiful dancer," Mrs. Salisbury said.

Thalia smiled at Henry. "So I have observed before. I should be happy to dance with you, H—Mr. Salisbury." She tucked her arm through his and followed him to the dance floor.

Henry bent his head toward hers. "I do think you ought to call me Henry. It would be so much easier, now that we're going to see much more of each other."

Thalia willed herself not to blush. "Very well. Then you ought to call me Thalia."

"After the muse of comedy?" Henry said. "Your sister told me that."

See? Thalia thought at the absent Mrs. Salisbury. *He does pay attention.*

"A rather poor muse for me," Thalia said, smiling up at Henry. "My brother will tell you that I have little capacity for humor."

"Is this the same brother I met?" Henry asked. "I must beg to differ: You may not have a bent for farce, but you have a gift for wit. In any case, I am not sure your brother would know humor if it bit him on the nose."

Thalia burst out laughing. It felt good to laugh, though several matrons turned severe looks on her. A young lady did not indulge in emotional outbursts in public.

"I like your laugh," Henry said, smiling at her as he swept her into the set just forming. He was not much taller than she was, but she liked the frank openness with which he met her gaze.

As Thalia had remembered, Henry was a capable dancer, smooth and firm in his leading, without ever making Thalia feel as though she were being dragged across the floor. More than that, though, he was comfortable to be with: They could talk or not talk, and Henry seemed to enjoy both equally.

Thalia only wished that *she* did not enjoy their dance quite so much.

It would never do to form a *tendre* for her employer's fiancé, not to mention her own sister's former suitor. Even if Henry were free, Thalia reminded herself, she did not mean to be distracted from her work a second time by romantic imaginings. Nor was Henry at all the sort of man she'd want to encourage even if she was open to romance—he might be kind, funny, and comfortable, but he was hardly someone who could support a poet. *If* she fell in love again, it would be with someone who understood her work, who challenged her ideas, and who inspired her to be better at her life's calling.

Having thus sensibly enumerated a trio of reasons why she should not find Henry too agreeable, Thalia was able to sink back into the pleasures of dancing with him.

CHAPTER NINE

Eleanor

I am proud of my heart alone, it is the sole source of everything, all our strength, happiness and misery. All the knowledge I possess everyone else can acquire, but my heart is all my own.

—Johann Wolfgang von Goethe, *The Sorrows of Young Werther*

The night air was bracing, and Eleanor drew several long breaths, letting the chill scour her lungs. Music tinkled faintly from the ballroom.

A gentle touch settled on her arm.

"Are you all right?" Anne asked. "My mother was—What she said was inexcusable."

"I'm all right." Eleanor forced herself to smile. She had never thought much of Anne's mother, but it would not help Anne to voice those thoughts. "And you? Are you feeling better than you did this morning?" Was it only that morning? It felt eons ago.

"I—" Anne puffed out a breath. "I don't know. I had hoped that coming to London would lift some of this heavy fog that seems to hang about me, but it has not."

For a brief moment, Eleanor was back in Albert's house (*her* house now, though it seemed strange to think of it), strolling the darkened hallways in increasing anxiety. She twitched, rubbing at her bare forearm.

Anne continued, "Some days I wish I could shed my life as a snake sheds its skin—here, under my mother's shadow, I find it hard to be anyone other than the anxious, unhappy creature my mother believes me to be."

Eleanor grasped Anne's hands. "Let us run away together. Let's travel across Europe, sail to Greece, tour Istanbul. We could travel incognito—no one needs to know who we are." For a moment, the vision unscrolled before her, dazzling and delightful.

Anne laughed lightly and pulled her hands free. "I do not think Henry would like it if you ran away with me."

Henry. Eleanor blinked. Her supposed fiancé. For a moment, she wanted desperately to tell Anne the truth—but Anne was not a great actress, too prone to let her emotions show on her face, and for this to work, for George to believe her truly engaged, Anne would have to believe so too. She would deal with the repercussions later.

"Then let us run away for a night. Perhaps a masquerade? We could don costumes, pretend to be anyone."

"Mama will not allow me to go to a masquerade—she says such things are not suitable for young women."

"Then," Eleanor said, grinning at her friend, "we shall have to sneak out. I do not currently know of any masquerades, but I shall find one, and we shall slip away under cover of night." The prospect sent tiny prickles of anticipation through her, the first such she had felt all evening.

Anne took a long breath, and Eleanor thought she meant to refuse her. Then: "Very well. A masquerade it is!"

A few minutes later, the two young women returned to the ballroom. And though Eleanor danced most of the remaining sets—with

Henry, and then with a succession of men whose names she could not bother to remember—nothing else about the night set her blood pumping as that secret plan had.

Thalia dropped into an open seat beside Eleanor, flushed and smiling from the most recent dance.

"Are you enjoying yourself?" Eleanor asked.

"Tremendously," Thalia said. "But are you sure I am not failing in my duties as a companion? I've hardly kept you company."

Eleanor waved one gloved hand. "It doesn't signify. You're here to lend me countenance, and it hardly seems fair that your only task should be to watch *me* dance." Doubly unfair, since Eleanor had sent half a dozen of her own would-be dance partners on to dance with Thalia.

Their host Mr. Dolland approached them, two gentlemen in his wake. After performing introductions, he left the gentlemen to escort Thalia and Eleanor in to the dance.

The music swirling around Eleanor was beautiful and perfect, but it seemed to rest against her skin without penetrating to her heart. She talked and laughed, but she felt as if she was performing a role.

A small, traitorous part of her brain reminded her that she had told Anne that one's emotions were not biddable, but she brushed that away. The thought of London's glittering *ton* and society parties was the one hope that had pulled her through those long, dark months of mourning. She could not admit, not even to herself, that her happiness was a veneer—a thin gold fabric stretched bright and taut across an empty drum.

The next morning, Eleanor found Thalia already at breakfast, humming an air Eleanor recognized from the cotillion the night before—one of the dances Thalia had danced with Henry.

"Good morning," Eleanor said brightly, helping herself to some toasted bread and spreading a thin layer of marmalade on it.

"Good morning." Thalia smiled up at her. "What plans do we have for today?"

"I have some letters to write this morning, so you may have the time for yourself, though I do hope you will share whatever poems you come up with during that time."

"They will likely be terrible."

"All the more reason to hear them," Eleanor said, and Thalia grinned.

"Are you sure you do not want me to write out the letters for you?"

Eleanor shook her head. "No. I'm afraid I must face this bear down myself."

But half an hour later, staring at an intimidatingly blank piece of paper, Eleanor wondered if she should take Thalia up on her offer.

Mr. Jones's last words echoed in her ears, his refusal to help her. Perhaps she could find someone else in the city who would assist her with Albert's papers, but she didn't want to. She wanted Mr. Jones. That is, she wanted his assistance. She did not know him well, but she had seen his protectiveness of his sister, and she sensed that he was kind. That was what she wanted. Someone kind, who would not laugh if it turned out that Albert had had a higher notion of his abilities than was warranted. Someone who would not laugh at her for knowing so pathetically little of her husband's work. Someone who would not judge her for having married a much older man—because *he* was kind.

But now she had to conjure words out of ink to tell Mr. Jones as much, to persuade him to come back when it was her own relative who had insulted Miss Montgomery.

Dear Mr. Jones—

She paused. The nib of her quill dripped, splattering ink across the rest of the line. Eleanor stuck the quill in the ink pot, crumpled the paper, and drew out a fresh sheet.

I am sorry for the reprehensible behavior the other day of my nephew by marriage. I want you to know that I knew nothing of his actions, that I—

No, that was wrong too. One should not begin an apology by making excuses, even if they happened to be true. She started again.

I am deeply sorry for Mr. Lockhart's actions and for my own part in bringing you in contact again. I have told Mr. Lockhart he is not welcome in my house. I hope his dismissal will make you feel more welcome here—and I would very much like to persuade you again to work for me in presenting my husband's work to the public. Not only do you understand his research, but you seem to have the compassion and generosity I would wish for in someone approaching a dead man's work. Please reconsider.

Before she could rethink her phrasing, Eleanor added her signature, folded up the sheet, and affixed sealing wax to it. She summoned a footman to deliver the letter to a postbox, and then bit her lip to keep herself from calling him back.

Owen's answer returned by the evening post, just as Eleanor was sitting down to dinner.

> *Dear Mrs. Lockhart,*
> *I am flattered by your estimation of my abilities and*
> *character, but unfortunately, my answer remains the*
> *same. I suggest you make inquiries of the Royal Society.*
> *Your sincere well-wisher,*
> *Mr. Owen Jones*

Eleanor read the letter twice before fully comprehending it. She had been so certain that she need only appeal to his good nature, and now his refusal hit her with the force of a blow to the gut.

"Eleanor?" Thalia asked. "Is it bad news?"

Eleanor folded the letter and slid it into her pocket. "It's nothing," she said. "Only an answer I was not expecting."

Tomorrow she would call on Mr. Jones—surely he would not be so quick to refuse her if she made her appeal in person.

The Joneses' jewelry shop was much as Eleanor remembered it: sparkling, mullioned windows, and even more brilliant gems and jewelry arrayed on velvet inside. But when she stepped through the door, she found no familiar faces—only a young woman in a neat apron, standing behind the counter.

"May I help you?" the young woman asked.

"I—" Eleanor's courage abruptly deserted her. "I am looking for something for my friend's birthday." Anne's birthday was not for another four months, but the shopgirl could not know that. Eleanor wished that she had not sent Thalia off on another errand. She had not wanted Thalia to witness her begging, but perhaps she would have felt braver if she was not alone.

The shop assistant asked several questions about her friend, about her age, her tastes. Then she drew Eleanor's attention to several lovely pieces, including a teardrop amethyst on a gold chain, and a delicate cameo of two women. They looked as though they might be sisters—or good friends.

"I'll take the cameo," Eleanor said. The golden brown would look lovely against Anne's coloring, and when she wore it, perhaps she would feel the warmth of Eleanor's regard. As she pushed some bills across the counter toward the girl—Albert would say that paying one's bills promptly was decidedly middle class, but some habits were hard to break—Eleanor asked, "Is Mr. Jones here today?"

The girl wrinkled her nose. "I believe so. Let me just check." She walked to the hallway extending from the main room and shouted, "Mr. Jones!"

A door creaked open, followed by footsteps. Eleanor's pulse picked up.

The middle-aged proprietor poked his head around the corner. "Yes, Sally?"

"Patron was asking for you," the girl said.

Eleanor flushed. "I'm very sorry—I meant Mr. Owen Jones."

Both the shopgirl and Owen's father frowned at her. "Well, then, you should have said so," Sally said, at the same time as Mr. Jones asked, "What do you want Owen for?"

"Is he here?" Eleanor asked.

"He's minding the books," Mr. Jones said. "But you haven't answered my question."

"I was hoping he might help me with a mathematical quandary," Eleanor said.

Mr. Jones raised his eyebrows. "A flash lady like yourself? Surely you have a secretary or some such to help you."

"That's just the thing," Eleanor said, smiling her most winning smile at him. "I haven't any such helpful person, and it would be the greatest favor if I could speak with your son."

Mr. Jones shrugged and disappeared down the hallway.

A few moments later, footsteps sounded again. This time, Eleanor could hear the difference: Owen's footsteps sounded steadier, more solid than his father's.

When Owen Jones appeared, he looked resigned rather than surprised. Eleanor could only suppose that his father had described her to him.

"If you've come regarding that other business," he said, "my answer hasn't changed."

"Please," Eleanor said. "Is there somewhere private we can speak?"

Sally's eyes went wide.

"On business," Eleanor hastened to add.

A glint of something that might have been amusement flickered in Owen Jones's eyes. Eleanor's heart thumped with hope. If he was not too offended to be amused, perhaps she had some chance of persuading him.

Then he sighed. "Very well. Follow me." He led her down the hallway, past a studio where his father was working on some bit of jewelry, to a tiny office. A small desk, covered in documents, filled half the room. On the opposite wall hung two shelves crowded with books and loose scraps of paper.

Mr. Jones followed her gaze around the room. "I own it looks a mess, but I've a system to this—I've not yet lost one of my father's bills or payments."

"I trust you," Eleanor said, realizing as she spoke the words that she meant them. Something about Mr. Jones, big as he was, felt as comfortable as a well-loved quilt.

Mr. Jones straightened a few papers on the corner of the desk. "What is it you wanted to ask me?"

"Will you please reconsider? If not for my sake, then for the sake of my deceased husband and his work. Perhaps there is nothing truly new in his ideas—but if there is, wouldn't you feel ashamed to deny that to the world?"

"My refusal does not deny your husband's work to the world. I am hardly the only mathematician in London." He looked up from his papers, and there was that gleam of amusement in his eyes again. "And appealing to my emotions through a reference to your dead husband was a rather low blow—not to mention obvious. I may be thick, but I am not stupid."

Eleanor's cheeks burned. "I never thought that you were. I'm sorry if my words implied otherwise. If I did not hold your intelligence in great esteem, I would scarcely be asking this favor of you."

"You might find me intelligent but still think me lacking in sense. Unfortunately for you, I possess both, and have the wit enough to refuse. I'm sorry, but knowing who your nephew is, I'm afraid I cannot trust you."

Eleanor nearly stamped her foot in frustration. "George Lockhart is not my nephew, but my husband's. We have nothing in common but our surname."

"And your religion, your wealth, your class, and your nationality," Mr. Jones pointed out.

"You know very well what I mean—that in terms of temperament and ideals, we are nothing alike."

"Then perhaps you should have said as much. I am a fan of frank speaking."

He had said no, Eleanor noted, but had not yet sent her packing. Her hope began rising again. "You do not, I presume, mean the language once spoken by the Franks?"

A grin spread across Mr. Jones's face. Eleanor suspected he was rather reluctant to give room to that emotion, as the grin hitched once or twice. She smiled sunnily back.

"And now you have caught me out in being imprecise in my language as well. Nicely done, Mrs. Lockhart."

"Please, won't you call me Eleanor?" she asked.

A frown shuttered down on his face, wiping out the lingering traces of his grin. "That does not seem appropriate, given the differences in our station."

"What differences?" Eleanor asked. "Because I married a wealthy man and you must earn your living, does that mean we are so very far apart? I mentioned, when I came to your store looking to have my necklace repaired, that my mother had died when I was young. I did not mention that I am the natural daughter of a stranger—my mother never spoke of my father, and no one seems to know who he was, though he paid for my schooling at a private school until I was sixteen."

Mr. Jones's expression softened. "And when you were sixteen?"

Eleanor swallowed, tears pricking the backs of her eyes. "At sixteen the payments stopped, as did my schooling. I had met Albert at the school a few times—he was friends with the mathematics instructor." Albert had caught her crying in the garden after the headmistress told her she would have to find new lodgings and employment, and it had not taken much for Albert to coax the story from her. Eleanor had been educated as befit the daughter of the gentry, with few practical skills. She had no notion what she was to do, where she was to go, or how to provide for herself. Albert's offer of marriage had seemed like a sensible solution for them both: Albert's first wife had died childless a year or so earlier, and he was still hoping for an heir. And Eleanor—Eleanor had desperately wanted the security of a home.

She shook herself. Best not to dwell on the past.

But perhaps Mr. Jones could sense some of what she did not say, because his voice was devastatingly gentle. "That sounds difficult."

Eleanor swallowed. She would *not* cry. "I managed."

"Had you no friends to help you? No other family?"

Anne Salisbury had been her only true friend, the only one to stand by her once her pecuniary situation had been made clear. But Anne had been scarce more than a child herself, wholly dependent upon her mother's caprice, and Mrs. Salisbury had been unwilling to bestir herself for someone who was not her own child. Eleanor had not yet forgiven Mrs. Salisbury for the look she put on Anne's face, when Anne had to say she could not help Eleanor. If Eleanor did not care so much for Henry, she would go through with the marriage just to punish his mother.

Eleanor forced herself to smile. "It was ages ago now. As I said, I managed."

"Ages ago?" Mr. Jones's eyebrows lifted. "If you are more than twenty, I shall eat my hat."

"I am nearly eighteen," Eleanor said.

Mr. Jones studied her for a long moment, his dark eyes warm and searching. Eleanor flushed under his scrutiny, but met his gaze, resolutely ignoring the internal quaking that accompanied this move.

"All right," he said at last. "I will help you."

"You will?" Joy, threaded with relief, was the first emotion that went singing through her. But a cold rush of doubt chased it. "Wait—are you only agreeing to help me because you feel sorry for me? Because if you are, I shall—" *Bite you* did not seem particularly appropriate or dignified. Besides that, curiously, the thought of biting Mr. Jones stirred up a strange sensation that was decidedly *not* vengeful.

"You shall what?" Mr. Jones asked, amusement glimmering in his eyes again.

"I shall do something too terrible to name," Eleanor said, feeling that her threat lacked teeth—both literal and figurative.

Mr. Jones laughed. "Well, you shall not have to do anything very terrible to me. I promise you, I do not feel sorry for you. Say rather, I admire your tenacity."

Eleanor smiled back at him, reassured. Tenacious was all right. Far better than being an object of pity.

"When do you wish me to start?" Mr. Jones asked.

"When can you begin?"

"Monday next, if that is convenient for you?"

Eleanor ignored the tiny dip of disappointment at the day he named, some four days hence. "That will do admirably."

CHAPTER TEN

Thalia

My lady Beatrice sat spinning in her tower,
Surrounded by her maidens, peace filling every hour.
From moor and mount, from town and farm, suitors drew around,
To hear the voice and see the face for which she was renowned.

Daily listened Beatrice to praise and veneration—
Even her unliving shadow garnered adulation—
And wondered that no one could see the soul behind her face.
Until one morn my lady woke to find that in her place
Her shade held court without her—and no suitor marked the trade.

—Thalia Aubrey

"Are you sure you will not come with us?" Thalia asked. Beside her, in the open door, Freddy cleared his throat, ill-concealing his impatience.

Eleanor, standing on the lowest rung of the stairs leading to the second level, smiled at her. "I am sure. I have a touch of a headache, so I shall content myself with some tea and an early bedtime."

Thalia searched Eleanor's face. Eleanor's expression was strained, but the headache could easily explain that. But there was something else—Thalia could not precisely tell what—that sent a thrill of unease up her spine. "You would be most welcome," she said.

"So you have said. But truly, I shall be content at home, dreaming happily by the time you return."

"Thalia," Freddy murmured, and she let the matter drop.

Eleanor had most generously loaned her carriage to the Aubrey siblings, so it was but a few minutes' drive until they reached the town house on Great Russell Street, not far from the British Museum, where the salon was being held. The rooms were above a corner shop, now shuttered for the evening. Lamplight guttered as they passed from the carriage into a shadowy hallway and up a flight of stairs.

Thalia suppressed a flicker of misgiving: This was not a fancy *ton* party in a well-lit mansion, with footmen waiting to open the doors and escort them into the room. She clutched at Freddy's arm. "Where have you brought us?"

"You'll see," Freddy said, grinning back at her as he climbed the stairs. "I can promise you this—the gathering tonight will be more engaging than any of your stuffy society parties."

Thalia did not want to imagine what Freddy might find more engaging, but already her brain was throwing lurid images at her: scenes of debauchery and wine, cards and cigars. She shook herself. Freddy might be a harum-scarum, scatterbrained young man, but he was not so lost to propriety as to bring his sister to a bacchanal.

On the landing, Freddy knocked at a door. It was flung open, releasing golden light and warm laughter into the dim stairway. Freddy was hailed almost at once and drawn into the room by an untidy, cherub-faced young man Thalia did not recognize.

Thalia hesitated at the entrance. The interior was full of candlelight and shifting bodies and laughter. She felt all the awkwardness of entering a space where she knew no one save her brother. Freddy's assurance that they were welcome suddenly seemed a rather thin support.

As voices rose and fell around her, Thalia squared her shoulders. The men and women gathered might not wear the finery of the *ton*, but they appeared respectable, clustered together in cozy groups on comfortable-looking chairs and couches, talking in animated fashion over and about one another. She had nothing to fear here but her own insecurities.

Though Thalia did not recognize anyone, Freddy had promised there were other authors present. This was part of the literary world she meant to enter. Last season, the literary circles of London had felt like James's circles, and it had taken her nearly a twelvemonth to feel that *she* might have some claim to them as well.

Only, what to do now? She supposed she might follow Freddy to his corner, but that seemed odious: She hated playing the part of the trailing little sister.

While she stood dithering, an older woman with dark curls framing a round face approached her and drew her gently into the apartment before shutting the door behind her. "Good evening, my dear, and welcome. I don't believe we have met. I'm Mary Lamb."

Thalia stared at her. "Not—not Mary Lamb, the authoress of *Tales from Shakespeare*?"

The woman smiled. "The very same. Are you familiar with the stories?"

"My father used to read them to me as a child." Just as he now read them to Edward and Urania. "I was—am—very fond of them."

"That's kind of you to say. And you are?"

Thalia flushed. She'd been so struck at meeting an author she admired that she'd forgotten the most basic of manners. "I am Thalia Aubrey. I came here with my brother Frederick." She nodded toward Freddy, now deep in a coterie of young men, their cheeks and eyes bright as they argued.

"Well, you are very welcome. We are an informal group here, so you needn't bother with introductions and the like. There are some refreshments on the far table, though they are rather plain: just bread and cheese and good English beer."

"Sometimes the simple pleasures are the best," Thalia said, earning another smile from her hostess.

"I quite agree. Now, do you know any of our party?"

When Thalia shook her head, Miss Lamb began to point out some of the attendees: Her brother, Charles, was the rather spare man talking to a musician. The cluster of young men around Frederick included Leigh Hunt, who had a head full of curls and an expressive mouth and was the editor of the *Examiner*; as well as a rather intense-looking man with unkempt hair, somewhat older than the others.

"William Hazlitt the essayist, you know," Miss Lamb said, and Thalia thrilled because she did, indeed, know. She had been sorry her arrival in London was too late to hear the lectures he had given on the English poets at the Surrey Institution. The newspapers had suggested they were brilliant, if sometimes controversial because of his politics.

"And the young man beside your brother is Mr. John Keats."

Another thrill darted through Thalia. "But I know him! That is, I don't know him, but I have read some of his work. Did not Mr. Hazlitt call him one of three young poets to watch?"

"I believe that was Mr. Hunt, but yes."

Thalia winced. She had meant to appear so informed, and already she was mistaking her authors. Still—these men were real writers and poets, artists whose work appeared in magazines and books that Thalia had read. In fact, Mr. Keats's newest book, *Endymion*, lay in all its new-book splendor on her bedside table. The opening lines came back to her:

> *A thing of beauty is a joy for ever:*
> *Its loveliness increases; it will never*
> *Pass into nothingness.*

His words carried a depth and mood that hers still seemed to lack, though he could not be above three or four years older than she. True, the poem was not always consistent, but there were glimmers of brilliance that she envied.

"Would you like to meet him?" Miss Lamb asked. Without waiting for an answer, she took Thalia's unresisting arm and led her across the room. Catching snippets of conversations as they passed, Thalia could not help thinking that for all James's proud insistence that he was part of the literary heart of London, he had never introduced her to so many luminaries in one room. The poets of James's circle were aspiring poets—these were *published* poets.

Mr. Keats was speaking as they drew near. "I admit that Wordsworth has written some fine passages, but should we be bullied into accepting the philosophy of an egotist because of that? Poetry should be great and unobtrusive—a thing which enters into one's soul and does not startle it or amaze it with itself, but with its subject."

"Hear! Hear!" said Mr. Hazlitt, raising a glass of amber liquid. "Though when I tried to say as much in my lecture, I thought the crowd was liable to tear me from the stage. Our good host did not approve." He cast a swift glance toward Charles Lamb.

Next to Freddy, Mr. Hunt said, "And yet, you were bitter not to be invited to dine with Mr. Wordsworth last time he visited the Lambs, were you not?"

Mr. Hazlitt pointed an angular chin at Miss Lamb. "I was sorry to have been left out, yes, but not on Wordsworth's account. It was entirely the food and good company I missed."

"Your poetry is not unobtrusive—that is not to say it lacks merit, only we do not always need to be obvious," Mr. Keats said to Mr. Hunt, and the young men were off again, speaking across one another in ways that made it hard for Thalia to follow them, though she did admire their energy.

Freddy, at last, seemed to notice Thalia. To his credit, a faint color swept across his cheekbones as he realized his abandonment of her. In the first pause in the conversation, he said, "Gentlemen, may I present my sister Miss Thalia Aubrey. A poetess in her own right."

"Oh?" Mr. Hunt said, looking interested. "Have you published anything?"

"A few poems only," Thalia said, then pressed her lips together in vexation. This was not the company in which to make light of her gifts—she did not think any of these men would admire her more for being modest. Miss Lamb pressed her arm once in reassurance and then drifted away.

"I do not believe I've heard of you," Mr. Keats said, "though I do not mean to fault you for that. My own first volume of poetry dropped into obscurity nearly at once through the ineptitude of my publishers. I am indebted to friends who continued to trust in me."

Thalia smiled uncertainly, not sure if the second part of his statement robbed the first part of its sting.

Mr. Hazlitt said, "Let us pray your newest work does not do the same—the *Quarterly Review* does not think highly of it."

"It's easier to say what poetry should or should not be than to write it," Keats said, shrugging dismissively.

"Do you mean *Endymion*?" Thalia asked. "I have not finished it, but I am enjoying the poem so far."

Mr. Hazlitt laughed. "The reviewer did not finish it either!"

Ignoring Mr. Hazlitt's dig, Keats turned to her eagerly. "Are you? And what do you like about it?"

Feeling a trifle caught-out, as she had not yet decided what she thought about the poem, but had only meant to make Mr. Keats less uncomfortable, Thalia said, "The words are very evocative—there is a great deal of feeling and vivid imagery." The same might be said of almost any poem. These men must think her a fool.

"It's not merely feeling," Freddy said, "it's pure sensation. Reading your poem, one feels transported back to a freer, purer time, where men and nature existed together in perfect harmony."

Did such a time even exist? Thalia wondered, but she held her tongue.

But Mr. Keats appeared to see nothing wrong in Freddy's statement. "Precisely! We are moving away from the current school of poetry, which concerns itself too much with the politics of the moment, and back to an older epoch when poetry was more manly, more sensitive to the beauty of the external world. Poetry ought to be an expression of the truth that is beauty, not about the worldly concerns of men."

Thalia could feel a frown gathering again and tried to smooth it away. Mr. Keats was a far more experienced poet than she was, but what did he mean, to suggest poetry should be *manly*?

"Yes," Freddy said, clapping Mr. Keats on the back. "You've mastered that truth brilliantly in your work."

"Careful," Mr. Hunt said dryly, "or you'll give Mr. Keats a head so big he will not fit through the doorway tonight."

"It's not about my vanity," Mr. Keats said. "It's about the work. About beauty finding expression through words. About simplicity of form and earnest, rustic strength. I believe we have lost that strength in England today, in our arts and poetry, and we must recapture it."

Thalia's question burst from her. "Must poetry always capture strength? Must it always be manly? What then of the poetess? If women are seen as neither manly nor strong, are we therefore already doomed to second place in the annals of literature, as we are similarly condemned in society?"

Drat. She should not have said that. For a moment the four men stared at her. Then Mr. Keats said, "I suppose a female poet should concern herself with what is feminine. Whether or not her work is second-rate depends on the quality."

Thalia struggled inwardly for a moment. She desperately wanted the approval of these men, which she would not earn by challenging them—what man liked to be challenged by a woman? But they were wrong. A rising sense of injustice burned through her. She tried to keep her voice steady. "And what do you suppose a feminine subject is?"

"How should I know?" Keats asked. "Do I look like a woman?" His friends laughed.

Freddy, perhaps trying to help her, said, "Oh, domestic scenes and the like. Children and home and hearth. You know."

The burning inside her grew hotter. "So a poet, if he is a man, has the whole spectrum of human experience before him: history, myth, love, war, science, art. He might even write about the domestic, as Wordsworth has done. But a female poet must confine herself only to what is deemed feminine? How is that fair?"

"A woman's experience is not so broad as a man's," Keats said, in such a reasonable tone that she wanted to hit him. "How does one write about that which one has not experienced?"

"Such as Greek myths?" Thalia asked sweetly, then, when Keats flushed, wished she had bitten her tongue. *Endymion* was drawn from such a myth, the story of a handsome shepherd beloved by the moon goddess.

Freddy glared at her. "Myths are only exterior trappings for deeper truths—it is the truth of the myth that matters, not the actual story."

Mr. Hazlitt said, "What does it signify, so long as the words are good and the sensations evoked real?"

And with that, her argument was dismissed. The discussion moved on to Mr. Hunt's current work. Thalia blinked back a sudden sharp stinging in her eyes. Not one of them understood what she meant; not one of them had *tried* to understand what she meant.

Perhaps Mr. Hazlitt was right. She would have to ensure that her words stood on their own merit. But a small part of her still wondered: If her work was judged against a "manly" standard, would she ever be able to meet it? Her very sex would work against her.

She slipped away from the poets, to join Miss Lamb and her brother, listening to a discussion of music until it was time to go.

"Was that not amazing?" Freddy enthused as their carriage pulled away from the Lambs' rooms. "Such brilliance! Such energy!"

Thalia brushed raindrops from her sleeves and stifled a sigh. She would not spoil Freddy's enjoyment of the evening with her own misgivings. "Yes. The Lambs were very kind to have invited us."

"Oh, 'twas not the Lambs. I happened upon Mr. Hunt some time back and he invited me. Said the Lambs would not mind."

He invited me. Thalia swallowed a twinge. At this rate, she would have indigestion from all the things she could not say, all the things she would not allow herself to feel. She *was* glad to have gone, to have met so many writers. She would not regret it simply because *she* had not been formally invited.

Freddy leaned back in his seat and looked at her. "You were fairly pert, though, Thalia. What got into you? Why would you challenge Mr. Keats before his friends like that?"

She had been *pert?* Not, *The men were dismissive of women's writing?* "I did not mean to be rude," she said, as evenly as she could. "I was merely trying to understand the standards they set for poetry."

"Well, you are lucky they are the understanding sort. Mr. Hazlitt thought you showed good spirit."

Thalia could not decide whether this was flattering or insulting.

Eleanor's coachman dropped Freddy off before his hotel, then swept Thalia home.

Thalia darted from the carriage to the door, rain splattering against her exposed skin.

At her knock, the door was opened by the butler, wearing a dressing gown and holding up a lantern. She entered, shaking water from her skirts. "Good evening, Mr. Davis. Thank you for waiting up for me. How is Mrs. Lockhart? Has her headache improved?"

Mr. Davis twitched his mustache. "I presume so. She went out, some two hours past."

"Out?" Thalia echoed, bewildered and a trifle alarmed. "But she said she was unwell, that she meant to rest. Where could she have gone?"

"I really couldn't say, Miss Aubrey. No one seems to have seen her leave. Her absence was only discovered when her maid went to help her dress for bed."

Something about this was ringing all the alarm bells in Thalia's head. Had Eleanor slipped out past dark in secret? Why should Eleanor feel the need to hide her actions? Thalia tried to calm herself: Eleanor was a grown woman, and her employer besides. She had not hired Thalia to be her minder.

Still. She would sleep better if she knew where Eleanor had gone. Perhaps Miss Salisbury would know.

"Can you rouse one of the footmen, Mr. Davis? I should like to send a note," Thalia said.

"Very good, ma'am." Mr. Davis's eyebrows drew together in disapproval, but he did not refuse her.

While Mr. Davis went to wake the unfortunate messenger, Thalia scribbled a quick letter to Anne Salisbury. Pray heaven she knew where Eleanor was, and that it was only a little mischief she was into, and not some great trouble.

CHAPTER ELEVEN

Eleanor

*'Tis an old observation, and a very true one; but what's to be done, as I said before?
how will you prevent people from talking?*

—Richard Brinsley Sheridan, *The School for Scandal*

At precisely 9:40 p.m., on an overcast Friday evening in late April, Eleanor Lockhart slipped unnoticed from the servants' exit of her own town house, as if she were a thief. Her heart certainly pounded as though she were.

It was exhilarating.

Eleanor stood for a moment in the darkened mews behind the house. She adjusted the folds of the black domino that she wore over her costume, an elaborate gold brocade gown with a pointed ruff collar protruding above the cape. She had teased a red-gold wig into a crown about her face, and the satchel she carried bore an actual crown to be donned later for her role as Queen Elizabeth. Her fingertips brushed the edge of the mask she wore, still secure over her upper face.

When she was sure she would not be recognized by any member of her household, she made her way from the mews toward Curzon Street. She garnered a few curious looks, but it was the height of the season, and a masquerading woman was not so unusual.

"Where to, lady?" one particularly adventuresome gentleman asked. "I would follow you, and you would let me."

Eleanor only smiled—she hoped enigmatically, like the *Mona Lisa*. She wished she could have a witty repartee that conveyed her disapproval at being addressed so familiarly while still remaining aloof. Still, it was nice to know that she looked well.

She had not gone more than a block or two when she came upon what she was looking for: a hansom cab to take her to Anne Salisbury's, and then on to their destination.

As prearranged, Anne was waiting for her on the corner, a few houses down from the home she shared with her mother and brother. Like Eleanor, she wore a domino and mask. Unlike Eleanor, her domino was white, setting off her strawberry-blond curls. Beneath the domino she wore a red velvet gown encrusted with paste pearls along the bodice and stomacher, as Queen Elizabeth's cousin and sometime rival, Mary, Queen of Scots.

It was just beginning to spit rain as Anne climbed into the vehicle, and Anne shook a couple of diamond-like drops from her hair.

Once Anne was secure in the carriage, it was but a short drive to the Argyll Rooms where the masquerade was being held. It was pure luck that Eleanor had overheard two gentlemen speaking of the masquerade at the Dollands' cotillion, just after promising Anne she would find one. This was precisely the sort of thing to lift Anne's spirits, and a masquerade held among the *ton* would not have the atmosphere of the more scandalous romps that sometimes overtook Vauxhall Gardens, with their more liberal admissions. A romp would only make Anne more anxious, not less.

Once Eleanor knew about the masquerade, it had been easy enough to send Thalia off on an errand while she procured the tickets to the ball. The man at the Argyll Rooms had seemed surprised at her purchasing the tickets herself: No doubt he was more accustomed to seeing a footman dispatched for such errands. But Eleanor did not want any of her servants to know where she had gone—largely because she did not want to risk Thalia getting word and relaying it to Henry, who might try to stop them. Or worse, join them.

But also, she admitted to herself, the secretive, almost illicit nature of her errand made it much more exciting.

Anne's eyes sparkled behind her mask. "I am so glad you arranged this, Eleanor. I have been anticipating it all day! Do you suppose we shall dance much?"

"I am confident you shall dance every dance, if you wish it," Eleanor said. "And there was no trouble with the gown?" She had ordered the costume for Anne, knowing that it would cause questions were Anne to try to do so herself.

"None. It fits like a dream, and the courier delivered it directly to me, just as you instructed. Mama knows nothing about it."

"And Henry?"

"He has no idea either! I told him the package was comprised of ladies' underthings, and he lost interest immediately." Anne's smile deepened, revealing a dimple much like her brother's.

Eleanor laughed.

The coachman helped them dismount from the carriage and agreed to return at half past midnight. Eleanor and Anne darted up the stairs to the doorway as the rain was coming on heavier now, gave their tickets to the doorman, and entered the famed Argyll Rooms, which had once belonged to the Duke of Argyll.

The entrance featured high Corinthian columns and gilt lamps, and past the entrance were a series of smaller supper rooms, and beyond that the ballroom, with its three tiers of boxes and a stage at the far end. Red-velvet-covered benches lined the walls where there were no boxes, and eight elaborate glass chandeliers sparkled overhead.

The ballroom was moderately full, though it was still early. Anne pointed out, with delight, that the gentlemen outnumbered the ladies nearly three to one.

"We shall not have to sit out a single dance!"

Curious, Eleanor thought. Admittedly, she had not been in London long, but she had not attended a single society event with such a composition. But then, she had not yet been to the races—presumably gentlemen outnumbered ladies there too.

Assailed by a sudden qualm, though she could not say why, Eleanor found herself longing for a glass of ratafia or punch to fortify her courage. She led Anne through the ballroom, conscious of the eyes following them and the low murmurs of approval, and back to one of the supper rooms—a lovely space with gray-papered walls and scarlet curtains—where they found a table, covered with a dainty white cloth and groaning under the weight of a punch bowl and various hors d'oeuvres.

Eleanor secured a glass of champagne from an attendant and felt her worries lift as the liquid settled inside her. There was nothing to be afraid of. Likely, it was the presence of so many masks that had given her a temporary sense of danger. A mask could make anyone seem strange: Even Anne, whose face she knew almost as well as her own, had an uncanny, almost fey appearance, her blue eyes glittering behind the lace-edged mask.

The young women made their way back to the ballroom just as an orchestra on the stage began playing the opening strains to a waltz. Eleanor looked at Anne, feeling a faint blush rise in her. The waltz had been considered too fast for her country town when she was a girl, and even now, a waltz could only be danced at Almack's if one had the patronesses' approval. Eleanor shook herself: Hang needing approval. Why should she suddenly feel like a fussy matron who needed to guard Anne's respectability? It was only a dance, and it *was* danced at Almack's.

Before long, two gentlemen were bowing over their hands, requesting the dance. Anne's partner was the shorter of the two, with a wide gleaming smile. Eleanor's partner was taller and thinner, with brown hair curling above his mask. He wore no costume beneath his domino but instead elegant evening clothes.

They took their places in the circle forming on the floor, and then her partner rested his right arm lightly across her shoulders and took her right hand in his left. As they spun into the figures of the dance, his right arm moved to the small of her back, and Eleanor caught her breath.

She was not used to being held so close by a man. Even Albert had not generally done so, though they had danced together a mere handful of times before he had fallen ill. Eleanor nearly bowed out of the dance. The closeness left her feeling exposed and vulnerable.

Eleanor glanced across at Anne, who was laughing, and steeled herself. She was doing this for Anne. She would not ruin the night for her friend.

Her partner was speaking. "Are you enjoying the dance, Miss—?" His eyes, behind an elaborate silver mask that covered three-quarters of his face, were a pale blue. His voice was husky and rough, as though he had just recovered from a cold. Or was he trying to disguise his voice?

She smiled, though her lips felt stiff. "I will not be caught so easily, sir. Is not the point of a masquerade one's anonymity?"

He returned her smile smoothly. "I apologize. Social habits are hard to overcome. And yet there is something familiar about you. I fancy I could put a name to you if I tried."

Something cold slithered through her, and she tried to shake it off. After all, what did it matter if someone recognized her? "You have me at an advantage then, sir. I do not believe I know you. But it seems rather unsporting of you to try and unmask me."

"You are quite right." He spun her through another circle of the dance, his hand still hot at her waist. "Let me compliment you instead on your costume—Elizabeth, is it? The Virgin Queen. A brave choice for this company."

Eleanor nearly stumbled, her face heating. Her glance swept the room. There were a dozen or more couples in their circle, and more watching as they chatted or sipped glasses of champagne. "This company? Are you suggesting, sir, that this society is not respectable? Is that not presumptuous, as you also are here?"

He deftly shifted positions, raising their linked hands above their heads. "Ah, but I never claimed to be respectable." He paused a moment, then asked, "Do you?"

Eleanor disliked the direction of this conversation. "I—if you please, I'd rather discuss something else."

Her partner was quiet for a moment, then said, "Your friend is rather lovely. Who is she meant to be?"

"My cousin Mary, Queen of Scots. We meant it in jest, as we are rather better friends than those two were."

"You do not, then, intend to behead her when the night is over?"

At this, Eleanor did laugh. A rush of gratitude filled her, that her partner had sensed some of her discomfort and worked to assuage it, and that she could, after all, still find enjoyment in this room crowded with strangers.

"No, indeed," Eleanor said. "That would be a rather sad loss for both of us."

"Queen Mary," her partner said musingly, his eyes following Anne for a moment. "Now there was a woman who enjoyed the company of men."

And just like that, Eleanor's brief moment of enjoyment shattered. She should leave this man on the floor, embarrass him before the assembled company for his audacity. Two things stopped her. First, the certainty that should she do so, Anne would also interrupt her dance to find out what had happened. Second, she doubted that this man could feel shame, so it would be a wasted action on her part.

"Because we happen to be dressed a certain way does not give you license to imagine crude things about us, sir. Pray confine your remarks to unremarkable topics."

Her partner bobbed his head. "You ask a great deal—it is hard to confine myself to unremarkable things when the woman in my arms is rather remarkable."

Eleanor sighed. She was just going to have to endure the dance.

At least he kept his hands confined to their proper positions during the movements of the set. His silly words she would simply have to ignore. "I am no more remarkable than any other woman living, and it reflects poorly on your judgment to presume to know so much about me upon a ten minutes' acquaintance."

"Perhaps," he said, and a tiny smile played about his thin lips.

He had thought she looked familiar. *Did* he know who she was? Her gaze snagged on the brown curls at his crown. She did not think she knew any men of this height and build with that coloring, at least not well. Not Freddy or Henry, certainly, nor Mr. George Lockhart. Owen was as tall, but he was broader, and his hair was darker, and she could not imagine him at a ball like this. Though perhaps her partner wore a wig, as she did.

The dance drew, at last, to an end, and Eleanor's partner bowed before her. She scarcely knew what she said as she tugged her hand away, already searching the room for Anne.

But it was Anne who found her, drawing up in a whirl of brocade, her cheeks prettily flushed. "Oh, Eleanor! Is this not magical?"

Before Eleanor could answer, her former partner was bowing before Anne. "May I have this dance?" His bow was the picture of elegance, and Eleanor could see Anne melting before it.

Now there was a woman who enjoyed the company of men. The man's words echoed in Eleanor's head. She remembered the way he had looked so admiringly at her friend. "Anne—" she began, but Anne was already moving away from her, her fingers resting on the stranger's arm.

Eleanor tried to follow Anne, but another man stepped in front of her. This one was not so tall as her former partner, but broader, dressed in a vaguely Roman toga that revealed an uncomfortable expanse of chest, covered in dark hair beginning to gray. His laurel leaf wreath tipped drunkenly over one ear. She tried to skip around him, but he moved with her, listing a bit. His crown, she realized, was not the only drunken thing about him.

"Where are you off to, pretty lady?"

"If you please, I must reach my friend—"

One thick hand closed around her arm. "Am I not good enough? I would be a friend to you—a very good friend."

Eleanor wrinkled her nose. "I beg your pardon, but I really must—"

His other hand encircled her waist, drawing her to him so that her front was pressed against his belly. He smelled of sweat and brandy. He swung her around, not quite in time with the music, and she stumbled after him, struggling to stay on her feet. She tried to break away, but his grip was too strong.

She thought of Mr. Jones suddenly, and wished he were here. He was bigger even than this man, but he would not mistreat a lady. Eleanor kicked out with one slippered foot. The man did not even appear to register her kick, but her toes began to throb.

They were not, she realized suddenly, moving into the throng of dancers, but toward the curtains flanking the stage, where the lights were dimmer.

"Unhand me, sir," she said.

"Oh, you mustn't play coy," the man said. "It's not attractive at a dance like this. Won't send the right message."

"It sends exactly the right message," Eleanor said, feeling more exasperated than frightened. "I would like you to let go of me."

She craned her head around to try to see Anne, but her cursed ruff prevented her from turning her head more than a few inches and then her assailant jerked her forward and she fell against his stomach. He dropped a rather wet kiss on her cheek, having aimed for—and missed—her lips.

Eleanor brought her foot down, as hard as she could, on the instep of his boot.

Startled, the man loosened his grip on her, and Eleanor pulled free. "Hey, what'd you do that for?"

Eleanor spun away, her brocade skirts *shushing*, eluding his fumbling reach for her. She slipped past clusters of men ringing the dance floor, still trying to spy Anne. Was it the masks that made everyone suddenly so much more forward? Or the abundantly flowing punch and champagne? Perhaps they should not have come.

There was Anne, flowing through the steps of the dance like grace incarnate. Her partner bent to whisper something to her, and Anne dimpled up at him.

Well, at least one of them was enjoying this ball. Eleanor caught a glimpse of white and turned to see the toga-clad man stumbling along the edges of the room. Best to escape his notice for a while, she thought, and beat a hasty retreat from the ballroom toward one of the supper rooms.

Once in the safety of the hallway, she began to breathe a bit easier. Laughter echoed from one of the card rooms, along with distinctly masculine cursing. In an alcove along the hallway, a couple were engaged in strenuous kissing. Eleanor averted her eyes, feeling rather shocked at the open display, and then feeling frustrated with herself, because such shock only betrayed her own country naivety. And she had wanted to appear so smart in London.

Eleanor passed a woman laughing up at a gentleman, and blinked. The woman's white cambric dress was nearly sheer—had she *dampened* it? Eleanor had heard of such things but had never witnessed it. She had thought that such behavior was more in line with the demimonde—those expensive mistresses that gentlemen were widely known to keep—than with polite society.

But then, apparently there was much about society that she was still learning.

In the supper room, Eleanor found a tray of pastries that melted in her mouth in a swoon-worthy burst of butter and golden crust. She had just selected her third when a voice sounded at her ear.

"I admit, I came into this room looking for something to eat, but I did not imagine I would find anything so delectable as you, my dear."

Eleanor stiffened. Where *did* these men get their affrontery?

She turned, slowly, to find yet another man beside her. This one was neither tall, nor short, but rather middling, with hair neither blond nor brown. Forgettable, if his speech had not been so laughable.

"Do you go in for cannibalism, then?" she asked, hoping the question would offend him into leaving her alone.

Undeterred, the man laughed and said, "A wit! I do like a woman with wit. A witty woman." And he laughed again.

"That is rather unfortunate," Eleanor said, backing away from the table. "Witty women, as a rule, tend to prefer wit in their gentlemen."

Her tongue was going to get her in trouble one of these days. She should not have said anything at all—better not to engage, but leave at once and find Anne. But perhaps he had not understood her.

No—there was that flash in his eyes, a tightening of his lips beneath his mask. "Do you insult me?" he asked, stepping toward her so that she was forced to back up again.

Don't engage. Eleanor tried to sidestep the middling man, but he was quicker than she was, being unencumbered by ridiculous skirts. He pushed forward until he had her backed against the wall, continuing, "You, who are no better than you should be?"

Eleanor's resolve to stay silent evaporated.

"I think you forget yourself," Eleanor said. "I am a lady, and you should at least pretend to be a gentleman."

He laughed again, and this time there was nothing humorous about the sound. "You may call yourself whatever you like, but I assure you there are no ladies here." He thrust out his hands, thumping them on the wall on either side of her head.

Eleanor tried to duck beneath the block of his arms, but between her stiff ruff and heavy dress, she could not do it. The man shoved one hand beneath her chin and forced her head up.

"I shall have to teach you not to insult me," he said, sliding a finger along her chin. Eleanor shivered. "But I do admit I find the prospect exciting."

She had to get out of there. She would find Anne and beg her to leave, no matter how much Anne was enjoying the dance. There was something wrong with this place, with these men. It did not matter that their coach would not return for an hour or more—they would walk the streets until they found another cab, even if the rain ruined their expensive gowns.

Though would that not be, perhaps, as risky as the ball had proven to be?

The middling man traced her upper lip with his thumb.

Eleanor thought, for a fractional second, about biting him. But she did not want to sink her teeth into a stranger's pink flesh.

Instead, she kneed him between the legs.

CHAPTER TWELVE

Thalia

Some men wear masks of gilded satin
To hide their faces as they play.
Some men wear masks of iron,
To cover their hearts in shades of gray.
But you wear a mask of light and smiles,
To fend all nearing souls away.

—Thalia Aubrey

A light tap at the drawing room door brought Thalia to her feet, but it was not the messenger returning with a note from Anne Salisbury.

It was Henry Salisbury himself.

Though not Henry as she had ever seen him before. His hair appeared its usual, well-behaved self, but Henry seemed to have dressed at random: unexceptional trousers of a cream color, with the most lurid pink coat she had ever seen. The shoulders were padded to excess, and it did not seem at all the thing for a polite visit.

Thalia shook herself. "Henry! Why have you come all this way? A note would have sufficed."

"Anne is missing."

Thalia stared at him, her heart falling. "Missing?" She had been so sure that Anne would know where Eleanor was. No, that was still true. Anne undoubtedly *did* know where Eleanor was; they were likely together. Though where that should be, Thalia had no idea.

"She went to bed early, claiming a headache. When your note came, I went to rouse her, and found her bed had not been slept in. A search of the house did not reveal her." Henry stalked to the mantle, where a few embers still burned in the grate.

"Where could they have gone?" Thalia asked.

Henry slammed his hand against the mantle—a most un-Henry-like move that made Thalia jump. "Damn it! Do you think I would be here, dragging you into this, if I knew?"

Thalia blinked. "I'm sorry that I cannot magically tell you where they are. What do you want me to do?"

"I want you to think!" Henry gripped his hair with one hand. "I cannot seem to think at all."

Something about the plaintive note in his words softened her irritation. Henry was not angry, but frightened for his sister, and lashing out in that fear. Suddenly, she wanted to put her arms around him, an urge so overwhelming that for a moment she could not seem to breathe.

She drifted closer to him. "It will be all right, Hen—Mr. Salisbury. Eleanor and Anne are likely together. Perhaps it is not so bad—only a bit of mischief."

Henry whirled to face her, his cheeks pale. "And what if it is not only mischief? What if something has happened to them?"

"Then we shall find them," Thalia said soothingly, setting her hand on Henry's arm, feeling the muscles of his forearm bunch as his fingers clenched and unclenched.

Henry shook her hand off. "Please don't touch me."

Thalia's face burned, the heat scalding to the top of her head. "I'm sorry. I only meant to help." *Think.* Henry did not need or want her emotions.

"Did none of your servants see anything?"

"No, none." Henry turned back toward the fire, scuffing one booted toe against the carpet.

"No one saw Eleanor leave either. Whatever they are doing, it must be something they imagined we would protest. That rules out the usual society events: the opera, the theater, any private balls or musicales. Did anything unusual happen in the last few days—did Anne receive a message of some sort that she tried to hide?"

The tense line of Henry's shoulders softened as Thalia reasoned out loud. "She did receive a package that she would not let me see. Said it was ladies' undergarments." He turned back to Thalia, his eyes narrowing. "The box was rather a large one. I assumed it was a dress, until she said otherwise."

"Hmm. If it were an ordinary dress, she would have had no objection to showing you. Perhaps she and Eleanor have donned men's clothing and gone to see a cockfight? Or some such?"

Henry rubbed a hand across his face. "God forbid. But no— Anne cannot abide the sight of blood, and Eleanor, for all her faults, is a loyal friend. I cannot see her risking anything truly scandalous that might tarnish Anne's reputation."

"Such as sneaking out alone at night?" Thalia asked.

"They are not alone, and Eleanor may claim that her widowed status makes her companion enough. No, I think we may discard the theory of men's clothing."

"A costume, perhaps?" Thalia asked. "Or a domino?"

"Do you think they've gone to Vauxhall?"

"In this weather? They'd have a rather miserable go of it, I'd think."

"But where else could they—" Henry broke off. "Is Eleanor's driver here?"

"Yes, I believe so." Thalia sent a maid to fetch the driver and watched Henry pace the room as they waited.

When the driver, a stout middle-aged man, appeared, Henry asked him if he'd taken Eleanor or any of the servants to the Argyll Rooms that week.

"Aye, I took Mrs. Lockhart," the man said. "She stopped only a minute."

"Oh, Lord," Henry said. He looked at Thalia. "I think I know where they went."

"A Cyprian's ball?" Thalia asked, once they were settled in Henry's carriage and rattling down the streets. "I'm afraid I don't know what that is."

Gaslight striped through the window. Henry wouldn't meet her eyes.

"A Cyprian is—well, a woman who—dash it, Miss Aubrey, I don't think I ought to be explaining that to you." Was Henry blushing?

"If I am about to be surrounded by such women, I dashed well think you can," Thalia said. "If you mean to say mistress, you might as well say so. No need to be mealymouthed about it."

"I mean—I did not know if young ladies were taught such things."

"We are not *taught* such things, precisely," Thalia said, a wicked part of her enjoying Henry's discomfort, "but one does hear things. Are young men taught them?"

This time, Henry was definitely blushing. He didn't answer her question. "Miss Aubrey, I must apologize for my behavior earlier." He sat very stiff and formal.

"You were worried for Anne," Thalia said.

"That is no excuse. I have never in my life behaved so unmannerly before a lady."

Thalia frowned. "Not even as a child? I used to fight something dreadful with my siblings."

Henry shook his head. "Mama didn't like it."

Thalia could imagine such a childhood: a quiet, restrained thing, stripped of any of the joy and fun and, yes, occasional fights, that should have filled it. Her heart ached. "We are friends, are we not, Mr. Salisbury? You do not have to pretend with me."

"Don't I?" There was a rather wistful note to his voice.

"No, indeed. In fact, it is rather refreshing to know that you too have a temper. My sisters tell me I have an abominable one."

"Would that temper add to my reputation as a gentleman?"

"Perhaps not. But you got angry, and you apologized. It's all right to be angry sometimes."

"I am not certain that it is. To expose our friends to such callous, unthinking behavior? How can it ever be acceptable?"

Thalia peered at him. She could not quite read his expression in the intermittent light of the streets. "Do you believe I might think less of you because you were angry?"

"Don't you?"

Thalia spoke slowly, working out her thoughts. "I find I am often the angriest with people I—" She stopped. *With people I love.* "With those I am most comfortable around, because it is safe to show my feelings, because they will still care for me despite my flaws. I said we were friends, did I not? True friends value one another for who they are, not simply what they do. An occasional disagreement will not make me think less of you—unless you think less of me, knowing that I have a temper?"

"No, of course not. How could I?"

"You do not have to be perfect, you know."

"I wish you would tell that to my mother," Henry muttered, dropping his head back against the seat. He sat up almost at once. "Please pretend you did not hear that."

"Hear what?" Thalia asked, trying to keep her voice light, as, for the second time that night, her heart cracked for Henry Salisbury. She had always taken him for a genial, rather amusing fellow—the consummate gentleman, but with little behind his pleasing manners.

But she, of all people—she, who meant to be a writer and a student of human nature—should know that people did not always match the facade they presented to the world.

The rain had mostly stopped by the time they reached the Argyll Rooms, and Thalia followed Henry up the steps, past a doorman who asked them for tickets. Henry handed him several bills, and the doorman did not impede them further.

They had just entered the hallways when they heard a cry from a room down the hall. Without even looking at Thalia, Henry raced into the room. Thalia followed.

The first thing she saw was a table groaning with food.

The second was Eleanor, holding a gloved hand to a reddened cheek and glaring at a gentleman who was bent over, also groaning.

"You little—"

Whatever else he meant to say was lost as Henry strode across the room and interposed himself between Eleanor and the angry gentleman. Eleanor released a tiny sigh and tucked herself behind Henry. The open relief on her face, the way her entire body seemed to relax at the sight of Henry made Thalia's heart hurt. Mostly for Eleanor—but a little for herself.

"I beg your pardon," Henry said in frigidly polite tones. "Kindly desist from attacking my fiancée at once."

"Your fiancée?" the man echoed in astonishment, straightening. His eyes flickered up and down Henry, hitched a little on the pink coat, but returned to meet his gaze. "But you are a gentleman."

"Indeed. Perhaps you should leave now."

"But I thought—"

"I know very well what you thought," Eleanor said tartly, coming around Henry's side to face him, "and it does you no credit."

"But you were here, on this night—"

Henry cut across him. "I believe I asked you to leave."

The man gathered his ruined dignity and fled from the room.

Henry turned to Eleanor, his fingers gently tracing her cheek where a bruise was starting to form. "Are you injured?"

Eleanor's hand covered Henry's. "Not badly, no. But I am glad you came when you did."

Thalia looked away, studying the lace covering the table beneath the food. It didn't seem right to be an audience for such tenderness. The least she could do was turn her eyes away, so she could not see whatever look or touch Henry gave her employer.

Henry said, "I am not at all certain you needed my rescue."

"Perhaps not," Eleanor said. "But I am glad to see you. No doubt it would have been even more unpleasant on my own."

"Where's Anne?" Henry asked.

Thalia glanced up from her study of the table to find Henry looking about the room as though he might discover his sister hiding behind a plate of sliced ham.

Eleanor hung her head. "Dancing. Oh, Henry, I am sorry. If I had known what sort of ball this was, I would never have brought your sister here. I would not blame you if you hated me and wanted nothing more to do with me."

"Eleanor," Henry said, very gently. "I could never hate you."

Thalia stared fixedly at the delicately painted line of green leaves rimming a china tray before her.

"What did you know of the ball before you came?" Henry asked.

"Only that it was a masquerade. I heard two gentlemen talking about it and thought it must be all right, if gentlemen were attending."

"The kind of men who attend a ball looking for their next mistress are not the sort of gentleman I aspire to be." Henry's voice was very dry.

"I realize that now."

"Come, let's find Anne."

Thalia turned away from the table to follow them from the room, noting, despite herself, the way Eleanor linked her arm through Henry's, the way they leaned in toward each other as they walked with the deep affection of old friends—of lovers.

It took a few minutes to find Anne among the throng of dancers, most of them in masks and costumes. Thalia found she could not blame Eleanor for not knowing that this masquerade was meant for men and their mistresses—the women were every bit as elegant and bejeweled as the women of the *ton*. Indeed, she had seen women dressed more scandalously at society events. Only the preponderance of gentlemen offered any hint—she had never seen so many gentlemen enthused to be present at a marriage mart event.

They found Anne at last, twirling in the arms of a tall brown-haired gentleman with a silver mask covering all but his mouth and angular chin. There was something a bit familiar in the way he moved, but Thalia did not know who he was. When Anne caught sight of her brother, she missed her step in surprise. Admittedly, Henry was hard to miss, unmasked as he was and in that ridiculous coat. Thalia would have to ask him how he came by it.

Anne left the dance at once and approached them, her partner trailing behind.

"Henry! However did you come here?" Her bright eyes found Eleanor's, dipped to the red mark on her cheek, and Anne frowned. "What happened, Eleanor?"

"A lucky guess," Henry said, just as Eleanor answered, "A minor fracas. I'm fine."

"We've come to bring you home," Henry continued.

Anne folded her arms. "Then you can take yourself right back. I'm not going. I've been having a splendid time. You cannot imagine how nice it is to be myself for once, free of judgmental eyes, free of *Mama*'s eyes."

"Can I not?" Henry asked mildly, but Anne did not appear to hear him.

"I have met the most interesting gentleman," Anne went on, turning, as if she would introduce her partner. But her dance partner had vanished during their conversation.

"We really should go," Eleanor said, a bit apologetically. "I am happy you have enjoyed the ball, but truly, it is not a place I would ever have brought you had I known what it was."

"Why? What is wrong with this place? It is beautiful, and my partners have all been most agreeable."

Eleanor grimaced slightly but said nothing. Thalia suspected that Eleanor had not shared Anne's experience.

"It is a ball for the demimonde," Henry said. "By coming here, you and Eleanor have raised speculation that you are, um—" He broke off, changed tack. "You expose yourself to insult."

Anne's eyes widened, and she cast another look around the room. Apparently deciding that there was, perhaps, something in her brother's words, she deflated. "Very well. Only I was having the most wonderful time. What does that say about me that I have enjoyed this masquerade much more than a truly genteel party?"

She spoke as if daring Henry to criticize her. But Henry said only, "It says that you are a generous girl without an ounce of snobbery."

Anne relented and took Henry's free arm, offering him a small smile, and they walked out of the ballroom into the night.

Thalia trailed behind the trio. She should have been glad Eleanor and Anne had been found safe, that it had been mischief only and they'd come to no real harm—and she was, she told herself. Truly, she was.

But it was lonely too, trailing behind the others and realizing how very far she was outside the cozy circle of those who knew Henry best.

In the end, it was Anne who asked Henry about the coat.

"Is this supposed to be a costume?" Anne asked, as the carriage rolled away. She pinched the bright fabric between her fingers dubiously.

"Alas, I was not so clever," Henry said. "I had no notion of your being at a costume ball when I put it on. I had already dressed for bed when Miss Aubrey's letter arrived, and when the servants brought word that you were nowhere in the house, I could not get my coat on without my valet's assistance, so I grabbed something from my closet that I could put on myself."

Thalia began to laugh. "Is *this* the monstrosity your tailor made, that your valet threatened to quit over?"

"Quite," Henry said. His eyes met hers, bright with merriment.

Two mysteries solved in one night. That was a rather good achievement, even for her. Added onto an evening where she had met the famous Lambs and Mr. Keats, and it was no wonder that her limbs were heavy with exhaustion.

Henry escorted her and Eleanor into the house while Anne

waited in the carriage. He did not stay long, but pressed a quick, chaste kiss to Eleanor's cheek and nodded at Thalia before returning to his sister.

Eleanor stripped her gloves off in the vestibule. "Well," she said, and hesitated, as though she would say more.

"Is there anything you need?" Thalia asked, when Eleanor made no move to fill the silence. It was the wrong thing to say. Eleanor's soft, tired face hardened and closed like a flower against the night.

"No," Eleanor said. She lashed the gloves against her open palm. "It was kind of you and Henry to come for us."

"I—we—were worried about you."

"You needn't, you know. I am perfectly capable of taking care of myself. I hired you to lend me respectability, not to mind me."

Thalia felt as though she had been slapped. She had thought, for a moment, that Eleanor was about to open up—to share something of the thoughts she kept so closely guarded. Instead, Eleanor had put Thalia back in her place.

"Yes, Mrs. Lockhart. I apologize." Thalia dropped a shallow curtsy and moved past Eleanor toward the stairs.

Eleanor caught her hand as she passed. "Thalia—"

Thalia paused, waiting.

"Nothing," Eleanor said, releasing her. "It's nothing."

CHAPTER THIRTEEN

Eleanor

When falsehood can look so like the truth,
who can assure themselves of certain happiness?

—Mary Shelley, *Frankenstein; or, the Modern Prometheus*

Eleanor added one lump of sugar to her breakfast tea, then a second. She studied Thalia covertly across the table, but the young woman was rather ostentatiously reading a book of poetry and would not look up. Eleanor dropped in another lump of sugar, watching the crystals dissolve in the heat.

It was the third morning since their midnight adventure, and their interactions since had been clipped and exquisitely polite. Eleanor knew she should not have spoken to Thalia as she had that night. Thalia had only meant to help—and indeed, despite Eleanor's words to Henry, it was good that they had arrived when they did. Eleanor had seen the look in her assailant's eyes after she kneed him, seconds before he boxed her ears, and she was certain he would have hit her again had he not been interrupted.

Eleanor had been tired and snappish when they arrived home—the more snappish because she knew she had been wrong, and she did not like being in people's debt. She should have apologized to Thalia, but could not find the words. And now so many days had passed, she could not do it. She did not know how to show vulnerability, or let people close to her. Doing so generally led to disaster and heartbreak.

So she said nothing. She lifted her cup, sipped, choked, and put her drink down.

The tea was teeth-achingly sweet.

Thalia closed her book. "Shall you be needing me this morning?"

Eleanor shook her head. "Mr. Jones is coming to help with my husband's papers. You are free to write, or whatever it is you wish."

Thalia inclined her head and rose.

"Oh," Eleanor said, a thought occurring to her. "Should Henry and his sister come, would you entertain them for me? I shall deny myself to other visitors, but I do not think it quite right to simply turn them away. If Anne comes alone, I shall see her myself."

"But not Henry?"

Eleanor sighed. "I suppose I must see him for a few moments. But I would rather not, today."

She did not look at Thalia—she did not want to see the young woman's judgment. Eleanor could not truly explain it herself, but she did not want to see Henry while Owen—Mr. Jones—was at her house.

Mr. Jones arrived promptly at ten, as he had said he would. Eleanor laid down her stitching—abysmal stuff, but it was something to keep her hands occupied—and led him down the hallway from the drawing room to her study.

"How should you like me to start?" he asked, filling the doorway of the small room.

"I think you are a better judge of that than I," she said, gesturing at the boxes of paper around the room. "Start where you like."

Mr. Jones nodded and slid past her, so close that she could feel the heat from him. It brought an answering warmth to her cheeks. What was wrong with her? She was behaving like a missish schoolgirl.

He paused for a moment, just beside her, and raised his hand. His thumb swept across her cheekbone, so lightly she wondered later if she had imagined it. "What happened?"

Eleanor fought a fleeting impulse to lie, to brush it aside, to bury what had happened. "I, um, kicked a man and he retaliated."

Owen frowned, his heavy eyebrows drawing together. "A man *hit* you?"

Eleanor tried not to feel pleased at his instinctive concern for her. "It's all right. I handled it." With a bit of help from her friends.

"I trust he looks worse than you do?"

For the first time, recalling that incident was not wholly terrifying. Eleanor smiled. "I believe he does."

"Good. Any man who dares lay a hand on you deserves no less."

Mr. Jones settled into the chair behind the desk and pulled the nearest box toward him. When Eleanor did not move, he looked up at her questioningly.

"Do you . . ." She hesitated, gathering her courage. "Do you think I might assist you? I have nothing else this morning, and if I cannot understand math, I can, at least, follow directions. If you tell

me what and how to sort, or what to fetch and carry, I can do it."
Anything was better than unfilled time.

Owen smiled, a slow, warm smile like honey. "If you'd *like* to do
so, I would be glad of the help."

She observed Mr. Jones for a while, as he read through several
papers, trying to get a sense for what her husband's work involved.
She liked watching him, liked the swift flicker of emotions across his
face: the faint frown of puzzlement, the clearing of his brow, the way
his eyes narrowed with interest, or his lips pursed.

As he began shuffling the papers into different stacks, he said, "If
you have pencil and paper, perhaps you might tally what we find so
that we can stay organized?"

Eleanor jumped up to find blank paper and sent an unsteady
stack careening to the floor. She scurried to put it to rights, conscious of Owen's eyes on her.

When she straightened, Mr. Jones held out his hand. "Capital
idea, Mrs. Lockhart. We'll go through those papers next."

After a while, they settled into a pattern. Mr. Jones would skim
over a document, then write a letter and number on it: a letter for
the general topic, the number for the page. Eleanor would write the
same letter and number on a pad of paper she had found, with some
notation about what the paper contained.

"See, here," Mr. Jones said. "Your husband has begun collecting
parish data: births, deaths, marriages, illnesses, and the like. You can
see a story emerge from the numbers, clear as a story you might tell
with words."

"And what story is that?" Eleanor asked, more because she liked
to hear his voice than because she cared about the numbers.

"A typhoid plague that hit the village some decades back, by the number of deaths. And here, a rash of April weddings following a long winter."

Eleanor blushed again. She knew what that meant. But she began to see what Mr. Jones meant too, how numbers were not just marks on paper, but they could tell you about a community, about trends that might help you predict later events.

"Is that why you like numbers?" she asked. "Because of the stories they tell?"

"That—and because there's a beautiful order and clarity to numbers. Numbers will always behave as you expect them to."

"Unlike people, then?" Eleanor had never been especially partial to mathematics herself, but she liked that Mr. Jones was. His eyes sparkled as he spoke.

"People are awful."

Eleanor couldn't help laughing at the fervor in his tone. "Awe-full: both great and terrible?"

"Mostly terrible. They are predictable when you don't want them to be and unpredictable when you do." Faint color washed along Mr. Jones's cheeks, and he looked back down at his papers. "That is— *you* are not terrible."

"Only predictable?" Eleanor smiled.

"That's not what I—" Mr. Jones cleared his throat. "Dash it, Mrs. Lockhart . . ."

Eleanor held up her hand. "It's all right. I'm only teasing you. I know what you mean. But I rather like people."

"Do you?" Mr. Jones looked up again, one eyebrow raised. "Why?"

"I like that people are unpredictable. I like that there are end-less variations of humans, endless reasons why they behave one way and then another, endless varieties in their interests and dislikes. It's true that some people can be terrible"—she remembered, briefly, the masquerade—"but most are not. Being around people makes me feel more myself. More alive." *And less lonely.* Eleanor only just caught the last thought from escaping her lips.

"Being around the right people, I can grant. But all people? Mrs. Lockhart, I'm afraid you're teasing me again."

"Indeed, I am not! I—"

A footman scratched at the door, interrupting Eleanor. "Beg pardon, Mrs. Lockhart, but there is a lady to see you."

"Tell her I am not at home to visitors."

"I did tell her, but she insisted on seeing you, and she is a count-ess, ma'am—"

A countess? Eleanor did not know any countesses. She exchanged a quick glance with Mr. Jones, who looked more amused than any-thing, and she rose.

"Very well," she said. "I will see her."

She had scarcely settled on a chair in the salon when the door opened and the footman announced, "The Countess Lieven."

Eleanor nearly fell out of her chair.

She recognized the countess, of course, though she had never spo-ken to her. The Countess Lieven was one of the famed patronesses of Almack's, a hallowed portal that admitted only select members of the *ton*. The countess was a rather beautiful woman, with shining dark hair and brown eyes, a narrow nose set in a brilliant complexion. She carried herself with the confidence of a woman accustomed to the possession of power, given that her husband was the Russian ambassador to the English court.

What could such a woman want with her? Eleanor had been offered vouchers to Almack's, by way of George, and he had shredded them in a fit of pique when she stood up to him. She could not imagine that she would be given a second chance at them.

Eleanor rose and bowed before the lady, then ushered her into a plush chair that was the most comfortable in the room before taking her own seat again.

"How is your ladyship?"

The countess studied Eleanor for a moment without speaking. "Members of the *ton* call me Lady Lieven. Only servants and shop-keepers call me 'your ladyship.'"

The rebuke was delivered in a gentle tone, but Eleanor's cheeks burned. She ought to have known as much. "My apologies, your— Lady Lieven."

The countess nodded acceptance. "I see it is true what they say, that you are a rather pretty young widow. Is it true, also, that you have a considerable fortune from your late husband?"

Eleanor thought such topics were considered rude in polite company, but if a countess was asking, surely it must be all right? "I am comfortable, thank you."

"So long as you do not marry, I am told. And yet you are engaged?"

Eleanor stiffened. "I beg your pardon, but might I know the purpose of your questions?"

"I am merely trying to understand you. I was told you were a respectable, genteel sort of girl, and yet rumor has reached me that you were in attendance at a rather unfortunate event this Friday past."

Eleanor gripped the arm of her chair. How had *that* particular rumor reached the countess?

"Is it true that you attended the Cyprian's ball?" Countess Lieven demanded. "Do not lie to me. I shall know if you do."

Eleanor would have sworn on her life that Henry and Anne would not betray her, as Anne would be implicated in the scandal if word got out. And Thalia had not left the town house except in Eleanor's company. With an increasingly sick sensation, she thought of the brown-haired man who had baited her, hinting that he knew who she was.

"I was there," she said. "But I had no notion what kind of ball it was."

The countess snorted, a rather unladylike sound, but one that gave Eleanor the first glimmer of hope she'd felt in this interview. "Well, I suppose that does rather support the idea of your being genteel. Only a sheltered ninny would not know what a Cyprian was. But how came you by the addle-brained notion to go alone? Any reasonable escort could have told you what you might expect."

Curious: Whoever had passed along the rumor had not known—or chosen not to tell—that Anne was with her. "You are quite right. It was foolish of me." Better to be thought a fool than a fast woman. Fools were richly represented in society; fast women were much less welcome.

The countess fished around in her reticule and pulled out two squares of paper. "I am charged with delivering these to you. I do so with some reservations, on the strict condition that you do not indulge any more gooseish behavior. Proper ladies do not indulge in adventures." She held the sheets out to Eleanor, who pinched them as though they might burn her.

Eleanor read the top card over twice without comprehending. *Ladies Voucher: Almack's. Tickets for the balls on Wednesdays, 1818.* Her name had been written in an elegant hand. Then she looked up. "You are giving me vouchers? To Almack's?"

"For you and your companion, as I do not wish you to appear alone. I had thought your nephew might escort you, but he tells me you have had a falling-out." She fixed a stern eye on Eleanor. "That will not do, you know. Mr. Lockhart is popular in society, and he means well. You ought to reconcile with him."

Eleanor said nothing.

Countess Lieven stood, brushing her salmon silk skirts. "I hope you will take some kindly intentioned advice: Society's good opinion is fickle and easily lost. Do not trade it lightly." She nodded one final time at Eleanor and sailed out of the room.

Eleanor sank back into her seat with a sigh, setting the vouchers on the cushion beside her.

The door opened again, and Eleanor bolted upright, wondering what the countess had forgotten.

But it was not the countess, it was Mr. Jones, and he was frowning.

"Why do you let such people order you around so? I heard some of what that woman said—you let her pronounce judgment on you. And she defended your nephew, when we both know what kind of man he is."

Eleanor spread her hands wide. "What else am I to do? That was Countess Lieven. If she chose, she could bar me from polite society with a word."

"Perhaps," Mr. Jones said, still frowning. "But I do not under-stand why you care so much for society. It is not the society you were born to, and it does not seem to make you happy. You never talk of it without a heaviness in your eyes. You claim to like people, but you do not appear to enjoy the company of *these* people."

"And how would you know?" Eleanor fired back, lashing out as she had not been able to lash out at the countess. "Have you seen me at a ball? Or at the opera? No—because that is not the strata you inhabit."

Mr. Jones retreated a step, his face shuttered. "You're right. I apologize." He held out a scrap of paper. "I only came to bring you this."

Eleanor took the paper and watched him walk from the room, her heart aching though she could not quite say why.

At the doorway, Mr. Jones turned. He released a long exhale. "My sister, Sophia, has urged me to invite you to join us for some tea and cakes this afternoon. I am certain you have better things to do, but my sister will not let me rest until I have delivered the invitation. Now I have done so. I will continue the work I have committed to do, but I will not disturb you again."

He left the room.

Eleanor looked at the paper in her hands. It trembled like a leaf in the wind. She forced her hands to still.

The paper was in Albert's spidery writing, near the end of his life. *To my dear wife Eleanor, I leave all the worldly goods with which I endowed her at our wedding. My estate, my fortunes, all that I have.*

A will. Albert had been drafting—or redrafting?—his will. But this was not a finished will, not signed and notarized, not even dated. It would not be legal in any court.

One hot tear dropped from her eyes to the paper, smudging the ink. She scrubbed at her eyes with her free hand.

She had not cried when Albert died, nor at the reading of the will with its devastating clause: Maintain the wealth she had married into and resign herself to a life alone, or seek love and lose the security she had fought so hard for. Why should this small note affect her so?

And what had happened to change his mind?

George, most likely. Mr. Lockhart and his poisonous tongue, telling Albert that if he did not add such a clause, Eleanor would not wait a week, a month, before marrying again. Perhaps he had convinced Albert, that poor, brokenhearted man, that she already had someone in mind. As though she would be so faithless.

Well, Eleanor would not marry again. Not Henry, after George had tired of his games. Not—anyone else.

And if Owen thought her a snob, well, she would disappoint him. She would accept his invitation, and he would see that she was as comfortable with an actress as with a countess.

CHAPTER FOURTEEN

Thalia

I wear words like a crown, glittering and gold,
And drape myself in syllables, shimmering and sleek.
This word set to catch your eye, that to turn away.
This to draw attention, that to show I'm meek.
Words are cheap and precious, a mask made up of art.
Men who take them casually, think they've found my outer shell.
When in fact I have quite openly given them my heart.

—Thalia Aubrey

Thalia was writing at the desk in the drawing room, breathing the spring fragrances blowing in from the open window, when Eleanor popped her head in.

"I am going out," she said, an unnecessary declaration as she tied the ribbons of a bonnet beneath her chin. "Mr. Jones invited me to take tea with him and his sister."

Thalia could just see Mr. Jones through the open door. His face was grim, and he did not look particularly excited at the prospect of Eleanor's company. He looked, rather, like a man facing his own execution. Why on earth had he extended such an invitation? Or perhaps Eleanor had inveigled it. She seemed awfully drawn to the man, for a woman who was engaged to someone else.

Stop. Thalia ground the nib of her pen into the paper, leaving an unseemly ink splotch. It was not her place to judge Eleanor's choices. Even if she did not agree with them.

"Perhaps you would like to join us," Mr. Jones offered.

Eleanor scowled at Thalia. "No doubt Miss Aubrey has work she needs to attend to."

"Indeed, I do," Thalia said, though she might have said yes out of pity for Mr. Jones if Eleanor had not made it so clear she was unwelcome. Eleanor and Mr. Jones continued on their way, and Thalia went back to her poem, diligently expanding the ink blot she had just created.

But not five minutes after their departure, the footman opened the door of the drawing room to announce, "Mr. Henry Salisbury."

Her pen skipped across the paper, creating three more ink blots to join the first. A veritable ink family. Thalia wondered if Eleanor's injunction to entertain Henry while Mr. Jones was here still held, as neither of them were around.

"Eleanor has gone out with a friend," Thalia volunteered, and waited for Henry to withdraw.

Henry began walking across the room toward her.

Thalia did not want to spend a quarter hour alone with Mr. Salisbury. That is, she very much *did*, which was precisely why she ought not.

"Is Anne with you?" she asked, trying to slow his approach. Clearly, his sister was not with him, but perhaps the question might recall him to the intimacy of their situation.

"My sister has gone to walk in Hyde Park with a maid," Henry said.

"Do you want me to leave a message for Eleanor?" Thalia asked, a trifle desperately. *For your fiancée?*

"You may tell her I called," Henry said, as though it were no great matter.

He had reached the desk.

Thalia wondered if she could sink into the floor if she only willed it enough.

"Is this some of your poetry?" he asked, looking at the pages scattered across the desk. She had finished one poem that morning and begun another. He nudged the ink-splattered page with a finger.

"That is my ink family," Thalia said, then wished she had bit her tongue instead. Better to have blood coming from her lips than idiocy.

"I see," Henry said, with a lift in his voice that told her he was amused. "They do propagate most alarmingly. I have many myself."

Thalia sat, lumpish, wondering why her normal trade in words tended to abandon her just when she most wished for the right ones.

Henry said, "May I read one?"

"If you must."

"I won't if you don't like it," he said, and she knew he meant it.

"No, it's all right." Suddenly, she wanted him to read it. The scansion of the first poem had been off somehow. Maybe if someone else looked at it, he could help her spot it. She handed him the poem.

Henry read in silence. Thalia watched him for a moment, then decided that trying to decipher the minuscule expressions of his face was unbearable, and looked out the window. There was a bird dipping up and down in the sky that demanded her attention. Henry cleared his throat.

Thalia turned back, her heart beating painfully. Rejection of her words was more unbearable than rejection of herself—her body was only the outward case she used to move her words through the world. Her words were *her*.

"It's good," he said. "This line particularly." He pointed it out to her.

"And this line?" Thalia indicated the line that had given her trouble earlier.

Henry frowned, thoughtful. "I don't think 'reprobate' rhymes well with 'debate.' Too many syllables. Perhaps 'ingrate'?"

"Ooh—and that's a better fit for the meaning. Adds an interesting twist of ingratitude." Thalia beamed up at him. "Thank you!"

Henry settled himself on a chair near the desk, where he could face her without towering over her. "I am always happy to be your muse, Miss Aubrey."

Her muse. She flushed. He was not her anything.

"You have other poems too, I noticed."

She nodded. "I mean to make a book of them."

"Will you tell me about them?"

Thalia blinked at him for a moment. Papa had always encouraged her writing, as had Kalli and Charis. And they were more than willing to *listen* to her talk about her writing, but she could not remember them asking outright, inviting her to talk. She supposed she was rather like Charis in her passions: One had to be careful what one asked Charis as one was liable to get an answer that outstripped one's inclination to listen.

"Do you truly want to know?"

Henry met her gaze unwaveringly, hazel eyes with a ring of green and flecked through with gold. "I truly want to know."

So Thalia told him—about the different themes she hoped to pick up, about why societal roles were so different for men and women, about the challenges of ambition, if one was a young woman expected to want only a family and children. Henry didn't interrupt her, didn't challenge her, but simply listened quietly. Occasionally, when she stopped for breath, he asked a question that showed he had actually understood what she was trying to say—or was earnestly trying to understand.

It was, quite honestly, the most intimate thing Thalia had experienced—even including the kisses James had given her when he persuaded her to elope with him.

She tried to remind herself that Henry was engaged to someone else, but it was no help. The quiet he gave her to work out her thoughts in was a gift, and she would prize it no matter how it came.

So engrossed was she that she did not hear the door opening until her brother came bounding across the room. He must have told the footman he'd introduce himself. Thalia shoved her chair away from Henry—how had they drawn so close as they talked? What would Freddy think?

Freddy, it seemed, thought nothing. Barely glancing at Henry, he joined his sister at the desk. "How are you, old chap?"

"As I am neither old nor a chap, I don't know how you expect me to answer that," Thalia said. "What are you doing here?"

"I was with Sophia, you know," Freddy said, his expression softening as it always did when he mentioned Mr. Jones's sister. "But she kicked me out. Said she had a guest coming for tea and cakes. Could have blown me over when I saw who it was—your Mrs. Lockhart! So I figured that if she was *there*, you were here by your lonesome and might be wanting company."

From this, Thalia deduced that Freddy was hungry. "Shall I have a maid bring up some cakes?"

Freddy could not quite hide his eagerness from her. "That would be first-rate! I mean, if you haven't already eaten. I mean, it would be all right with me."

Thalia's stomach grumbled. When was the last time she had eaten? Breakfast? She went to the door and gave directions to the footman waiting there.

When she returned to her desk, Freddy was reading one of her poems, half under his breath so both she and Henry could hear him. He was getting the cadences wrong. Nor had he asked her if he could read, as Henry had.

"I say, this isn't half bad," Freddy said.

"I thought it was rather excellent," Henry said.

Freddy gave him a pitying smile. "I wouldn't expect you to have the refined judgment of an actual poet."

Thalia wondered how much of Henry's esteem she would lose if she kicked her brother. *An actual poet.* Had Freddy ever written anything other than love poetry for Sophia? And that girl back home—what was her name?

"You know, I could read your other poems too, if you like," Freddy said. "I know you've been working on a book. Be happy to give them a look, tell you what I think."

Thalia reflected for a moment. Did she trust Freddy's judgment?

In most things, likely not. But in this—he had been to Oxford, and she knew that his tastes in poetry had often matched with hers growing up. Perhaps he would spot things she had not seen?

"I went out with Keats, the other day," Freddy continued. "Met his publishers, Mr. Taylor and Mr. Hessey. We had lunch together, talked about Keats's work. My work too, if you must know. It went quite well. I could put in a good word for you."

Thalia tried to ignore the sudden surge of jealousy in her gut. Freddy had talked with actual publishers? Men who would not give her the time of day if she appeared in their offices, most like. She exhaled. Well, what could it hurt? Perhaps Freddy's insight would be helpful, perhaps not. But even if not, Freddy had connections she did not. And he'd offered to speak for her.

"All right," she said. "I'll give you my spare copy." After her experience with Edward's illustrations, she had begun making dual copies of each poem she wrote, so she would have a spare even if she sent them off to publishers. "Only do not lose it."

"My life on it," Freddy promised.

A maid came in carrying a tray with sliced cake on plates. Henry rose—was it only Thalia's wishful thinking that he rose reluctantly?

"I had a splendid visit, Miss Aubrey," he said. "I enjoyed our discussion. But I imagine I have quite overstayed my welcome, and you must wish to speak with your brother."

He hadn't, and she didn't, but Thalia would not tell him so.

"As did I," Thalia said.

Freddy mumbled something, his mouth already full of cake.

"Are you sure you won't stay?" Thalia asked.

"I'm sure. But thank you."

149

After Henry left, Thalia turned back to find Freddy watching her. He brushed a crumb from his cheek. "I say, I'm not sure it's all the thing to be cozied up to your employer's affianced."

A thousand different things bubbled up to Thalia's lips: It was none of Freddy's business; nothing had happened; it didn't matter because he had proposed to Kalli once and even if he wasn't engaged to Eleanor, he would not want to propose to an Aubrey again. But she reminded herself that Freddy wanted to read her poems for her and might even speak to publishers on her behalf.

She said only, "Oh, Freddy," and went upstairs to fetch her poems.

CHAPTER FIFTEEN

Eleanor

As soon as they were all seated round the table, my friends returned to the parlour. The tea-table now made its appearance, and never did a meal seem so delicious; so true it is, that by letting others participate in those blessings Providence has assigned to us, we increase our own enjoyment of them.

— Mary Mister, *The Adventures of a Doll*

The flat Sophia shared with Owen was not a large one, but it was comfortably appointed and cozy. Sophia laid out a pretty china tea set, with delicate pink roses. Not expensive, like the set in Eleanor's town house, but good quality.

What had Eleanor expected? That they lived in poverty because they were not upper class? Eleanor buried her nose and her shame in the steam rising from her cup. Suppose she had found they did live in poverty? Eleanor had been poor for much of her life. Had she been less worthy when she had nothing than she was now? Many people might think so. Did she?

She hardly knew what to think, and it was perplexing and disturbing. She and Owen—Mr. Jones—had scarcely spoken on the cab ride to the Joneses' flat, but when Eleanor had reached their rooms, she had been enveloped by Sophia in a warm, lavender-scented hug. She really was a beautiful young woman, almost dazzlingly so up close, with thick eyelashes that brushed her cheeks and strawberry-red lips.

"I am glad Owen persuaded you to come," Sophia had said. "I am a most excellent judge of character, and I have thought from the beginning that we should be friends. I suppose it comes from being an actress: I can tell when someone is playing a part or being herself."

"And me? Am I playing a part?" Eleanor could not help asking.

"You?" Sophia laughed, a warm, tinkling sound that made Eleanor want to laugh too, though she was a little worried at what the joke might turn out to be. "You, my darling, are a terrible actress, which is why I like you."

"I am not very forthcoming," Eleanor confessed, which was unlike her. She never admitted to her faults.

"Precisely. If you were a better actress, you should pretend to be more forthcoming. Society does love those sorts: the ones who seem to spill their innermost secrets, but then you find, upon reflection, that they have really told nothing at all. Your secrets are more precious, because they are more rarely shared."

Sophia turned to catch her brother by the arm, drawing him into their little circle. "Do you not agree, Owen?"

"About El—Mrs. Lockhart?" Owen asked. "I do not think it's my place to have an opinion."

Why should that little slip of the tongue make Eleanor's heart sing?

"That only confirms my point," Sophia said. "You are two of a kind: both of you so protective of your innermost hearts, like burrs guarding a chestnut."

"Brrr," Owen echoed, growling like a bear and rubbing his nose into Sophia's cheek. She laughed and pushed him away.

Eleanor stared at him in fascination. She hadn't seen him behave in any fashion that might be considered playful. As though feeling her eyes on him, Owen looked at her and flushed, color washing in a wave from his chin to his hairline.

He was a different person here, in his own home. More relaxed, somehow. Softer, as if he were used to holding his largeness stiffly, so as not to infringe on people. Eleanor relaxed too, listening to Sophia and Owen banter: Sophia telling stories about rehearsal and Owen teasing her about her beaux. (Mr. Lockhart was notably *not* mentioned.)

Eleanor found herself missing a sibling she had never had. To be sure, she had Anne and Henry, but their sibling banter was seldom this relaxed, not with the shadow of their mother hanging over them.

Owen mentioned Thalia's brother Freddy.

"I had to chase him away before you came over," Sophia said, sighing. "Freddy's a nice boy. He'll make someone a fine husband when he outgrows his boyish earnestness."

"Poor Freddy," Eleanor said, remembering his passionate attack on George, when he believed Mr. Lockhart had insulted Sophia.

"You should be careful," Owen said. "He's liable to do something reckless if he believes he still has a shot at winning you."

"Unlike you?" Sophia said, smiling. "You've never done a reckless thing in your life." She turned to Eleanor. "Even as a child he was careful, counting out pastries and cutting them so we should always have exactly the same, organizing my books by size and subject."

Eleanor could picture Owen as a small child: all round cheeks and knees, the same intense look on his face then that she'd seen when he was studying her late husband's papers.

Owen shook his head. "That's not true. I've done at least one reckless thing." His gaze flickered—briefly, so briefly—to Eleanor.

Her heart skipped a beat.

She caught his gaze, determined not to be cowardly just because it terrified her to look at him like this, to let him look at her, as though he might see something inside her she had never shown to any man.

"I do reckless things weekly," she blurted out.

The sudden, alarming tautness between them shattered with Sophia's chuckle. "Do you? Pray, what was the most recent?"

Eleanor found herself telling Sophia and Owen about her disastrous visit to the Argyll Rooms.

As soon as she mentioned the Cyprian's ball, Sophia sputtered her tea. "No, you didn't! Dear one, how did you not know?"

And somehow, in telling of the horrible moments from that night, they lost some of their sting. The memories were still offensive, but it was easier to see now that it was not her fault—that being in the wrong place did not mean she deserved to be treated as she had been. When she got to the part where she kneed the middling man, Sophia laughed out loud.

"Well done, Eleanor! May I call you Eleanor?"

"I was not entirely unscathed," Eleanor said, pointing at her cheek. "And yes, you may."

The conversation moved on after a moment, Sophia talking about a new play she was studying, and her fear that she would not be able to master the nuance needed for the part.

"You have not yet failed at anything you set your mind to," Owen said. "I believe you can do it."

"I have only seen one of your performances," Eleanor said, "but it was masterful."

"Thank you," Sophia said, beaming at her.

They sat in quiet for a moment, sipping their tea. Silence often disconcerted Eleanor, giving her too much space in which to confront herself and her thoughts. But here it felt peaceful. Welcome, even.

"And what of you, Eleanor?" Sophia asked after a moment. "Have you any grand ambitions?"

"None," Eleanor said. The word came out too fast, too loud, so she forced herself to smile. "Only to finish my husband's project and enjoy the Season." *And retire with enough wealth to never again want.*

"How fares your project?" Sophia asked. "Is Owen proving helpful?"

"I could not do the work without him."

"You rate me rather too highly, Mrs. Lockhart."

"Nonsense!" Sophia said. "You're brilliant, Owen, and someday the whole world shall know as much." At a raised eyebrow from Owen, she amended, "At least, the entire world of mathematics."

"I wish I could believe you," Owen said. "Sometimes I fear that I shall spend my life living my father's dream, not my own. That I shall never be able to do the work I feel called to, but spend my days cobbling together other people's financial records."

"I won't let you," Sophia said. "If I have to drag you screaming from our father's shop myself."

"Do—do neither of you wish to be wealthy?" Eleanor asked. The people around her had always seen wealth and status as the highest goal, and Eleanor had never questioned that. But Owen and Sophia both spoke of dreams that had nothing to do with money—or, only a little to do with money.

"I should not complain if I were to become the next Mrs. Siddons," Sophia said. "But so long as I have sufficient money for my needs and some of my wants, I would rather spend my energy on the things that make me happy."

"What makes *you* happy?" Owen asked Eleanor. His tone was abrupt and his eyebrows drew together, but Eleanor got the impression that he was curious and intent, not accusatory.

Eleanor blinked. Had anyone ever asked her that before? As a lonely child first coming into boarding school, she would have said friends. When she grew a bit older, old enough to know that friends could not always feed you or keep you clothed, she would have said wealth. When Albert died, she believed it would be London. Now she had lived in London for some weeks. Was she happy?

Yes—she was happy *here*, now, if happiness felt like a warm belly and the company of people who required nothing of her other than that she *be*. But she could not say that. She did not want that to be true.

"I like pretty things," she said at last. "Fine dresses and sparkling jewels, well-matched horses and gleaming carriages."

The intentness in Owen's face faded. His eyebrows smoothed out and his pursed lips relaxed—was he disappointed in her answer?

"I—I am not sure what makes me happy," she continued. "I am not certain that it matters. I know what makes me unhappy: poverty, and want, and uncertainty. So long as I do not have those things, I must be happy."

"Those are hard things," Sophia said sympathetically. "But I know that I am happiest when I am most myself, when I am fully in my body—when I stand on a stage and become, for a moment, someone else, and that transformation moves others. When I am home, with good friends and good food. When I get to see new places and find new friends."

"Mathematics make me happy," Owen interjected. "A well-wrought formula, the satisfaction of wrestling complicated ideas into a neat line of figures." He paused for a moment, then added, "Food is all right."

Sophia leaned toward Eleanor. "My brother does not like people."

He had said as much earlier.

"I do not like *most* people," Owen corrected. "The few I like, I love."

He was not speaking to Eleanor, but she felt herself flush all the same.

The Jones siblings' confessions broke something open in Eleanor. "When my husband was sick, and dying, I dreamed of London. Of fine balls and fancy dresses and rich food and beautiful music—and I would imagine all of those things so that I could stay beside my husband, and hold his hand, and not grow sick with fear and grief. But now that I am here—sometimes I stand in a ballroom and feel as I did at the Cyprian's ball, as though I am wearing a mask and a costume, pretending to be the person that everyone sees, but meanwhile no one sees me."

Eleanor stopped, wide-eyed. She sniffed her tea surreptitiously—perhaps Sophia had dropped some liquor in it. But all she smelled were the slightly earthy notes of the tea and the sweetness of the honey Sophia had added liberally.

"Then take off the mask. Be yourself," Owen said.

When she thought of it, a great yawning panic opened up inside her. *I can't.* "It's not so simple," Eleanor said.

Sophia, watching her with gentle eyes, said, "Stop badgering her, Owen. We have fatigued Eleanor long enough. It's time for you to return her to her home and for me to prepare for the stage."

Eleanor, startled, glanced at the window, at the gold-tinged light of early evening. When had it grown so late?

She accepted Owen's escort home, and they talked of innocuous things—of the weather, of poetry they had both read.

Owen helped her from the carriage and walked her to the front door. As Mr. Davis opened the heavy door, Owen took her hand and pressed it lightly.

"I like you better without the mask, Mrs. Lockhart."

How did one remove the mask she had been wearing for so long?

That thought rang in Eleanor's head two days later, standing in line for a country dance at Almack's, watching a pair of dancers move up and down the dancing line. Her partner—she had already forgotten his name—smiled toothily at her from across the gap, and she smiled back, but she felt as though she were the puppeteer pulling strings on a marionette. Or perhaps she was the marionette. She moved, but the movements felt divorced from herself.

When the dance finished at last, Eleanor thanked her partner, checked the ballroom to make sure that both Anne and Thalia were happily occupied (when had she added Thalia to her mental list of people she cared about?), and made a beeline for the refreshments in a small room off to one side. True to its reputation, the refreshments at Almack's were dreadful: watered-down lemonade, tea, and orgeat, with only thinly sliced bread and cake without icing. Eleanor scarcely tasted her lemonade though. She simply needed something to do, an excuse to move through the room and not think about how little the glitter around her touched her. To not think about how much happier (she was beginning to hate that word) she had been at Sophia and Owen's.

Eleanor finished the last of her watery lemonade and handed the cup to a passing servant. Nothing else on the table tempted her, so she reluctantly returned to the ballroom. At the same time, George Lockhart emerged from the card room that had been set up in a neighboring room, and she nearly backed up into the refreshment room.

But no, she would not be so craven.

"Good evening, Mr. Lockhart," she said. There, that was civil.

"Good evening, Mrs. Lockhart," he said, with an unsettling smile. "How is your evening?"

"Well, thank you. And yours?"

"Quite good, thanks."

"I take it you've had a run of luck at cards," Eleanor said. She was rather surprised he endured the gaming tables at Almack's—they could scarcely be called such, as the patronesses did not allow cards to be played for anything but paltry chicken stakes.

"I have not. As a matter of fact, I've been losing rather dreadfully. But I've made some progress in a venture that cheers me immensely."

Eleanor wanted to ask him what venture, but she would not give him the satisfaction of fishing for information.

"How are your marriage plans proceeding?" Mr. Lockhart asked. "Where is your fiancé, anyway? Ah, there he is—dancing with Miss Aubrey. If you're not careful, Eleanor, your own companion will cut you out and then where will you be?"

"My plans are none of your business."

"Do you know, I believe they are? Your marriage directly affects my material prospects. I have seen no announcement in the *Times*, heard no whispers of banns being called. I am beginning to believe your engagement is a sham, meant only to tease me."

Eleanor stilled. "Ask Mr. Salisbury, if you don't believe me."

"Perhaps I will." He stroked his chin, as if in thought. "If you are so in need of a husband, you might marry me."

"I've already told you no. If this is your idea of a jest, I find it in poor taste."

"I did not jest then, nor do I now. Perhaps after some consideration, you might find we'd suit."

"I would rather," Eleanor said with careful enunciation, "strip naked and run through Hyde Park, before all of fashionable London, than marry you."

He shrugged. "I could arrange that for you, if you like, but I daresay it would be rather drafty."

Eleanor walked away, George's soft laughter trailing behind her.

Her hands were trembling, and she clasped them together to still them.

She found Anne just leaving the dance floor and persuaded her friend to take a turn about the room with her. "I spoke with Mr. Lockhart just now," Eleanor said. "He was—" What could she tell Anne? She could not say that he had proposed to her again, not without explaining that he believed her engagement to Henry was false. "He was rather disagreeable."

"Mr. Lockhart?" Anne asked. "You always find him disagreeable. I am beginning to suspect you of prejudice."

"My prejudice is rooted in long experience," Eleanor said. "He wants the money Albert left me, and he will not stop harassing me until he has it."

"I'm sure it was not easy for him to have had such expectations until his uncle married a young girl."

Eleanor stopped walking. "Anne, whose side are you on? Mine, or his?"

Anne flushed. "Yours, of course. Only you do go on about him so."

"I'm sorry," Eleanor said. "I didn't realize I was boring you."

They walked on for a few moments in prickly silence. Eleanor waited for Anne to say something, to reassure her, but Anne said nothing.

As they reached the corner of the room, Anne pulled away. "I must go, Eleanor. There's someone I must speak with."

"With whom?" Eleanor asked, but Anne was already gone, a flash of cream and gold in a sea of dresses.

Eleanor went back to the refreshment room. Between Anne's odd behavior and George's unsettling offer, she was in no mood to dance.

What would George do if he knew her engagement to Henry was truly a sham? Renew his offers? Try some other stratagem to marry her off? And what if she were simply to call off her wedding? Then nothing would protect her from George's persistence.

The image of a large, gently smiling man flashed into her mind. If she called off her engagement to Henry, she could—no, she could do nothing. Would do nothing. Eleanor would not risk her future security on something so insubstantial as mere feeling. Owen Jones was only a friendly acquaintance, one who was helping her with her dead husband's life's work. Nothing more.

And Eleanor meant to keep it that way.

CHAPTER SIXTEEN

Thalia

Round and round at Almack's we go,
Where we'll stop, nobody knows.
I'll partner with him,
He'll partner with her,
We'll swap through the dance
And end back where we were.

—Thalia Aubrey

Thalia swirled through the steps of the dance in a haze of pleasure. She loved dancing—the movement of her body, the swell of rhythmic sound, the ebb and flow of people around her. It was one of the few occasions in her life where her mind and body felt united, rather than discrete parts of her. Henry Salisbury met her for their partnered steps, and they moved through the music together. His gloved hand was firm beneath hers. She caught his glance, warm and open, as they spun.

Memory washed through her, drenching her in a rush of old feelings. She had danced with James just so, a year—a lifetime—ago. She had intercepted just such glances from James, felt those casual touches as promises of something more. She had read all the signs as closely as she might a book: rejoicing that he thought her pretty, that their steps paired together so well, that their thoughts seemed so in harmony. Everything seemed to augur their happiness together, and nothing had come of it but heartbreak.

Stop. She was doing it again, trying to read meaning into casual touches that was not there. Henry was not James, and Henry was engaged to Eleanor. He was too honest a man to let her believe he felt anything he could not, in honor, offer her.

They took up their positions in the line of the dance, facing each other, not touching, and Henry smiled at her. Light from the chandeliers overhead glinted gold in his hair, and the smile he tossed toward her was a gleaming arc.

Thalia caught her breath.

She had been evading self-knowledge for days now, but she had fought it, not wanting to know what slammed into her now with the force of a heavily laden carriage.

She was falling in love with Henry.

She had thought she had loved James, but some of that had been dazzlement, that someone who seemed so clever admired her. Some of it, undoubtedly, had been his kisses.

But she had never kissed Henry, never touched him except in casual brushes, as part of the forms of a dance. She was not dazzled by him—in fact, she had thought him dull at first, and it had only been as she had seen more of him that her impression had begun to change. She knew him to be kind, and loyal, someone who could listen without being asked—someone who did not ask more of her than she was willing to give.

Thalia took a long, slow breath. Henry was engaged to Eleanor, even if she suspected, sometimes, that his heart was not similarly engaged. Even were he free, he could hardly want to be with some-one as difficult and sharp as Thalia.

It did not matter what Thalia felt. She would master this emo-tion, as she had mastered her heartbreak after James. Anyway, she was not interested in romantic love. She meant to be wedded to her work. Her poetry would not disappoint her in the way a lover could, and romance would only distract her from writing. When she had believed herself in love with James, she had stopped writing entirely, her belief in James's opinion stronger than her own belief in herself. She would not make that mistake again. She would not give her heart, her self-worth, into someone else's keeping again.

And then, at once, her mind was full of words, so full of shapes and sounds that she would burst if she could not spill them. She suf-fered through a pair of indifferent partners, and when Henry came back to meet her in the dance, she grabbed the lapels of his coat. "Henry, have you a pencil and paper?"

"Don't tend to carry such things on the dance floor," he said, shrugging an apology.

"I must write," Thalia said.

"Now?"

"Would you ask me if I told you I needed to breathe?"

"All right!" Laughing, Henry ushered her from the dance, ignor-ing the curious glances of those still in the dance formation. Henry led her to the master of ceremonies, who sent a servant away to fetch the necessary supplies. Thalia fairly burned with impatience. She knew, from sad experience, that when inspiration struck so forcibly, any delay meant she risked losing the words. She did not want to wake tomorrow remembering that she had *almost* written something spectacular.

When the paper and pencil were produced, Thalia grasped them as though they were sustenance and she had not eaten for a week. She was vaguely aware that Henry followed her as she searched out a quiet corner and a chair, but when he tried to pull up a chair beside her, she waved him away.

"Go dance with Eleanor or something," she said. "I must write."

"Will you let me read it when you're done?"

"This poem? No." Henry featured too prominently in the poem taking shape in her mind. She could see that he was hurt by her abrupt answer, but, dear heavens, she did not have *time* to deal with his feelings at the moment. "It's private," she said. "It will likely be terrible."

It would not be terrible. Sometimes the words struck her with such rightness that she felt as though they came direct from some external source, and she was only the conduit.

"There will be other poems," she said, desperate for him to go. She loved him, yes, and he could not love her, and her heart would likely break over it, but right now she needed to write a poem.

When he did not move, Thalia bent her head low over the paper in her lap and began to scrawl the words as they seared through her. If she had to live with heartbreak, she might as well make poetic use of it.

> *I cannot name the moment when I fell.*
> *Love came upon me by degree, so slow*
> *I might have outraced it, might have quelled*

Desire before it bloomed, the faint glow
Of fire snuffed before it kindled red.

She did not notice when Henry left. She wrote until she had no words left to give, and then looked up in a daze to find herself sitting alone.

She quashed a faint surge of disappointment. It was better this way.

After breakfast the following morning, while Eleanor was supervising Mr. Jones's work on Albert's papers, Thalia returned to her room to reread the poem she had scrawled at Almack's. She made a few changes, then set it aside. She picked up the sheaf of papers that represented the rest of her poems and read through those as well.

They were not perfect, but they were good. As good as she was capable of. She would wait to hear Freddy's opinion, then set about securing a publisher, God willing, with Freddy's help.

Her stomach fluttered, but it was a pleasurable kind of discomfort. Exciting, even. She allowed herself a few minutes of daydreaming of her poetry finding popular acclaim. For those brief moments, she even forgot about Henry Salisbury.

Her equanimity suffered a blow when she returned downstairs to the drawing room to find Henry waiting there.

Her traitorous heart thumped, and blood flooded into her cheeks. She reminded herself that he was not waiting for her, but the heat in her face remained.

"Why are you—" she started.

"How is your poem?" he said at the same time. Then, "I'm waiting for Eleanor to finish her work. We are supposed to go driving this morning. You are welcome to come with us."

And watch Henry play gallant to Eleanor? "No, thank you. I'm afraid I have other work today."

"You did not tell me how your poem writing went last evening."

"Well, I believe," Thalia said, and she could not help smiling at the memory of that rush of words. "Most often I have to go digging for inspiration like a miser searching for gold, and sometimes, if I am very lucky, my efforts turn up something good. Very rarely does inspiration strike like it did last night, like lightning, all at once."

"You speak of your poetry like a saint who has just had a vision. I wish I had a hobby or vocation that drove me like that."

"Do I?" Thalia asked, rather pleased by the idea. She had seen a drawing, once, of an Italian sculpture of Saint Teresa during an ecstatic vision. Perhaps she would write a poem about that. Then Henry's meaning settled in, and she frowned. "Is there nothing that you care for passionately?"

"There are several things I care for mildly," Henry said, shrugging. "Perhaps I am not meant for greatness."

"*Some are born great, some achieve greatness, and some have greatness thrust upon them*," Thalia murmured.

"That sounds deuced uncomfortable," Henry said.

"It's Shakespeare."

"That accounts for it then."

"I think you underrate yourself," Thalia said. "You are a gifted friend and brother—you make a great effort to make the people around you comfortable."

Henry looked mildly disgusted. "That's no gift. That's common human decency."

"Maybe, but a good many people make little effort to act accordingly. And not all gifts look the same. I happen to have a visible one, as does my cousin Charis with her obsession with science. But what of Kalli? Like you, my sister has a kind heart and a knack for caring for those around her, for making ordinary spaces inviting and home-like. Are her talents less valuable than mine because they are less easy to measure?"

A strange expression crossed Henry's face at the mention of Kalli. Did it pain him, still, to think of Kalli's rejection? Perhaps Thalia ought not to have mentioned her.

She hurried on. "But if caring for others is not the vocation you want to pursue, what do you like? Hunting? Racing horses? Perhaps you fancy boats."

Henry raised one eyebrow at her. "If you added pugilism, gaming, and women, you'd have named every hobby attributed to sporting men. Am I so predictable as all that?"

"Well then, perhaps art? Or music?"

He shook his head. "I take a mild interest in most of those things—enough to converse with any person I might happen upon at the club or at a party. But none of them make me look as you did just now talking about that poem. What was it about, by the way?"

Thalia shook her head. "I will not be so easily distracted, Mr. Salisbury."

"You called me Henry last night. Can you bring yourself to do so again?"

Thalia did not even remember doing so. "If I was so forward, I must apologize. I don't believe it would be right for us to be so . . . intimate, when you are engaged to my employer."

Henry's cheeks pinkened. "You're right. I'm sorry. I should not have asked."

"In any case, we were not finished talking about you. What is it you do when you have no one to please but yourself?"

He only pressed his lips together and shook his head.

Thalia was about to inquire further when the drawing room door opened. It wasn't Eleanor, whom she had been half expecting, but Freddy. He clutched a stack of papers in his hands and his cheeks were red. He looked guilty, but what did he have to be guilty of?

"I've brought your poems back," he said.

She waited for the *but* that she could hear in his voice.

"I'm afraid I spilled a little chocolate on some of them."

Thalia laughed. That accounted for the guilty look. "It's all right—this is why I keep a copy. Though I do not believe your chocolate is any match for Edward's sea creature." To Henry, she explained, "Our younger brother found a collection of my poems once and turned them into drawing fodder."

"He sounds precocious," Henry said. "How old is he?"

"Five," Freddy said, just as Thalia said, "Seven."

"No," Freddy said. Then, "Is he?"

"I like children," Henry said, and Thalia had a sudden picture of him surrounded by a pair of ginger-haired children, a boy and a girl, the three of them laughing at something. He would be a good father, much like her own father had been. Still was.

"He can be sweet when he is not being a nuisance," Thalia said, and she and Freddy grinned at each other in shared memories.

"Here," Freddy said, shoving the poems at Thalia.

She took them, noting with some amusement the large brown stain spreading across the top page. Freddy had not spilled *a little* chocolate. He appeared to have spilled the whole cup.

"Well?" Thalia asked. "What did you think?"

"They were all right," Freddy said. "Some of them were rather good, though of course they still need work—more vivid images, stronger words here and there. Several of the themes seem a bit immature. I've marked a few spots, though the chocolate may make my notes hard to read."

"Oh," Thalia said, her heart sinking. She forced brightness into her voice. "Well, thank you for reading them! I am sure you have other demands on your time besides helping your sister, so I do appreciate it."

Freddy shrugged vaguely. "It did not take me long. And I daresay you would do the same for me. At any rate, I must be off. I'm meeting Sophia for lunch."

And then he was gone. Thalia stared down at the stained pages. Was it possible the spot was growing? It seemed about to swallow everything in her vision.

She couldn't look at Henry.

Then Henry was beside her, ducking a little so that his friendly, beloved face was in her line of sight. "Thalia," he said gently—*Thalia*, not Miss Aubrey, and Thalia's heart twisted. "Will you look at me?"

When she did not move, he continued, "I know that man is your brother, and I have not met him above half a dozen times, but I am fairly certain he is not the only, or even the best, judge of poetry."

Thalia knew that. Which was to say, her head knew that, but her heart did not seem to agree. What if Freddy was only voicing what most of his literary friends—Keats, and the others—would say when they read them? That her themes were immature, that she hadn't the control or range that she needed. *They were all right.*

Her daydream of a published volume of poems seemed suddenly laughable.

"Don't listen to Freddy," Henry said. "Trust yourself—trust whatever inspiration hit you like lightning last night."

What if inspiration was only a particularly spectacular form of delusion?

"Thalia, are you all right?" Henry asked, when she still did not say anything.

She wanted to speak, but her throat was tight, and she was afraid if she said anything about her poetry she would start to cry. "I'm fine," she managed. "Pray excuse me to Eleanor."

Before Henry could say anything else, before his kindness could dissolve whatever fragile barrier she'd constructed, she had hugged her manuscript to her chest and slipped out into the hallway.

She raced up the stairs to her room, shutting the door behind her and leaning against it. She held the manuscript away from her, staring at the still-spreading stain.

Perhaps she should just burn it.

But even as she thought that, the words beneath the stain seemed to emerge. She read through them once, a second time. She still liked them—something in them still sang to her.

Perhaps they *were* immature and undeveloped.

But Freddy was not a publisher. His opinion was not the only opinion that mattered. Perhaps even Thalia herself was not a capable judge of her own work. She would write out a clean copy and send it to Mr. Taylor and Mr. Hessey. If they did not want it, she would send it somewhere else. And she would keep sending it out until someone wanted it—or it became clear that no one did.

If that happened, she would figure out a new plan.

But for now, she set to work.

CHAPTER SEVENTEEN

Eleanor

Where a whole heart is given, there should be a fair return;
neither eyes nor ears for any than the favored object.

— Miss Byron, *The Bachelor's Journal*, 1815

It had been just over a week since that singularly cozy encounter at the Joneses' when Owen had asked Eleanor to take off the mask she wore in society. A week in which she had seen him every day but Sunday, and a week in which Eleanor had said absolutely nothing to Owen about that conversation.

At first, she had not quite known what to say, or how to feel, and then after George's unpleasant speech at Almack's, she had realized how close she had come to falling for Owen, to giving up everything she had sacrificed so much for.

It was easier to pretend that nothing had happened, that the time she had spent with Owen and Sophia—one of the pleasantest experiences of her life—was only a dream. A lovely interlude, but not part of her real life.

Now, when they spoke, they were polite acquaintances. Owen had stopped telling her stories; Eleanor had stopped trying to draw him out. She refused to admit, even to herself, that she missed his tales, missed him even when he was present in the room with her.

This particular morning, as Owen sat engrossed in a piece of Albert's writing, Eleanor realized that she was trying to memorize the contours of his face. She set down her paper and pencil.

"Do you need me today?" she asked.

"You pay my wages," Owen said. "I believe that gives you the right to set my terms as you see fit." When she only stared at him, he smiled a little. "I can manage without you."

She nodded, wondering why his admission made her heart twinge.

Eleanor left the room and found Thalia working on something in the drawing room. "I'm going to call upon Anne Salisbury," she said.

Thalia looked up. "Do you want me to come with you?"

"No, it's all right," Eleanor said. She hoped to persuade Anne to a stroll on that clear, early May morning, and Anne was unlikely to agree if she brought Thalia. As she left the house, Eleanor wondered how it was that she had invited so many people into her life who seemed perfectly happy in their own independent sphere. Why could none of them need her as she seemed to need them?

She found Anne sitting in the drawing room with her mother, picking at some embroidery, her lips drooping.

Mrs. Salisbury looked up as Eleanor entered. "Henry is not here, Mrs. Lockhart."

"I'm here to see Anne."

Mrs. Salisbury's eyebrows lifted in vague surprise, as if she had forgotten her own daughter. "Anne?"

"I was hoping she might come for a walk with me."

"I suppose she may, provided she wears a bonnet. The sun is so injurious to one's complexion." Mrs. Salisbury put one still-smooth hand to her own cheek. "And Anne is particularly susceptible, as you can see."

Anne colored, an uncomfortably mottled red and white.

"I think Anne is lovely," Eleanor said, trying not to glare at Anne's mother.

She whisked Anne out of the house as quick as she could.

"I do love my mother," Anne said as Eleanor's carriage lurched away from the house. "But I cannot say I like her. What kind of child says that?"

"Anyone with a mother like yours might find loving her a hard task," Eleanor said. She wondered what her own mother had been like.

Perhaps Anne read something of her thoughts in her face, as she covered her mouth with her hand. "Oh! I am sorry. How thoughtless of me to complain about my mother when you must frequently wish for yours. Let us speak of something else."

It was too early in the day for the fashionable set to be seen in Hyde Park, so Eleanor and Anne found the green paths delightfully empty. They climbed down from Eleanor's carriage and wandered arm in arm down a trail at random, admiring the azaleas and bluebells growing up between the verdant trees.

"How is Henry?" Eleanor asked. "I have not seen him these past few days."

"Shouldn't you ask that of Henry?" Anne asked.

"Of course I will, but I've been busy."

"With a certain handsome mathematician?" Anne sighed. "Are you certain you know what you're about, Eleanor? You know I love you like a sister and would rejoice to have you as my sister in truth—but do you love Henry?"

For a heartbeat, all Eleanor could see was Owen's face, his eyes warm as they met hers. She shook that image away. "Of course I love Henry." It was even true—as a dear friend. She bent to inspect a cluster of rhododendrons. "Henry has nothing to worry about—nor do you."

Anne relented. "Henry is well. We went sketching the other day in Regent's Park."

"Henry? Sketching?" Eleanor tried to picture this and failed. "I didn't know he was artistic."

"Well, I went sketching and Henry decapitated flowers while I worked. He was very likely bored, but he did not—" Anne broke off.

"Anne?" Eleanor looked up at her friend to find Anne staring at wisteria curling around the walls of a nearby cottage, color washing up her cheeks. This was not the mottled embarrassment she'd shown before her mother, but a gentle flush that suffused even her ears.

"Anne?" she repeated.

Anne glanced behind them, to where Eleanor's coachman was following slowly with the carriage. She leaned close and whispered, "I kissed someone."

Eleanor could only stare at her. Anne had never been one for the violent crushes of most schoolgirls—she had never so much as expressed interest in holding a man's hand.

"Don't tell Mama," Anne begged. "I was walking here in this park with Mary—my maid, you know—and we came upon him. He began to walk with us, and I sent Mary behind, and then he swept me behind a bit of wisteria and kissed me."

Eleanor flashed back to their night at the Cyprian's ball. "Did you kick him?"

"Why would I—oh, you are misunderstanding me. It was not someone I'd just met in the park, but someone I have known for some time, only I never dreamed he thought about me in any particular fashion. But he said he has wanted to kiss me since meeting me."

"Who?" Eleanor demanded.

"I can't tell you yet," Anne said. "I want to. Soon. It's only that it's still new, and I'm afraid that if I speak of it, I shall somehow spoil it." She pulled her arm free of Eleanor's. "You disapprove."

Eleanor tried to wipe the expression from her face. "How can I disapprove when I do not know the man? I only worry a little, is all. I don't want to see you hurt."

Anne's face softened. "It's all right. He is a gentleman, truly." She linked her arm through Eleanor's again.

"Will you tell me about him? Not his name if you don't wish, but what sort of man is he?"

Anne blushed again. "I would say he is perfection, but that would not be true. But his imperfections make him all the more delightful. He is tall, and handsome, and speaks with a perfect mix of propriety and passion. And he says he finds me lovely!"

"So you are," Eleanor said. If she worried that Anne's descriptors only touched on surface things, she kept that thought to herself. It was early stages yet. She squeezed Anne's hand, unable to find the right words that were supportive without being false. She settled on: "If he makes you happy, then I am happy for you."

"I am perfectly happy," Anne said. She poked Eleanor in the side. "You never told me that kissing was so delightful!"

Eleanor tried to remember if she had ever kissed Henry. She remembered kissing Albert: quick, dry kisses that were not unpleasant, but not particularly moving either.

Anne's eyes widened. "Henry has not kissed you? I shall tell him that he is failing his duties as a fiancé. How can you agree to marry someone if you do not even know you like their kisses?"

"Not everything in marriage is about kissing."

"But surely some parts are," Anne said. She bent down to pluck a white daisy from the grass, then set about systematically pulling the petals from it. "You say that you love Henry, and I believe you, but something has been troubling me. I just now realized what. Since that kiss, I have spent every day thinking of the man I love, scheming and wondering how I am to see him again. But you and Henry—neither of you act like you particularly care if the other is present." She tossed another white petal to the ground. "Is there something you are not telling me?"

The temptation to share everything was so strong Eleanor could nearly taste it: to tell Anne about Albert and the will, about George Lockhart and his relentless pressure, about Henry agreeing to a fake betrothal to buy her some time. But Anne would be hurt that she had not told her earlier, and she did not want to burden Anne with any more worries than she already carried.

"Nothing," Eleanor said.

Their talk turned to other topics, and they emerged onto a more frequented path, where they spotted a few acquaintances.

One young man pulled up beside them. "Good morning, Miss Salisbury, Mrs. Lockhart." Eleanor tried to place him—she thought he was one of Henry's friends. "I say, is that nephew of yours all right?"

"What?"

"Mr. George Lockhart, he's your nephew?"

"My husband's nephew, yes. What has happened to him?"

"Oh, nothing fatal, I daresay. Only I heard he had lost his shirt in a card game the other night."

"'Lost his shirt'?" Eleanor pictured George wandering around London in his smallclothes and trousers. Aside from the temporary discomfort, she wondered why that fact should be alarming.

"A great deal of money," the young man clarified. "Over a thousand pounds."

Beside her, Anne gasped.

"Goodness," Eleanor said. It *was* a small fortune, more than the yearly income of all but the most wealthy men. "Well, thank you for telling me."

In truth, she wished he had not. She did not know how George was to pay so great a debt, which meant he would shortly be darkening Eleanor's doorstep, begging for the money or encouraging her marriage.

If only she were done with him.

The party at John Soane's on a Wednesday evening in mid-May was not the usual *ton* party, but Eleanor had known it would not be when she accepted Freddy and Thalia's invitation. The party was to be composed of artists and intellectuals, and while Eleanor was not either, she thought that an evening of clever people she had not met yet seemed like a perfect way to keep herself too busy to think.

The evening had started well enough: They had arrived in a timely fashion, after the first wave of guests but not so late as to appear discourteous. They had met their host and toured his remarkable house, which he himself had designed: full of interesting angles and columned hallways, with strategically placed mirrors to magnify the light and give an illusory sense of space; domed rooms with richly colored salmon and green walls; rooms filled with bits of statuary and molding and other items Mr. Soane had collected. One entire room was devoted to pictures, including a few artists and works Eleanor recognized: Hogarth's *A Rake's Progress*, Canaletto's paintings of Venice. At the end of the tour Eleanor had been given a glass of good wine and was enjoying a conversation with a young architect when Owen Jones had arrived with his sister.

Eleanor choked on her wine, and the architect unhelpfully pounded her on the back. And of course the commotion had drawn Owen's and Sophia's attention directly to her. Sophia approached at once, and they had a pleasant short conversation before Freddy discovered Sophia's attendance and carted her off to meet all his poet friends. The architect drifted away, and Eleanor was left alone, acutely conscious of Owen talking to a middle-aged man in glasses.

She looked for Thalia, but could not see her, so she left the main drawing room and found her way back to the library she'd seen on the tour, a large room with red walls and dark wood bookshelves, cupboards overflowing with books and curiosities of all kinds. She had just opened an old volume filled with brilliantly colored illuminations when the door behind her opened.

"Mrs. Lockhart?" Owen shut the door quietly.

Eleanor froze, every muscle in her body going taut. Her brain screamed at her to flee, but she could not make herself move. This was dangerous. This was not her home and library, where she was protected as his employer. This was a neutral space, a new place where they had never before been together, which had no associations for her, no habits or customs she could fall back upon.

Anything could happen here.

"I've been hoping I could have a word with you," he said.

"Well, you have me now," Eleanor said, setting the illuminated book carefully back on the shelf. "My attention, that is." She gripped her hands together.

Owen paced toward her, stopped some three steps away. He was too close, but Eleanor did not back up. Her heart was pounding oddly.

"You've been avoiding me," Owen said. "Why?" Trust Owen to avoid the usual social niceties and cut right to his point.

"I have seen you nearly every day."

"*Seen*, yes. Spoken to, no." Owen shoved a hand through his dark hair, and one curling lock fell down over his forehead. Eleanor's fingers itched to push it back into place. "I—" He took a deep breath, his big shoulders rising and falling. "When you came to our home, you seemed to enjoy yourself. You seemed comfortable in a way you rarely seem to be, letting your entire self relax. You laughed and spoke easily. But since then, you have spoken to me only as needed. Have I offended you somehow?"

"Of course not. You've been nothing but kind to me." How could she tell him that it was not his behavior she feared, but her own? She was not sensible around him.

Owen frowned at her. "You're not happy. I know you said that happiness for you means avoiding want, but there is more to life than just existing. You are engaged, but in the nearly three weeks I have worked for you, you have not once mentioned the man you are to marry. You go from party to party, but none of these social engagements seem to touch your heart."

"Oh? And you are the expert in happiness now, are you? Tell me, what do you fill your hours with, besides work?"

Owen flushed. "At least I enjoy my work. Can you tell me that you enjoy this?" He gestured at the room around them, but she knew what he meant: the party unfolding outside the library.

Owen's own words echoed through her mind: *Then take off the mask.* Eleanor wanted, desperately, to relinquish the weight of her glittering facade. And if not with Owen, who seemed to want nothing from her, then with whom?

Eleanor dropped down into a nearby chair. "It's exhausting, sometimes," she said. "To track all these people and pretend to care for the things they care for, to smile and laugh at witless jokes."

"Then why do it?"

"It's the *ton*, isn't it? The highest society England has to offer. If I am accepted here, I am accepted everywhere." Her voice broke. "I can't go back to being that girl, alone, desperate, scorned, without a penny to her name. I can't go back to being nothing, having nothing."

Owen knelt before her so that his face was on a level with hers. He cupped her cheek gently in one big hand, his thumb brushing wetness across her skin. She was crying. When had she begun crying? When had she last let herself cry, before anyone? She did not think anyone had seen her cry since Albert had caught her in the gardens behind the school.

"You're not alone, Eleanor," he said gently. "You're not nothing."

Something in Eleanor cracked wide, and then she was crying in earnest. She leaned forward to bury her head in her hands, to hide this shameful burst of emotion from Owen, but he did not pull away. Instead, his arms went around her, and she buried her head in his shoulder, inhaling the ink and soap smell he carried with him. She could hear the soft, fast thumping of his heart.

All the invisible weights she carried with her seemed to evaporate as he held her. If she could spend the rest of her life here, with him, she would be content. But she could not—the gap between their lives was too big. She would lose Albert's estate, all that security—

Eleanor pulled back, swiping at her cheeks with gloved hands.

Owen's face was right there, only a hair's breadth from hers. His eyes, clear and honey amber, were fixed on her with an expression of compassion and concern she had rarely seen directed at herself. Her heart turned over and her gaze dropped to his lips. Were they as soft as they looked? If she moved the barest fraction, she could touch his lips with hers.

Later, she would blame her action on a temporary vulnerability— that whatever guard she had let down when she cried had robbed her of the ability to think. But that wouldn't be true.

In that moment, all Eleanor wanted was to kiss Owen.

And so she did. Leaning forward, she brought her lips to his, hesitated a moment so he could pull away if he wished, and when he didn't, she pressed her mouth against his.

His lips were soft and warm, and he followed her initial kiss with kisses of his own, his hand sliding back to cradle her neck, his mouth whispering her name against her lips. *Eleanor*.

Eleanor could tally the men who had kissed her on one hand, and they included that wretched man at the masquerade ball. Albert's pale, polite kisses faded into nothing beside this one, which overwhelmed her senses, flooding her with heat and a churning desire. She clutched at Owen's arms to keep herself upright, and then the kiss was deepening, and she was floating away on a wash of warmth, every nerve in her body coming to attention.

Anne had tried to tell her, Eleanor realized. But she hadn't known kissing could be like this, hadn't known that a simple touch, lips to lips, could remake the whole world, could turn it upside down and then make it right again.

And then at once, it was over. Owen pulled back so suddenly Eleanor nearly toppled from her chair. She shivered in the chill left in the wake of his warm body.

"Eleanor—Mrs. Lockhart, my apologies. I should not have done that."

"I kissed you," Eleanor pointed out.

The barest smile tugged at his lips. "Then you should not have done that."

"Why?" There were reasons why, Eleanor knew—good reasons. But all she could think of was how right it had felt to embrace Owen, how her heart, body, and mind had seemed united for one brief, glorious minute.

"You are engaged," Owen said. "And I am not the sort of man to dally with another man's affianced wife, though I know it is fashionable among your set."

Your set. Eleanor flinched. "An engagement is not a marriage. Engagements can be broken." What was she saying? But for the merest of moments, she let herself wonder what would happen if she told Owen the truth—that her engagement to Henry was only a sham, that she could be entirely free with a word.

What if she could take that moment at Owen and Sophia's and spin it into a life?

Owen sighed. "Even if you were free, this would be impossible. Your class, for one. My work, for another."

His words doused any lingering ember in her.

"Our class is not as different as you seem to think. And what has your work to do with anything?" Eleanor knew she was inviting more pain with her questions, but she couldn't seem to stop herself, like a child picking at a scab.

Owen was silent for a moment, then said, "When I was a child, my father worked long hours. Still does. My mother was a wonderful, warm-hearted woman who thrived on affection—affection my father could never seem to give her. In this, I am like my father. I am not a particularly demonstrative man, and my work often engrosses me. What kind of bargain is that in a husband? If I marry—which does not at all seem likely—it will be to a woman who understands what I am capable of giving. But you, Mrs. Lockhart, deserve so much more than that."

"I've seen you with Sophia. You're capable of generosity and affection," Eleanor said.

"But not romantic love."

Eleanor heard what he meant: *I do not love you.* He might desire her, but she knew enough of the world to know that was a separate thing from love. Embarrassment flooded through her, followed by hurt. She dug for words that would wound him too. "You're right.

This was a mistake. By your own admission, you are incapable of love. And even if you were not, how could I be foolish enough to jeopardize everything I have—my wealth, my place in society, my future? You have nothing to offer me that would make that loss worthwhile."

Owen met her gaze steadily. "You are not nothing, Eleanor Lockhart. But neither am I. You demean us both if you think that."

Then he stood and walked from the room without a backward glance.

CHAPTER EIGHTEEN

Thalia

A fire burned through me yesterday eve:
Red flames scour'd and devoured all in their path.
Numb, I could but trail the wreckage and grieve.
Nothing remained for kindling—or for wrath.
This morning I gathered my tools to try
Again to craft a poem or two.
But naught but ashes rained down from the sky.

—Thalia Aubrey

A tenor was singing somewhere near the front of the gold room, and though the voice was elegant and clear, Thalia was distracted. Eleanor had disappeared somewhere—not surprising, in this lovely maze of a house—and Freddy was up to something. He wore the exact smirk Edward had that time he hid the remains of a particularly sticky plum cake in his bed.

As she watched, Freddy led Sophia from the drawing room, trailed by a handful of his poet friends. Thalia slipped across the room to follow them. She found them in a neighboring salon: Mr. John Keats was saying something about his theory of art.

"A poet must strive after his negative capability," Keats said. "When man is capable of being in uncertainties, mysteries, doubts, without any irritable reaching after fact and reason."

"A sort of poetic mood, then?" Mr. Leigh Hunt asked.

"Deeper than a mood, I believe," Keats said. "A state of being, where one is fully receptive to the world around him but comfortable with uncertainties."

Well, thought Thalia, if that was what was required of a poet, it was no wonder that she was not one yet. She was fascinated by uncertainties, but she would not say she was comfortable with them. For instance, her impossible affection for Mr. Salisbury was distinctly uncomfortable. And contrary to expectations of women, she preferred to reach after fact and reason.

"I say," Freddy interjected, "I have some good news."

The others, a little startled by the disconnected interruption, turned toward Freddy.

"Taylor and Hessey have agreed to publish my first book of poems."

Have agreed to publish—

Thalia didn't hear what the others said, though she was distantly aware of them jostling Freddy, slapping his back and shaking his hand. A hot wave flushed through her, leaving a sharp sourness in her mouth. They had agreed to publish *Freddy*? And she had heard nothing from them yet, though she had sent them her manuscript earlier that month, despite—or perhaps in defiance of—Freddy's lukewarm praise.

She walked toward one of the windows, looking out on a darkened street. She tried to tell herself that she should be happy for her brother, that perhaps his poetry had improved in the last few years, just as hers had. She told herself to approach Freddy, to congratulate him before he suspected just how bitter his news was to her. But she could not bring herself to move.

Thalia took a long breath, then another. After several moments, she felt perhaps she could face Freddy.

She turned back, just in time to see Freddy kneel before Sophia and clasp her hands. His friends looked on with mixed expressions of bemusement, surprise, and mild contempt.

"Miss Sophia Montgomery, this achievement of mine would not have been possible without you—your very existence inspires me to reach higher. You are, indeed, a muse among muses."

Sophia was not as amused as Freddy's fellows. She tugged her hands away. "Freddy," she said, "don't be an ass."

"If I am a fool," Freddy persisted, reaching for her hand again, "let it be known that I am a fool for love. I hesitated to say anything when I had nothing to offer you, but now—Miss Sophia, will you marry me?"

"I do not think the sales of a single book of poetry will support a wife," Mr. Keats observed.

Freddy ignored him, continuing to stare up at Sophia.

Sophia sighed. "Freddy, stand up."

"Not until you answer me."

Thalia took a step forward. She was not entirely certain what she meant to do—join Sophia's pleas, pull Freddy from the room—but people beyond Freddy's circle of friends were beginning to notice the commotion and gather in the room.

"Freddy, you are a dear, ridiculous creature, and I like you very much, but I cannot marry you."

"Is it my lack of wealth?" Freddy asked, finally scrambling to his feet. "I assure you, this book is only the first of many."

"You might have a hundred thousand books and a hundred

thousand pounds, and I could not marry you," Sophia said. "I'm afraid I do not feel for you the way I hope to feel about the man I marry."

One of Freddy's friends clapped him on the back. "Tough luck, old chap."

Freddy looked dazed. "Sophia—you do not know what you are saying. I love you. I—"

Thalia intervened, taking her brother by the arm. "I do not think Miss Montgomery will like you more for claiming to know her mind better than she does," she murmured. She drew Freddy from the room, toward the library she had seen earlier, hoping to distract him.

Sophia mouthed *Thank you* at Thalia as they left.

They had not quite reached the library when the library doors burst open, and Mr. Jones stepped out. He nodded at them, his face drawn, and walked past without speaking.

Thalia reached for the door and opened it to find Eleanor standing alone in the middle of the room, her face in her hands.

Thalia dropped Freddy's arm and sprang toward the other girl. "Eleanor! What has happened? Are you all right?"

And Eleanor, for the barest moment, fell into Thalia's arms as though Thalia had come to rescue her from drowning. Thalia had just felt the trembling shaking Eleanor's entire body when Eleanor pulled back. "I'm fine. It's a headache only. Please, may we leave?"

A thousand questions burned Thalia's lips. She didn't ask any of them. Instead, she tucked her arm through Freddy's again, and they followed her employer from the house.

The following afternoon, Thalia was again working at the desk in the drawing room. Or rather, she was trying to work. But every time she set her pen to paper, she heard Freddy's announcement from the night before: *Taylor and Hessey have agreed to publish my first book of poems.* It was so very like Freddy to waltz into town, collect a passel of artistic friends, and have a contract handed to him. While Thalia had worked for months on her craft, and for what? She was still barred from intimacy with the poets Freddy had collected because she was a woman.

She sighed and set her pen down. Rising to stretch, she caught sight of a carriage pulling up before the house. Henry leaped out of the carriage, and her heart leaped with him. *Enough foolishness*, she told herself sternly. When Mr. Davis opened the drawing room door to admit Henry, she was tolerably composed.

"Good day, Miss Aubrey," Henry said. "I've come to take Eleanor for a drive—she said that she wished to speak with me in private. Am I in trouble?" But he smiled at her in such a way that she knew he did not really believe he was.

"Driving?" Thalia frowned a little. She had not seen Eleanor all morning, nor had Eleanor come down for luncheon. "Let me check on her." She could have sent a maid, but something did not sit right. It was not uncommon for Eleanor to spend the morning in bed, but not when she had an engagement.

Thalia left Henry to amuse himself as he would in the drawing room—perhaps it was a good thing, after all, that she had been unable to write a word that day. There was nothing incriminating among the papers on the desk, should he be tempted to inspect them. She made her way up the stairs to Eleanor's room and tapped on the closed door. "Eleanor?"

A muffled grunt reached her. Eleanor was awake, at least. Thalia opened the door.

The only thing visible of Eleanor was a mound on the bed, a few strands of brown hair tangled on the pillow. "Eleanor? Henry has come to take you driving."

Eleanor swore—not an aggrieved explosion, but rather in resignation. She rolled so she was facing Thalia, and Thalia saw the dark circles beneath her eyes. Had she slept at all? Something—was it Mr. Jones?—had happened to disturb her last night.

"I cannot go driving," Eleanor said. "Make him go away—tell him I won't go, or go with him yourself. I don't care."

"Do you want to talk about whatever ails you?" Thalia asked cautiously.

The words hung between them for an interminable moment. Then Eleanor released a gusty sigh. "It's merely a headache."

Thalia didn't believe her, but she wouldn't press. She returned to the drawing room. Henry was standing at the window by her desk, but he turned when the door opened. Her heart contracted. "I'm sorry, Mr. Salisbury, but Eleanor is indisposed."

"I'm sorry to hear that," Henry said, and he did look sorry, his eyebrows drawing together in a slight frown. Then—"Would you like to drive with me? It's a beautiful day and my horses are ready to go. It would be a shame to waste it."

Thalia nearly said no. She should not go driving with Eleanor's affianced, not when a drive promised so much time with Henry,

193

alone but for his coachman on the seat behind them. But she thought of Eleanor's words, *Make him go away . . . go with him yourself* and some perversity seized her. If Eleanor meant to stand up someone as kind and generous as Henry, Thalia would not.

"Very well," she said. "Give me a few minutes to make myself ready."

The day was as lovely as Henry had promised. A sky so blue it might have inspired the color itself, a gentle spring wind ruffling her curls as they drove. Thalia's spirits began to lift as they rattled down the streets, and she could almost—*almost*—forget about Freddy's publication.

She said, "Taylor and Hessey have accepted a manuscript of Freddy's poems." So she had not really forgotten.

Henry looked gratifyingly astonished. His eyebrows nearly disappeared into his hair. "Your brother Freddy? I had no notion he even wrote poems."

See? Thalia thought. "I did not know myself. He never truly applied himself at Oxford, but he must have learned to apply himself to writing."

Henry frowned at her. "And how do you feel about this? It must be disappointing, having worked as hard as you have, to have your brother achieve your dream first."

"Ah, I'm used to being eclipsed," Thalia said, striving for a lightness she did not feel. "Both my sister and my cousin 'took' last spring during our Season in London, while I, I'm afraid, did not."

"You spin a very pretty story," Henry said, still frowning, "but I question its accuracy. You forget that I am one of the few people in London who know that you nearly eloped. If you did not 'take'— what a loathsome phrase, anyway—it was by choice."

So much had passed between her and Henry since that failed elopement that it was almost like it had happened to two different people.

"We are friends, are we not?" Henry asked, echoing her own words to him. "You don't have to pretend with me."

She sighed. "You're right. It hurts. It hurts abominably. I have worked on my poems for years with very little to show for it, and it seems unfair that Freddy can simply waltz into town and achieve what I have been trying to do with no effort." She caught herself. "Perhaps that is unfair. Perhaps Freddy has been working harder than I give him credit for."

"That seems unlikely," Henry said, so matter-of-factly that Thalia was surprised into laughing. "I wish you could achieve everything you deserve—it's not fair that society does not reward people exclusively for merit and hard work."

"I can scarcely imagine what such a world would look like," Thalia said. "Certainly much different than the one we have now. Far too many people are born to a lot in life that they did not earn. Some to far more than they deserve, some to far less."

Henry grinned at her. "Next you'll be advocating anarchy." He drove in thoughtful silence for a moment, then slewed in the seat toward her. "I say, I have an idea. Will Eleanor miss you if you are not back for some time?"

Thalia thought back to Eleanor's scratchy voice rising from the bed. "I don't believe she will. What do you have in mind?"

It took them perhaps an hour to reach the small village of Highgate, along the edge of Hampstead Heath, with its riffling grasses and occasional glints of light across scattered ponds. It did not feel so long to Thalia, as they talked of everything and nothing, or sat in companionable silence watching birds fly overhead.

Henry did not stop to ask for directions, but pulled up before a rectangular, redbrick house with rows of square windows. He had refused to tell her where they were going, saying only that he wanted to surprise her. Curious, Thalia followed him down from the carriage and to the door, where Henry rapped smartly.

A neatly dressed maid opened the door. "Yes?"

"We would like to see Mr. Coleridge, if he is receiving visitors."

Black spots danced at the edge of Thalia's vision. *Mr. Coleridge?* As in Samuel Coleridge, author of *The Rime of the Ancient Mariner*, which she and Kalli had delighted in reciting to each other as children? She gripped Henry's arm. Surely they shouldn't be here.

But the maid only bobbed a curtsy and disappeared into the bowels of the house, leaving them to wait in the front hall. After a moment in which Thalia nearly lost her courage and pulled Henry out of the house, the maid returned to say that Mr. Coleridge would see them in the drawing room.

She ushered them into a pretty room, with white lace curtains at the window and a pair of red velvet chairs flanking a narrow sofa, upon which sat a middle-aged man. The man, white whiskers curling about his jowls, looked up as they entered.

"Mr. Coleridge, this is—" The maid hesitated and turned an enquiring look on Henry, who supplied, "Henry Salisbury and Thalia Aubrey."

"Do sit down," the gentleman said courteously, attempting to rise. His legs seemed to give out on him, and he sat back down rather suddenly. Thalia pretended not to notice as she followed his directive, perching on one of the chairs.

Mr. Coleridge studied them curiously. "Do I know you?"

"We met at a party, some months back," Henry said. "The Billingtons', I believe?"

Thalia felt a wash of relief. It was not so inappropriate for them to visit if Henry had met the great author.

"Oh, yes. I was there. I'm afraid I do not remember you."

"I'm afraid I'm not very memorable," Henry said, laughing ruefully. "It's good of you to see us."

"I meant to be writing, you know, but the words won't come today. Skittish things."

Thalia wanted to say something, to acknowledge a fellow feeling, but her words turned suddenly skittish on her tongue too. She could feel Henry looking at her.

The maid returned with a tray of pastries and tea, and Thalia took the teacup offered her with gratitude. She might busy herself for a moment and collect herself without appearing impolite.

"We were wondering," Henry began, with another sidelong look at Thalia, "that is, I was wondering, if you had any advice you might give an aspiring poet?"

Coleridge brightened, his slumping shoulders drawing upright. "Oh, you mean to pursue the elusive muse?"

"No, I—"

"Do you know, I wrote on this very topic for my *Biographia Literaria*. I believe a poet—any writer really—ought always to have some other means of making a living. A useful vocation will provide one with the money upon which to live, while the pursuit of writing offers a welcome respite from daily labors. I might recommend the church: It offers a suitable meld of intellect with the time required for writing. And one need not be a complete hermit—the undisturbing voices of a wife or sister in one's home will be like a restorative atmosphere."

As Coleridge waxed enthusiastic, neither Thalia nor Henry was able to say a word. When he paused to lift his teacup to his lips, Thalia and Henry spoke at the same time.

"I believe Mr. Salisbury was asking for me," Thalia said.

Henry said, "I would make a terrible clergyman."

Mr. Coleridge set his teacup down, only a slight waver in his hands. "I'm afraid I've been rather ill," he said. He blinked at them both a bit owlishly before focusing on Thalia. "*You* wish to become a writer?"

"A poet," Thalia said, a trifle defiantly, thinking of Coleridge's description of wives and sisters as gentle atmospheric noise. "And why not? There have been many fine women poets before me: Mary Sidney, Charlotte Smith, Joanna Baillie."

"No doubt, no doubt. A woman might, if she is very clever, pen some fine words. But one must first be certain that one is meant to be an author; one must take care to study the very best words on the subject. Too many a young author has intemperately published only to find their immature works exposed to ridicule. The German author Herder has perhaps said it best: *With the greatest possible solicitude, avoid authorship. Too early or immoderately employed, it makes the head waste and the heart empty.*"

Thalia set down the pastry she had just picked up, untasted. Something sour seemed to coat her tongue. Was she mistaken then, in her writing? Had she taken some youthful arrogance for skill, for a vocation?

Henry fidgeted in his chair, as though he were about to rise and thought better of it. He said, "Is it not equally likely that we have been denied works of genius by young writers who doubted themselves too early?"

"It is possible, of course, but I believe anyone truly meant to be a writer will persist despite discouragement."

Thalia took a long, slow breath, then released it. She wondered if Mr. Coleridge had any sense of the barriers that faced a writer who was not male, who did not have the support of her family. She listened as Henry got Mr. Coleridge talking about some amusing anecdote about the village, though she could not have said afterward what the point of the story was.

When their fifteen minutes had elapsed, Henry stood easily and helped her rise, and they left Mr. Coleridge still sitting on his sofa. Thalia had not said a word since her challenge to the poet had been rebuffed.

Once in the carriage, Henry turned to Thalia. "Are you all right? I've never seen you so quiet."

"I am fine," Thalia said.

Henry waited, eyebrows raised in doubt. The carriage jolted forward.

Thalia sighed. "What if Mr. Coleridge is right, that too many young authors attempt to publish in spite of talent or maturity? Should I give up writing now, before I embarrass myself?"

Henry took her hand in his. "Mr. Coleridge may be a celebrated writer, but he does not know everything. He has not read your poems. I have. I think you should write, and keep writing, as long as the words bring you joy."

Thalia didn't move. She didn't pull her hand away, as she knew she ought to. Instead, she left her fingers in the warmth of Henry's, and felt something small and tight start to unfurl inside her.

"I had hoped this visit would cheer you up, and in that, I seem to have failed. But Thalia, you really cannot let the opinion of someone unconnected to you or your happiness shape your belief in yourself. You have talent, I know you do. More to the point, *you* know that you do. I wish you would trust your own judgment." He hesitated for a beat. "At least, setting aside your appalling lapse in judgment in spending time with *me*."

Thalia laughed, as Henry had meant her to, and let the warm sun wash over her face. A similarly warm, melting feeling spread through her, making the tension in her body dissolve like sugar in butter over the stove. She wanted, suddenly, to kiss Henry.

She managed to restrain the impulse, but she left her hand in Henry's until they were nearly in sight of London. When she pulled her fingers away, Henry's fingers closed convulsively, as if they missed her weight. As if he missed *her*.

At such a traitorous thought, Thalia folded her arms across her torso, and tried diligently to think of Eleanor, and what she might require of her when she returned.

CHAPTER NINETEEN

Eleanor

A *forward* girl always alarms me.

—The Rev. John Bennett, *Letters to a Young Lady,
on a Variety of Useful and Interesting Subjects*

Eleanor was not often given to swearing.

It was not ladylike, so she eschewed it in company. But sometimes, in private, it was so very satisfying to release frustration with a few pithy syllables. At least Thalia was not present to hear her again—she was off somewhere with Henry.

"Damn it."

Eleanor set the latest of Albert's papers back on the desk. She had read over the article three times now and it made scarcely more sense than it had the first time. How was she supposed to organize these papers without Owen's—Mr. Jones's—help? There was no possibility of his help now, not after their last, disastrous conversation.

Damn him anyway. Why did he have to ruin everything by making her have feelings? Her life had been quite satisfactory before he showed up to spoil things.

She picked up another of Albert's papers. This one was easier for her to understand, about the effects of a gentleman's gambling debts on his family's finances. But the easier understanding did not make her feel better. It only reminded her of George, of the passing stranger's words about George's gambling debts. At least George had not tried to contact her—yet.

Eleanor forced herself to go through Albert's work for another hour, stopping only when she felt a resurgence of her headache from that morning. Thalia still was not back—where had the girl gone to? Perhaps it had been a mistake to send her with Henry. She had no doubt of Henry's loyalty—he would not jeopardize their fake engagement when he had agreed to it—but it would not do to generate talk. It would only encourage George to pester her.

Eleanor pushed aside a small qualm. Perhaps the drive would not harm Henry, but might it hurt Thalia? She had not missed the way Thalia watched Henry. No—Thalia could look after herself. She would not need—or welcome—Eleanor's interference. In any case, if there *was* something between Thalia and Henry, some test of that affection could only prove beneficial.

Shutting the door to the small study firmly behind her, Eleanor walked down into the kitchen for a cup of tea, scandalizing the cook and maids clustered there. "We would have brought it to you, ma'am," one of the maids said.

"I didn't want to trouble you," Eleanor said. She backed out of the room, clutching her teacup, feeling like an intruder in her own house.

The last time she had truly felt at home in her skin had been with Owen and Sophia, having tea together in their flat. But she wouldn't think about that. This was her home, her place. She was being ridiculous—a side effect of her headache.

Eleanor retreated with the tea to the drawing room and flicked idly through a ladies' magazine as she sipped. Her mood fell with each flicked page, and after half a dozen, she abandoned her tea and the drawing room. She needed to get out of the house, speak with a friend. A visit to Anne Salisbury would be just the thing to raise her spirits, she decided.

The Salisburys' butler ushered Eleanor into a gold-and-green drawing room in the Salisbury town house, where Mrs. Salisbury was sitting alone, reading a book of poetry on a gilded settee. The older woman did not look up as Eleanor was announced, but continued to read.

"Fetch Anne, would you please, Bardsley," Mrs. Salisbury instructed, then placed her finger in her book to mark her place and lifted her eyes to study Eleanor. "Good day, Mrs. Lockhart."

Was it only Eleanor's imagination that heard the slight emphasis on *Mrs.*?

"How do you do, Mrs. Salisbury?" Eleanor asked, waiting for Henry and Anne's mother to invite her to sit down. But Mrs. Salisbury said nothing, so Eleanor continued to stand, curling her hands into her skirts.

"Do you read much poetry?" Mrs. Salisbury asked.

"Some. My companion is a poet, did you know?"

"A lovely girl," Mrs. Salisbury said approvingly. "Did she come with you?"

"No—" Eleanor started to say *She's gone driving with Henry*, but caught herself. Even she could hear how that might sound to

Henry's mother. "What are you reading?" she asked, nodding at the book still clasped in Mrs. Salisbury's hand—as though Eleanor were merely a brief interruption, not a visitor.

"Oh, some book from the library. I cannot understand the half of it, but I'm told it's all the rage, so one must pretend." Mrs. Salisbury's pale eyes scanned Eleanor again, as though looking for something she could not quite find.

"Hmm," Eleanor murmured. She hoped Anne would hurry.

"There was one poem," Mrs. Salisbury continued, "about unrequited love. And do you know, it made me think of you and Henry. I have the oddest notion that the two of you are not as well suited as you may believe."

Eleanor's heartbeat picked up. "What do you mean?"

Mrs. Salisbury waved one slim hand airily. "Oh, you know. You do carry a whiff of the shop about you, dear girl. I mean no disrespect to your late husband, but really, who were his people? For that matter, who were *yours*? One hears such rumors."

What rumors? Eleanor thought, panic starting to close around her chest. Had someone been speaking of her? Had George? She had thought her past mostly buried after she married Albert. "If Henry does not object to my antecedents, ma'am, I do not see that it is anyone else's concern."

"Am I not allowed to worry about my son's happiness? I do not—forgive my frankness—believe that you will make him happy." Mrs. Salisbury hesitated for a moment. "I know you do not like me, Mrs. Lockhart. You think me heartless and shallow, concerned only for social standing. Perhaps that is so. Certainly, I was never taught by those who raised me how to care for other humans. Doubtless

I have made mistakes. But I'll be *damned* if I'll watch you ruin my son's life. Henry is a good boy, the most loyal of sons and friends. He would never cry off. So I am asking you to do so."

Spurred by an unexpected wrench of fellow feeling, Eleanor was tempted to tell the truth—that her engagement to Henry was a hoax, that Mrs. Salisbury needn't worry. But she pressed her lips together instead. She might owe Anne and Henry a great deal, but she owed Mrs. Salisbury nothing. What did it matter, what Mrs. Salisbury thought of her?

The door opened, and Eleanor turned toward it with relief. *Anne.* But it was only Bardsley again. The butler straightened his coat and said, "Miss Salisbury has gone out, ma'am." He bowed and left the room.

Eleanor looked back at Mrs. Salisbury. "If Anne is out, I won't disturb you any longer. I wish you good day." She dropped a brief curtsy and turned toward the door.

"Mrs. Lockhart?" Mrs. Salisbury's voice called after her. That rare moment of vulnerability was gone, and her voice was light and lilting again. "Do think on what I've said, will you, dear?"

Eleanor let herself out of the room without responding, everything she wanted to say tucked tight against her teeth.

Back home again, feeling drained and strangely sad, Eleanor made her way up the stairs to her small study. She stripped off her gloves and paused on the landing at the top of the stairs. She wanted nothing more than to crawl into her bed and pretend this day, this week, her fight with Owen, had never happened. Well, and why not? There was no one here to tell her not to squander her time.

She peeked into the drawing room, but Thalia was not at her desk. She must still be out with Henry. That realization added another layer to the pall clinging about her. She had lost Owen, she was losing Anne to her nameless beau, and even Henry and Thalia had no real need of her.

Eleanor shook herself. Now she was only being mawkish. She would *not* go to bed. She would do some work, like a reasonably grown woman, and feel better for it.

She made her way down the hallway to her study, opened the door, and stopped.

Owen sat behind the desk, humming softly to himself.

The tension and loneliness of her day lifted from her as though they had never been. How could just the sight of this man affect her so? Earlier that day, in her kitchen, she had felt like an outsider in her own home. And yet Owen's broad, familiar face in her study brought her back to herself. Her apartments didn't feel like home—*he did*.

That realization shot a bolt of panic through her. She turned to shut the door, to flee as far from him as she could, just as Owen glanced up to see her.

"Mrs. Lockhart? Are you all right?"

"What are you doing here?" she managed.

"I agreed to do a job for you. I was not aware that we had terminated that agreement, even if you—" His cheeks reddened. "If you do not wish me to finish this work, you have only to say so."

Yes, go, Eleanor thought. But she remembered her frustration of earlier that afternoon, that yawning despair of never finishing

Albert's work, and she swallowed her first words. "Thank you. That would be kind of you. I—" She stopped, took a deep breath, started again. "I could use your help."

A tiny smile flickered about Owen's lips, but he seemed to catch it and flattened it out as soon as he realized what he was doing. "Then I will finish the work. You needn't worry—I won't disturb you. Your butler can let me in, as he has thus far. Nor will I refer to that conversation which pained us both."

"Oh. Good." Eleanor felt ridiculous. Just when she wanted to appear cool and indifferent, all she could find were single syllables. Worse still was the tightening at the back of her throat and the stinging in her eyes. She would not cry in front of Owen.

In the doorway, she halted. "Do you ever wish that things could be different? I mean, between us? That you were not you and I were not me, and we could be friends—real friends?" Her question was nonsense, she could hear that even as it burst from her, but she knew what she meant: If there were not barriers of class and Owen's own constitution between them, could he have cared for her?

But why had she asked that? What possible answer could he give her that would satisfy her? "Forgive me—forget I asked that. It was wrong of me."

That barely there smile trembled around Owen's mouth. "If I were not me and you were not you, I very much doubt we would be having any kind of conversation." He rubbed his hand across his face, wiping away the smile. His eyes, when he looked at her, were so very kind that Eleanor wanted to cry again. "But we are friends, I hope."

"Yes," Eleanor choked. "Friends."

She shut the door and fled down the hallway, up another flight of stairs to her bedroom. She locked the door carefully behind her, folded back the cover on her bed, and lay down. She stared at the ceiling for a long time, until hot tears slid down her cheekbones and dripped into her ears.

Then, as though a dam were releasing, she flipped over and put her face in her pillow, strangling the sobs that escaped her. For a woman who never cried, Eleanor had twice been reduced to tears by Owen in as many days.

Damn him anyway.

And her too, for letting herself believe in romance, even for a moment.

CHAPTER TWENTY

Thalia

There are words we have for thieves:
For a friend who steals one's lover,
Whispering beneath the eaves.
For a silk-fingered touch in the darkness,
Stealing away one's gold.
But what do you call a brother
Who robs the words of my soul?

—Thalia Aubrey

Thalia walked up the stairs to Eleanor's town house in the early evening, still smiling, Henry at her side. They let themselves into the house. The front hall was dim and quiet, but a package the size of a manuscript had been left on a side table. Heartbeat quickening, Thalia inspected the address. It was to her, from Taylor and Hessey.

"Oh." The word escaped her almost as a cry.

Henry looked from the address to her face. "I'll go find Eleanor. You can tell me before I leave if it's good news or bad."

Thalia smiled a little wryly. "If it's bad news, I doubt I shall want to share."

"But we are friends, are we not? If it is bad news, I shall help you roundly abuse them for their lack of taste, and we'll both feel better for it."

"Thank you for the offer, but I should prefer not to need it."

Henry took her hand and squeezed it briefly. "Good luck," he whispered, though no one was around to hear them, and then went up the stairs to find Eleanor.

Thalia followed him more slowly, the weight of the package heavy in her hands. Surely it was not good news, if the publishers had chosen to return her manuscript. She took the parcel into the drawing room, to the little desk where she had written several of the poems. She pulled the knot binding the brown paper together, then peeled back the paper one corner at a time, as though unwrapping an anticipated gift.

There was a letter lying atop the manuscript. It looked as though it had been scrawled hastily, the letters jagged and quick, with ink splatters across the page. Not the action of a publisher who wishes to court the good opinion of a writer.

Heart sinking, Thalia picked up the letter and began to read.

Miss Aubrey—

No *dear*, no softening of the salutation.

We have received and reviewed your manuscript and find we are unable to publish it. You are young, and female, and so perhaps you do not realize that to imitate another's work so closely is a cardinal sin among writers. If this was meant as a joke, it is in poor taste. If it is not a joke, then we can find little excuse for you, other than a perhaps pardonable ignorance of your sex. We ask that you do not attempt to submit this work to another house, or we will be forced to bring legal action.

It was signed, curtly, *Taylor.*

Thalia blinked at the paper. She could not seem to make sense of the words. She read it a second time, then a third.

To imitate another's work—? But the words were hers. Whose work was she meant to be imitating? Some of her poems might be in the style of older poets, but surely that was no crime? Poets drew inspiration from one another all the time. And none were so close that she might be accused of stealing someone's words. No one had even seen these poems, really, except Henry and Freddy, and only Freddy had seen all of them.

An appalling suspicion darted into her mind.

Thalia dropped the letter back on top of the manuscript, chills prickling across her skin. *No.* It wasn't possible.

She thought of how Freddy had borrowed her manuscript, had claimed to read it but found little to admire in it. He had spilled chocolate over the pages. She had thought at the time it was an accident, but what if it had been deliberate, to force her to spend time recopying the ruined poems? He had had the manuscript for more than a week, plenty of time to make his own copy if he had wanted to.

Taylor and Hessey had offered to publish Freddy's poems—poems she had not known existed—and he had proposed to Sophia on the presumed merit of their publication.

No.

She must be wrong.

Even Freddy would not stoop so low.

Would he?

The door opened. "Eleanor's maid says Eleanor is still indisposed," Henry said, more cheerfully than a confession of Eleanor's illness warranted. "What do Taylor and Hessey have to say?"

He strode into the room but stopped as he registered Thalia's expression. "What is it? Bad news? I suspected the men had no taste after they offered to publish your brother."

"They don't want my poems," Thalia said. "But that's not—oh, this is impossible. I must talk with Freddy." She began to pace across the room, wringing her hands, too distracted to care that she was behaving in a most clichéd fashion.

"With Freddy?" Henry echoed, confused. "What has he to do—?"

Thalia spoke across him. "Oh, Henry, I do love you, but please stop talking! I must think."

Henry blinked at her.

Thalia stopped pacing, a slow flush burning up her throat, across her cheeks. What had she just said?

"What?" he asked.

"Don't mind me," Thalia said. "I hardly know what I'm saying."

Henry crossed the floor toward her and took her hands in his. Thalia snatched her hands back as though his were live coals, humiliation at her unthinking words overriding her shock at the publisher's letter. Henry made no move to reclaim her hands, but he didn't step back. He was so close she could feel the warmth of him, smell the faint, spicy whiff of his cologne.

"Thalia," he said gently, "slow down. Tell me what is going on. Let me help."

She shook her head. She didn't know how to give voice to her terrible suspicions. She both wanted Henry to go, to ease the shame scalding through her, and wanted him to stay, because his presence irrationally made everything better. She gestured, instead, at the letter that lay discarded atop her manuscript on the desk.

Henry picked up the letter, frowning. He scanned down it, and

Thalia began to pace again, moving away from his distracting nearness.

"But this makes no sense," he said, shaking his head. "Whose manuscript do they think you have copied? They must be mistaken."

Her heart hummed at his implicit faith in her, that his first instinct was to question the publishers, not her honor. She wet her lips with her tongue and said hesitantly, "I think, perhaps, they mean Freddy."

He looked at her then, his hazel eyes widening as he made the same calculations she had done. His voice sharpened uncharacteristically. "You think your brother stole your manuscript and submitted it in his name?"

Said so baldly, Thalia flinched away from the accusation. "No—I mean, perhaps. I don't know. It seems so unthinkable, but—I must speak with Freddy."

"Shall I take you to him?" Henry offered.

Thalia shook her head. "No, not yet. I won't deal well with him while I'm upset, and I must think what to say. Perhaps in the morning . . ."

Henry nodded his understanding. Thalia thought he might take his leave then—heaven knew, she'd monopolized enough of his day and he must have more important things to attend to—but instead he closed the gap between them, his bright eyes meeting hers with a steady, intense look that brought the flush back to her cheeks.

"Thalia, are you all right? Between Mr. Coleridge and this letter and your brother, that's a good deal of bad news to absorb."

"I—" Thalia drew a deep breath. "I will be. It stings, but it will pass."

He waited for a moment, not saying anything.

"No, that's not true. It hurts damnably. I have spent years working for this, dreaming of publication, and all I've found in London is rejection." To her own horror, her last words caught on a sob. She blinked hard but was too late to stop one hot tear from slipping down her cheek.

Henry caught the tear with his thumb, rubbing it feather-light across her cheek. Heat blazed in its wake.

"I'm sorry—" she began.

Henry shook his head. "You don't have to apologize to me. Didn't you teach me that true friends do not have to be perfect for one another? You do not always have to be strong or happy for me. I can handle your grief and your rage. I can even handle your ill temper."

"Good," she said, her voice still shaking. "Because I am not sad—I am angry. So damnably angry."

"Then be angry," Henry said, and he stood, unmoved, while she raged at the injustice of it, pounding her fists against his chest.

And then, when the worst of her fury had burned through her, he stepped closer. Thalia sighed a little—in resignation or relief, she couldn't tell—and let her cheek, instead of her fists, rest against his shoulder. His arms tightened around her, and the last of her resistance to Henry Salisbury dissolved entirely. No doubt he saw himself comforting her as he might his sisters, but how could she not love a man who was not afraid of the worst of her?

Henry murmured into her hair, "What was it you said earlier, before you asked me to stop talking?"

CHAPTER TWENTY-ONE

Eleanor

The regulation of the temper and passions, is a point of the highest importance to individual and domestic comfort . . . A sullen or obstinate temper . . . if indulged, may terminate in melancholy, malice, and revenge.

The Female Instructor, 1811

Eleanor awoke sometime later, her room full of a dimness that might have been early evening or might have been early morning, she couldn't quite tell. Salt from her tears had crusted on her cheeks and her hair was tangled about her ears. She got out of bed and splashed water on her face and combed out her hair, though she didn't put it back up. Her head ached again.

Peering out her window, she could see folks passing on the street below, including a gentleman and a lady dressed in evening finery. They did not have the seedy look of people who had been out all night. It was early evening, Eleanor concluded. She straightened her dress, wiped futilely at the creases in her skirt, and then went downstairs to see if Thalia had returned yet.

Eleanor passed her study with a painful self-consciousness—the door was shut, a slit of light just showing beneath it. Owen must still be working. She would have to remember to send a maid with some tea and a sandwich.

A low murmur of voices emerged from the drawing room as she reached it, and she eased the door open curiously. Thalia must be back, but who was with her?

It took her a moment to distinguish the two people in the room, so closely entwined were they. It took a beat longer to realize that the sandy head so close to Thalia's blond curls belonged to Henry.

Henry.

A barrage of conflicting emotions coursed through her. There was a flicker of shock, though there should not have been—Anne had tried to warn her, and Eleanor had seen herself how Thalia looked at Henry. The sense of betrayal was keener, as she had believed Henry to be loyal. She had even foolishly expected loyalty from Thalia, as much for the sake of her wages as for Eleanor's own sake. But why should she have expected that? Thalia would benefit far more as Henry's wife. Eleanor refused to acknowledge the glimmer of guilt, that her own choices had kept these two apart. Eleanor ignored her yawning sense of loss and loneliness. It meant nothing.

Instead, she focused on the anger, hot and swift, that hid everything else. Anger was clean and easy. Anger did not make her an object of pity.

"What is going on?" Eleanor demanded, and was gratified to see Henry and Thalia spring apart, their faces scarlet.

"I'm glad to see you seem to be feeling better," Henry said.

"Don't be a ninny," Eleanor said. Her head throbbed in time with every syllable.

"It's not what it looks like," Thalia said. "I received some upsetting news. Henry was comforting me. That's all."

"And you cannot find comfort anywhere but in the arms of *my* betrothed?" Eleanor asked.

Thalia cringed.

Eleanor summoned her iciest voice. "I don't think our arrangement is working, Miss Aubrey. I'll pay you through the next week, but I no longer have need of your services."

A savage satisfaction surged through Eleanor at the shock on both Thalia's and Henry's faces. Eleanor didn't need Thalia. She didn't need either of them.

"I understand," Thalia said quietly. "I'll go pack."

Thalia didn't even fight her.

"Wait," Henry said. "Eleanor, we need to talk."

Henry wouldn't fight her either—or for her.

Eleanor lifted her chin. "Do you mean to cry off too? Not very gentlemanly of you, Henry." Never mind that Eleanor herself had briefly contemplated crying off. A perverse part of her wanted to force Henry to say the words, to break their agreement so he could be the villain, not her.

Now it was Henry's turn to flinch. "Dash it, Eleanor, that's not—"

Henry broke off as the door opened. A footman entered, bearing a letter. "Not another damned letter," Henry said under his breath.

Thalia, nearly to the door herself, paused.

"A letter for Mrs. Lockhart," the footman said, holding it out.

Thalia left the room. Eleanor watched her go before extending her hand to take the missive.

She recognized the handwriting at once: George Lockhart. Her fingers trembled only a little as she closed them around the letter.

Eleanor had been expecting something like this for days now. Better to get the worst of it over with. "Henry, you should go."

"But—"

"We'll talk later," she said, pushing more firmness into her voice than she felt. Irrationally, despite everything, she wanted Henry to stay. Wanted Thalia to stay.

No, she reminded herself. She did not need anyone.

Not until Eleanor was alone in the drawing room did she dare open George's letter. *My dear Eleanor,*

Eleanor suppressed a shudder and forced herself to read on.

> *It may come as some surprise to you to know that I have eloped with your friend Miss Anne Salisbury. I say "may" because, though Anne assures me she has said nothing to you, I know how you ladies enjoy talking of your affairs. Perhaps you have suspected something. In any case, I hope you will wish us happy, as the happiness of at least one of us depends very much on your goodwill.*
>
> *I have incurred some debts that must be paid at once. And while Anne is a lovely girl possessed of a modest dowry, her dowry alone will not cover my debts. Nor, should friends (hers or mine) offer to cover those debts, would it be sufficient to finance our desired way of life.*
>
> *Your friend has confided her future to me. Now that future depends upon you, dear Eleanor. You have*

dithered long enough over announcing your engagement
to Anne's brother that I begin to wonder if you ever
intend to do so—more to the point, so do my creditors.
So, my proposal is simple: Marry Mr. Salisbury at once,
effectively returning my inheritance to me, and I shall
make an honest woman of his sister. Or, if Mr. Salisbury
was only a means to an end, you need not marry him
at all. Any good lawyer can help you renounce the
inheritance my uncle left to you and make it over to me.
Might I recommend Mr. Hawthorne, just up the road
from you, on Curzon Street?

If you choose neither course, then Miss Salisbury
and I will head abroad, to enjoy a pleasurable couple
of months before our affair meets its inevitable end.
In a year or two, when society has tired of the gossip, I
shall make my return. Your friend, I fear, may not be
so lucky.

The choice is entirely yours, my dear Eleanor.

I shall await word of your choice at the George
Hotel (a bit self-referential, I know, but I could not
resist) until midnight tonight, then Miss Salisbury and
I shall disappear.

> *Your dear nephew-in-law,*
> *George Lockhart*

P.S. You may, of course, choose to bandy this about. But
the scandal would only reflect poorly on you and your

friend. If anyone but you appears at the George tonight,
you will not see me, or Miss Salisbury.

Eleanor's stomach sank lower and lower as she read. By the time she finished, it was curled up in a tight, uncomfortable ball in her toes. She stared at the letter unseeing for a moment, then folded it back up and set it on the table, beside a stack of Thalia's poems.

She went through her options rather mechanically, her mind churning slowly, like unoiled clockwork pieces. She could go after Henry and beg him to marry her. Her skin prickled with distaste at the thought. After what she had witnessed between Henry and Thalia, she would choke on her own pride before begging him. Anyway, she didn't need Henry.

Eleanor thought of Owen down the hall, still working at Albert's papers, his quiet, determined dedication one of the things she loved—*liked*—best about him. (She did not love him.) For a brief, intense moment, she wanted nothing more than to lay this whole sordid mess before Owen and let his good sense sort it out.

No—she had already brought enough trouble to Owen. Besides, George had warned her not to involve anyone else.

This whole disaster was her fault anyway—if she had not taken Anne to that silly masquerade ball, where Anne had gotten her first taste of the thrill of an illicit romance, likely this never would have happened. And what of that masked man Anne had danced with? Had that been George, even then? His hair had been all wrong, but a wig or dye could easily account for that. She had thought the man looked familiar, and he had certainly seemed to know who she was.

Eleanor put her face in her hands and took a deep breath.

Courage, she told herself. She had weathered poverty before. She could do it again. Perhaps she could find a position as a governess or a teacher at some small girls' school. Barring that, she could clean or cook.

Letting Anne suffer through the scandal George threatened was not an option. Anne had been the only person supporting Eleanor during a very dark period of her life, and Eleanor would never forget that. She would be that person for Anne now.

She had known she would be from the moment she read George's poisonous letter. It was only fear that made her put off her decision so long.

Eleanor squared her shoulders and went upstairs to her room, to pack up the jewelry that Albert had given her. It was hers outright, not part of Albert's estate, and its sale would buy her some time to find her footing. She put on the plainest of her gowns and packed a spare. Her remaining clothes could go to Anne with the rest of her inheritance—they were nearly of a height. A good seamstress could adapt them for her.

Could Anne possibly be happy with a man like George? It seemed impossible, but Eleanor must hope it would be so. Anne thought herself in love with him, and Eleanor knew he could be charming. Perhaps, with money and suitable motivation, George would be no worse a husband than many a society man.

Eleanor fought off a wave of nausea. No good now, thinking how Anne deserved better. Anne had made a choice, and all Eleanor could do was see it was not made worse by scandal.

She could hear Thalia moving around her room and tamped down the urge to apologize. They had nearly been friends—sometimes Eleanor had thought they *were* friends—but what did that matter now? Eleanor had said too much, burned too many bridges.

Then she went back downstairs again, sliding as silently as she could past the closed door of the study where Owen was still working.

Goodbye, my love, she thought. She could call him that now, when it no longer mattered. She would never see him again.

She let herself out of the house, shutting the door with a small *snick* behind her.

She was never coming back.

CHAPTER TWENTY-TWO

Thalia

The world does not end in fire.
There is no grand conflagration,
No flaming, destructive desire.
There is only this:
A quiet room.
A shut door.
Silence.

—Thalia Aubrey

Thalia glanced around her room, taking in the lace-covered windows, the pretty little dressing table beside the bed. Her valise lay open upon the bed, nearly full. Thalia had not brought much with her to London, so there was not much to pack. The pair of dresses Eleanor had purchased for her should stay here—they belonged to Eleanor as much as to her.

She had been happy here—more happy around Henry than she deserved—but she could not fault Eleanor for letting her go. Even if Henry's hug was not the illicit embrace Eleanor believed, Thalia *had* betrayed her employer in her thoughts, if not in deed.

Perhaps it was as well that Henry had not heard her—*Henry, I do love you*—that they had been interrupted before she had to answer his clarifying question. Henry was engaged—what good would it do to tell him when he could not in decency respond in similar fashion? She knew enough of his kind heart now to know that it would only distress him to give her pain.

In any case, she would leave soon, tonight if she could, on the first morning coach if not. Henry and Eleanor would patch things up, and Thalia would go home to her family. The prospect of a second journey home beneath a cloud of humiliation, after her earlier failed elopement, was daunting, but Thalia reasoned that if the first journey had not killed her, this one would not either.

She had no idea what she would tell Mama and Papa, or Kalli, but she was a writer. She would find some words, somewhere, somehow, even if words alone could not capture the tangled mix of emotions she felt now.

Thalia gathered up a few stray poems from the desk by the window and thought of the manuscript she had left below. Hoping that Eleanor was no longer in the drawing room, she went downstairs to fetch it.

The drawing room was blessedly empty, and Thalia scurried across the carpet. She picked up her manuscript, along with the letter from Taylor and Hessey. In the rush of everything that had happened after, she had almost forgotten. She would have to delay her return home a little longer then—long enough to confront Freddy and figure out what to do. She could not, in good conscience, let him publish *her* poems and say nothing. Perhaps she could afford a hotel room for a day or two.

Her movements disturbed the second letter, which flipped over and fell open. Thalia caught the signature, *George Lockhart*, and something in her went cold.

It was not her business, Thalia knew, but some instinct made her set her poems back down and open the letter. It took but a moment to acquaint herself with the contents.

When she finished, she raced back upstairs, empty-handed, to see if she could find Eleanor. Eleanor would be angry that Thalia had read the letter, but Thalia couldn't be sorry. Whatever Eleanor thought, Thalia *was* her friend: She cared for her; she wanted her to be happy. And this letter threatened to make Eleanor profoundly unhappy.

Thalia knocked at Eleanor's door and, when no one answered, eased the door open. Eleanor's wardrobe stood wide, the clothes in disarray as if someone had rifled through them quickly. The small case that held Eleanor's jewels was missing.

Heart pounding, hoping she was wrong, Thalia ran back down the stairs. Perhaps the butler would know where Eleanor had gone, if she had indeed left.

She had just reached the hallway leading past the study and the drawing room when the study door opened, and Thalia nearly collided with Mr. Jones.

He caught her arms, steadying her. "Are you all right, Miss Aubrey?"

"Eleanor's not here."

He frowned at her. "I'm sure there's nothing in that to upset yourself. Perhaps she had an engagement—"

"She's taken every one of her jewels," Thalia said, "and this terribly threatening letter came for her."

"Tell me," Mr. Jones said, the expression on his face going taut and urgent.

Thalia took him into the drawing room and showed him the letter Eleanor had left behind.

"Eleanor thinks she has no one," Thalia said. "She's left to deal with this alone. She means to give everything up." She thought back to Eleanor's confrontation of her and Henry. She had thought Eleanor was rightly angry. But what if there was more to it—what if Eleanor was also afraid, and had pushed them away out of fear, not just anger? It would account for why Eleanor had not sought help, in spite of the letter's threats.

Owen beetled his brows at her. "Are you certain?"

"We can ask the butler if he knows where she's gone, but I think so. Don't you?"

"Yes, I do. Eleanor—Mrs. Lockhart—never could be persuaded that she had anything of her own self to offer." Owen sighed heavily and shoved a hand through disordered dark locks. "What do you propose to do?"

"Help her, somehow. Remind her that she has friends—you, me, Henry." Thalia paused, stricken. "I have to tell Henry."

Owen nodded. "I'm coming with you."

The Salisbury town house was ablaze with lights when Owen and Thalia pulled up, in Eleanor's borrowed carriage. Wherever Eleanor had gotten herself to, she had gone on foot or in a hired cabriolet. Eleanor's butler, when appealed to, had looked faintly surprised. Mrs. Lockhart had not told him anything of her movements.

The footman who opened the door to them looked a bit harried. "I'm not certain the family is receiving—" he began.

A familiar voice called out, "Who is it, Charles?"

Henry.

A door down the hallway opened and Henry emerged, his face brightening—or was that only Thalia's wishful thinking?—at the sight of them.

"I beg your pardon," Henry said. "We're all at sixes and sevens here. Anne's gone out and not returned, and no one seems to know where."

Thalia nodded grimly. "That's why we're here."

"You've seen her? Oh, thanks be—"

Thalia cut across his relief. "We haven't seen her. But we know where she's gone. May we come in? This isn't something we should discuss on your doorstep."

"Of course." Henry led them across the entry hall, up the stairs to a drawing room.

The room was not one Thalia had seen before, decorated in rich crimsons and gold. "Is your mother here?"

The faintest frustrated grimace settled across Henry's face before he wiped it clean. "She's gone to the opera."

"But she will want to know this—"

Henry shook his head. "Better if I can settle it before Mama has to worry herself over it."

Thalia took a deep breath. "There's no easy way to say this: Your sister has eloped with George Lockhart, and he is trying to blackmail Eleanor into giving up her inheritance before he'll marry Anne."

"I don't understand." Henry furrowed his brows at her. "Anne has eloped? But what has Eleanor to do with that?"

228

Owen spoke up for the first time. "Mr. Lockhart wants Eleanor to marry you or renounce her inheritance, or he will elope with your sister and *not* marry her, leaving her open to scandal and worse."

Henry's face paled. "You're not serious?" He caught himself almost at once. "But you must be—you wouldn't invent such stories." He looked around the room, his frown deepening. "But where is Eleanor? Why hasn't she come with you?"

"Eleanor has gone to answer Mr. Lockhart's demands alone," Thalia said.

"Then we've got to find them." Henry's face took on an unaccustomed fierceness. "By God, I would marry Eleanor a thousand times before I'd let anyone hurt Anne."

Thalia swallowed. Henry had only said what she expected him to say—*I would marry Eleanor a thousand times*. Why then did it feel as though he had aimed a thousand sharp knives at her heart, each word a painful, gouging blow?

Beside her, Owen balled his hands, but said nothing. Thalia could only guess at how he felt about Eleanor, but she would swear that hers was not the only heart breaking tonight. It was a sign of his concern for Eleanor that he did not protest.

"Mr. Lockhart waits for Eleanor at the George Hotel, until midnight tonight. He wrote to Eleanor that if she did not come alone, he would disappear."

"Then we must make sure we are not seen," Henry said.

"As to that," Owen said slowly, "I may have an idea."

The three of them took Eleanor's carriage to the theater where Sophia worked. The show had not yet begun, but theatergoers were already arriving in driblets. Owen led them unerringly through the lobby and down a side passage to a warren of crowded, narrow hallways and came to a stop in front of a nondescript room. At his knock, Sophia's voice returned, "Who is it?"

"Owen. I need your help."

Something rustled behind the door, and then the door was flung open to reveal Sophia, wearing a flimsy silk robe, her hair and makeup already done up for the night's show. She ushered them into her little dressing room.

"George Lockhart has eloped with Miss Salisbury," Owen said.

"My sister," Henry interjected.

Thalia explained, once more, what she'd learned from the letter in Eleanor's drawing room. Sophia listened intently.

"I detest that man," she said. "He said such pretty words to me, but he never saw me as anything other than an object to acquire. What is it you need from me?"

"Disguises," Owen said. "We need some way of getting into the George without Mr. Lockhart recognizing us."

"That I can do," Sophia said. "It will take me a moment. Wait here." She walked out of the dressing room.

While she was gone, Thalia studied the handful of wigs resting on a dresser. One was red gold, very nearly the color of Anne's hair. She spun back to the two men.

"Mr. Lockhart can't ruin Anne if she is not known to be missing," she said slowly, thinking out loud.

"But she is missing," Henry objected.

"I know that," Thalia said. "But society doesn't. Not yet. You said your mother was at the opera, Henry? What if Anne—or someone very like her—were seen to accompany your mother?" She looked at Owen. "Your sister is an actress, and of a height with Anne. Could she play a part, just for one evening?"

Owen looked doubtful. "She's got her own performance in less than an hour."

"What could I do?" Sophia asked, sailing back in with an armful of men's garments.

Her heart beating with hopeful excitement, Thalia outlined her plan. But before she'd finished, Sophia was shaking her head. "It's a good plan, but I cannot do it. My eyes and complexion are too dark, and I do not know Miss Salisbury or any of her friends. The trick would be up as soon as anyone spoke to me."

"Oh." Thalia sighed, deflating. "I had not thought of that."

"However," Sophia continued, "I might be able to make *you* look enough like Miss Salisbury to pass in a darkened environment like an opera house. Miss Salisbury is the young woman I met at Mrs. Lockhart's, yes?"

Thalia nodded. "Yes, but surely I am too tall to imitate Anne?"

"You'll be sitting," Henry pointed out. "And if I bring you to join Mama, no one will suspect a thing."

"Surely your mama will notice," Thalia said.

"As to that, I would not vouch for it," Henry said, rather dryly.

Sophia clapped her hands together. "Then it is settled! I will help you dress and make you up so your own mothers would not recognize you. Then I will come with you."

"But your show—" Owen began.

"I've already spoken to another actress in our company," Sophia said. "I told her it was an emergency, and she will cover for me." She began handing out clothes, directing her brother and Henry to remove their coats in favor of the shabbier, shapeless coats she'd found. Thalia took one look at Henry in his shirtsleeves, at the pulse beating at the base of his throat, now revealed by the removal of his cravat, and turned away abruptly just as the door opened.

"I beg your pardon," Thalia began, and stopped.

Her brother stood in the open doorway, a bouquet of flowers in his hand. His hopeful expression dropped away at the sight of her. If Thalia had entertained any doubts about Freddy, the half-guilty, half-defiant expression streaking across his face removed them.

"How could you, Freddy?"

He thrust the flowers at Sophia, ignoring his sister. "I brought these for you, for luck."

Sophia didn't move. Her eyes flickered from Thalia to Freddy.

Freddy's outstretched arms drooped, rather like the flowers.

Thalia took a step closer, and Freddy flinched back. "You copied my poems and sold them to Taylor and Hessey."

She heard a shocked gasp behind her—Sophia?—but kept her eyes fixed on her brother.

"I needed them," Freddy said. "I tried to submit a few of my own poems, but no one would take them. And you—your poems were all right, and I thought I might try. I needed a success so I could propose to Sophia."

"You—" Thalia forced herself to stop, to draw a deep breath. Her thoughts ran in several directions before tangling together. "You never asked me if it was acceptable to me. And your publisher refused my poems when I tried to send them, accusing *me* of trying to steal my own poems. You cannot do this, Freddy. You have to tell them the truth."

Freddy's bravado fell away, and he looked, for a moment, so like the scared young boy who had accidentally spoiled one of their father's favorite books with a spilled pot of ink, that Thalia almost felt sorry for him.

Almost.

"Thalia, I can't do that. They—they'd hate me. My friends would despise me. I'd have nothing left in London. I'd have to go home, covered in shame. Would you really do that to me?"

Thalia drew in another deep breath. She reminded herself that she had done nothing wrong, and she would not let Freddy make her feel guilty. "Freddy, *you* made the choice to be dishonest, to pass off my work as yours. Not me."

Sophia said, "Freddy, I was never going to marry you. You should not have cheapened yourself for me." Her voice was gentle, but Freddy seemed to droop even more.

"I didn't mean to hurt anyone," he said, looking at Sophia. "I only wanted to make you proud of me."

"Then you should do the right thing," she said.

"I've read your sister's work, you know," Henry said. "I'd be willing to sign an affidavit verifying that the poems are hers, if it comes to that."

Freddy turned back to Thalia. He didn't say anything, just gave her a beseeching look that she was only too familiar with.

"No, Freddy," Thalia said firmly. "I'm not going to make this easy for you. You stole my work; you need to return it to me and make things right with the publisher."

Freddy glanced around the room with the air of someone looking for an ally. Finding none, he scowled. "Fine. I will write your bloody letter. But . . ." He hesitated for a moment, then said, "Please don't tell our parents?"

Thalia sighed. "Fine. If you tell Taylor and Hessey the truth, I won't tell our parents."

CHAPTER TWENTY-THREE

Eleanor

Sister, I would have no solicitor in such a case.

—Daniel Defoe, *The Family Instructor*

Eleanor did not go immediately to the George Hotel after leaving her house. (No, not *hers*. Not anymore.) Nor did she look up Mr. Hawthorne, on Curzon Street, as George had suggested.

Instead, she went to her own, or rather Albert's solicitor, a short, thin man named Mr. Talbot. It was a small act of defiance—using her solicitor rather than the lawyer George had recommended—but it was the only one she had left. She could not tell Mr. Talbot the truth, of course, but she could take some comfort from his friendly face. Mr. Talbot had been putting his hat and coat on as she arrived, about to leave for the evening, but he sat down again in a polished wooden chair behind a tidy desk and indicated she should do the same. He listened to her gravely as she expressed her wish to make her inheritance over to Mr. George Lockhart.

When she finished, he templed his fingers together. "Are you quite certain this is what you wish, Mrs. Lockhart? Your husband was very clear when making his will—he wanted the bulk of his fortune to go to you. He did not believe Mr. Lockhart was to be trusted with such an estate, and he wanted to make sure you were provided for." He hesitated for a moment, then added gently, "Your husband cared for you very much."

Eleanor fisted her hands in her skirt. "Then why did he write his will such that the estate would pass to George if I were to remarry? Did he wish for me to spend the rest of my life alone, for the sake of his memory?"

Mr. Talbot frowned. "No, I'm certain that Mr. Lockhart expected that you would remarry, at some interval. He meant only to protect you from fortune hunters."

"And so he wrote the will in such a way to prevent my marrying at all?"

Mr. Talbot's frown deepened. "But that is not . . . my dear Mrs. Lockhart, what do you believe your husband's will said?"

"That in the event of my remarriage, the fortune he gave me should go to Mr. Lockhart."

Mr. Talbot did not respond at once, but instead rose from his chair and began sorting through some files in a cabinet behind him. At length, he withdrew a document and resumed his seat. He ran his finger down the small, precise lines of text. "Ah, here it is! You are partially correct, Mrs. Lockhart, but I believe your understanding is incomplete. Your husband's will does include a provision for his fortune to go to his nephew in the case of your remarriage, but that is *only* if the conditions of the will have not been met. Those conditions are, first, that you and your betrothed present to me written evidence of your intention to marry no less than six months before your wedding, and second, that your betrothed submits documentation to me that he can support you independent of your money.

Both stipulations are meant to deter fortune hunters, but so long as you meet them, you are free to remarry."

Free to remarry. The solicitor's words seemed to buzz about her ears. For a moment, Eleanor simply stared at him, and then a wave of emotion washed over her, so hot and thick that she could scarcely breathe. Albert *had* meant his will to protect her, not restrict her. If only she had known that before Owen—

No. *Might have been* didn't matter anymore. George would still be waiting for her answer; Anne's happiness still depended on her choice.

But how had she missed this? Eleanor tried to think back to the day the will had been read. It had been a sunny, cold day in January, she knew that. The sunlight had pooled across the Turkish rug in their library, and she had tried surreptitiously to stretch her chilled feet to catch the bit of warmth. Mr. Talbot had been speaking in his gentle, dry voice, and she had not listened to most of the small bequests to the servants. George had been there too, in the high-backed chair beside hers, sitting stiff and eager.

Then Mr. Talbot had read the bequest to her, the house and the land and a considerable income, and the cold inside her had receded, a little, for the first time since Albert died. She was not to be thrown out again. But then that dreadful codicil, that in the event of her remarriage she was to lose that security. She must have stopped listening after that, shocked by the unexpected clause. And afterward, when Mr. Talbot had asked if she had questions, she only shook her head, dazed.

It was George, she remembered now, who kept reminding her of the codicil, who kept saying that when she remarried, her fortune would revert to him. She had never challenged or questioned him.

But she understood now why he had pressured her so to go through with her marriage to Henry before too much time had passed, why he had eloped with Anne rather than risk Eleanor's remarriage under the correct terms.

Mr. Talbot cleared his throat, bringing her back to the present. "Mrs. Lockhart? How do you wish to proceed?"

"I wish to make my husband's fortune over to his nephew, Mr. George Lockhart," Eleanor said, with more certainty than she felt. She forced herself to think of Anne. Anne, who she would never see again after her marriage to George, as she was certain George would not allow it.

"But how will you support yourself?" Mr. Talbot asked. "I cannot advise you to take action against your husband's wishes."

Eleanor willed herself to smile. "I am engaged to be married! Only, you see, we cannot bear to wait, and so better to make over the fortune now for poor George, who will need it rather more than I." It was not all a lie; her engagement to Henry was not officially broken. Yet.

"It would revert to Mr. Lockhart soon enough," Mr. Talbot said, "if you were to marry against the stipulations in the will, which it seems you intend to. Will you not need the money to furnish your trousseau?"

"I have everything I need," Eleanor said. Each lie soured on her tongue, but she forced them out. "Please?" She hoped he could not hear the desperation in her voice.

Mr. Talbot heaved a long sigh, then reached for his quill and a fresh sheet of paper.

It was half past nine when Eleanor reached the George Hotel—a Tudor-style building that could do with a fresh coat of whitewash. She walked slowly to the taproom, wishing she had not made herself eat supper at the little hostelry where she had reserved her own room for the night, only a street or two distant from the George. The food sat like a rock in her gut.

The taproom was dim and a little smoky. Not the sort of place she typically frequented, though not particularly disreputable either. A safe choice for George; a gentleman of fashion wouldn't be especially noteworthy here, but nor would he run much risk of encountering other members of the *ton*. That, as much as the name, was likely behind his choice.

George spotted her before she saw him and waved at her from across the room. He was seated at a booth in one corner, an empty glass in front of him.

Eleanor's stomach tightened. She was actually doing this. She took a long, slow breath—and then started coughing when the smoke seared her lungs. When she had stopped, she made her way across the room to George, whose broad grin betrayed his amusement at her expense.

"Please, join me, Aunt Eleanor."

"I am not your aunt," she said, but the frost in her voice only made him laugh. She slid into the seat opposite him and reached for her reticule. Better to be done with this business at once.

George waved his hand at her. "No, no. There's no need to rush. Have a drink with me—celebrate my wedding!"

"No, thank you," Eleanor said, and then wished she could bite her tongue. She owed George no politeness.

George shrugged. "As you wish." He summoned a passing barmaid and ordered another brandy for himself. His cheeks were rather flushed, and Eleanor wondered how much he'd had to drink before her arrival.

"You're earlier than I expected," George said.

Eleanor said nothing.

"Of course I knew you would come. You and Anne are very close, are you not? She speaks highly of you."

"You don't have to do this, George," Eleanor said. "I do not believe you will make Anne happy, and surely she is not the type of woman to hold your interest."

"Ah, but I do. You have no idea the pressing nature of my debts. And I simply refuse to be poor." The barmaid arrived with George's drink, and he took a slow sip.

"Poverty is not the worst thing in the world," Eleanor said. "Better to be poor and have one's honor."

George laughed again. "Better to have money, I think. Honor is only a word. If you are worried for your friend, you may take comfort in the fact that your actions now will do more for establishing her happiness—even her honor, if you prefer—than anything I might do. Anne can expect to be as happy as any young lady. She'll have a fine home and the respect of good society."

"And you will have the fortune you always wanted." Eleanor took a breath to steady herself. "Don't do this. Take the money, if you must, but let Anne go free."

"I think Anne would object to that! She is quite set on me, you see.

And the money should have been mine from the beginning—Uncle Albert had no business marrying again at his age. Though I admit, when I first met you, I could understand the temptation." George's eyes dropped from her face to the lace edging the modestly cut bodice of her gown. "I even offered for you myself, but you turned me down. Twice. It's just as well. I admit that as much as I appreciate experience in a mistress, I prefer innocence in my bride."

Eleanor swallowed down bile. She was going to be sick. "Enough."

George waggled his eyebrows at her, continuing as if she hadn't spoken. "Though I always did wonder if you and my uncle actually consummated your marriage. Did you?"

"That is really none of your business," Eleanor said, opening her reticule and fishing out the document Mr. Talbot had prepared for her. "I've brought the papers making my fortune over to you. All we need is a pair of reliable witnesses."

George settled back in his seat with a wave of his hand. "Fine, have it your way. We'll be quick about this. You really do know how to spoil a man's fun, Eleanor."

Eleanor took another deep breath and pushed the papers across the table.

CHAPTER TWENTY-FOUR

Thalia

I am playing a part at the opera:
Not a singer or player, but a lady.
Elegant and gracious, who smiles just so —
But her words and expressions are not me.
Yet if I am not me, and I am not she,
Then tell me, if you please,
Who am I?

—Thalia Aubrey

Thalia caught a glimpse of her reflection as she and Henry mounted the stairs of the opera house and paused, shocked anew by the transformation Sophia had wrought. The red-gold wig had been carefully curled and pinned before Sophia had settled it on Thalia's head, and Sophia had managed to transform the contours of her face with clever application of makeup. A French silk cap nestled on her head, a pair of white feathers curling down her forehead and cheek to obscure part of her face. Thalia was still too tall, but she did not look like herself. She looked, particularly at a casual glance under the candlelight of the theater, like Miss Anne Salisbury. It disconcerted Thalia, to be both herself and someone else at once. She rather thought there was a poem in the concept, one that she would tease out when she was not so nervous.

She followed Henry to the box where his mother was expected to be and breathed a sigh of relief at the sight of Mrs. Salisbury's familiar profile, an ostrich feather dancing above her turban as she whispered to her neighbor. The seat on her opposite side was occupied by an older gentleman who looked up at their entrance, his face creasing with some vexation as he spotted them. He stood, bowing perfunctorily as he offered his seat to Thalia, and took up an open seat in the row behind Mrs. Salisbury.

Henry's mother did not even glance at Thalia as she slipped into the place beside her. Thalia's seat was at the end of the row, so Henry stood beside her and bent over her as he spoke to his mother.

"Mama, I've brought Anne to join you. I've an errand I must run, but I'll return to fetch you when I've finished."

Mrs. Salisbury waved one hand in acknowledgment but still did not look at her children. Her neighbor, however, leaned forward, dark curls springing at her temples as she moved.

Thalia stopped breathing. The woman on Mrs. Salisbury's side was none other than the Countess Lieven, one of the noted patronesses at Almack's. How well did the countess know the Salisbury family? Thalia gripped Henry's wrist.

"How well you look, Miss Salisbury," Countess Lieven said.

Thalia started to breathe again. She was not going to be discovered immediately.

Then the countess added, "You look different. I think perhaps you've grown taller?"

Thalia slid down in her seat a fraction, hoping the slouch might disguise her height. "I have done my hair in a new fashion," Thalia said, trying to mimic Anne's soft tones.

The countess dipped her head. "Perhaps that's it. It suits you."

Mrs. Salisbury finally turned toward Thalia. Her eyes flicked over Thalia, and she frowned.

Thalia held her breath as Mrs. Salisbury studied her, the divot between her eyes deepening. *She knew.* Thalia braced herself for Mrs. Salisbury to reveal their charade and ruin Anne's potential alibi.

But Mrs. Salisbury only blinked and shook her head slightly, as though trying to clear her head. "You've not been drinking your tea and honey, as I bade you. Your voice is still hoarse. Why would you change your hair without consulting me? I preferred your old style. That cap is ridiculous. Anyone might think you are an old maid rather than quite a young woman," she said. "And why could you not have sent word that you'd be joining me late? You've caused no end of inconvenience to me."

Thalia took a long, slow breath. She couldn't tell if Mrs. Salisbury had truly not noticed that she was not, in fact, Anne, or if Mrs. Salisbury had decided for inscrutable reasons to play along with their pretense. Whatever the case, Thalia was grateful for the reprieve.

"It's the privilege of the young to be thoughtless," Countess Lieven said, smiling to soften her words.

Henry said, "Countess, might I speak to you for a moment, in private? Then I really must be going."

The countess raised her eyebrows at his request, but she rose in a rustle of silk skirts and followed Henry from the box. Thalia tried to concentrate on the opera unfolding on the stage before her, but the lyrics were Italian, and the few phrases she knew were not enough to disentangle whatever impassioned scene was unfolding before her—a chaotic confrontation between several men and women. At least the music was lovely.

The countess returned after a moment, but only to fetch her wrap from her chair, whisper something to her husband, who sat at the far end of their row, and then leave the box again.

Beside her, Mrs. Salisbury sighed. "I do wish they'd hurry up and finish and get to the farces. All this yowling is a bit much." She patted her ears with some smugness, as if that physical sensitivity made up for her emotional insensitivity. Thalia hoped that Henry and Owen's rescue efforts were meeting more success than she was. It felt wrong to sit so passively when Eleanor was in trouble, important though she knew her role to be if they were to preserve Anne's reputation.

"You really must do something about that friend of yours," Mrs. Salisbury said.

Thalia, a bit bewildered by the change in subject, said nothing, hoping Mrs. Salisbury would add something more that would enable her to respond with a modicum of intelligence.

"She must not be allowed to marry Henry," Mrs. Salisbury continued. "She is not suitable for him." *Ah.* She was speaking of Eleanor. Thalia bit her lip. She wanted to defend Eleanor, but she had not observed Anne to stand up to her mother, and she could do nothing now that would imperil her disguise.

Mrs. Salisbury did not appear to expect a response, as she moved on again, pointing out a gentleman in the box opposite theirs who was sitting with a lovely young woman who *was not his wife*. Thalia, uninterested in Mrs. Salisbury's gossip, turned her attention back to the stage.

The main male lead sat alone at a table, eating. A figure all in gray—a statue?—approached him and the music around them crescendoed before the stage appeared to erupt into flames, orange and yellow silks spooling out around the actors. Thalia, at last, recognized the opera: *Don Giovanni*. This must be the final scene, where the titular libertine was dragged down to hell for his sins. She rather hoped the same fate awaited George Lockhart.

The opera concluded with a flourish, and new arrivals crowded into the pit below them for the farce that was to follow, taking advantage of the half-price tickets for the later shows. A familiar figure caught Thalia's eye—Freddy, along with a couple of his poet friends. Thalia sighed. Why had she expected Freddy might spend the evening at home, racked with guilt? Freddy had only been sorry at having been caught, not at having stolen her poems. Perhaps even now he hoped for some miracle to save him from himself.

Well, Thalia did not intend to ease his conscience. She murmured an excuse to Mrs. Salisbury, then went into the corridor outside the box to find an usher and asked him to bring her a pen and paper. She waited in the corridor, pretending to study the floor to discourage any passing society members who might feel inclined to talk with her.

When the usher returned, Thalia took the paper, scrawled a brief message on it, and then gave the man a coin to deliver it to "Mr. Frederick Aubrey, in the third row of the pit."

Thalia returned to her seat and watched Freddy. She observed him laughing with his friends, and the good-natured teasing he endured when the usher approached him with a letter. Perhaps they believed it was some flirtation—it was not uncommon for such notes to pass at the opera. She noted the moment when he opened the letter and scanned the message: *Tell Taylor and Hessey the truth, or I will.* Freddy's head went up, all humor gone from his face, and he scanned the boxes around them. His eyes passed right over her, dressed and painted as Anne Salisbury, without even hitching.

With a short word to his fellows, Freddy left the theater.

Thalia settled back into her seat, smiling for the first time since she had come home to that dreadful letter from the publishers, and let herself enjoy the farce.

CHAPTER TWENTY-FIVE

Eleanor

But may confusion still the wretch await,
Be poverty, disgrace, contempt his fate,
Who the just end and means can disregard,
Yet arrogantly hope the just reward!

—Samuel Jackson Pratt, *Harvest-home*

Eleanor watched George Lockhart run his eyes over the neat script of Mr. Talbot's document, his smile widening as he read. When he finished, he summoned a serving maid to their table and bade her to bring him pen and ink.

Eleanor dropped her gaze and ran her finger over a whorl in the wood. She could not bear George's smirk.

Before the serving maid could return, however, the noisy bustle of the taproom was split by a woman's carrying voice.

"*There you are*. Ravisher! Debaucher! Defiler of innocent women! Oh, my eyes bleed to see you."

Eleanor and George both startled as they turned toward the voice, emanating from a rather voluptuous young woman in a white gown, honey-colored curls spilling over her shoulder and onto the soft skin exposed by her low neckline. The crowd in the taproom seemed to give way before her as she surged through the room, heading for their table in the corner.

The woman came to an imposing stop before them, her bosom heaving with indignation. "You will pay for the wrong you've done me!" she said, pointing a dramatic finger at George. Her voice had the rounded vowels of the West Country.

George flushed, a mottled red creeping up his neck and cheeks. Most of the room was staring at them agog, their eyes flashing between George and the woman facing him.

"I don't even know who you are!" George spluttered. "What wrong could I possibly have done you?"

The woman turned back to the taproom, her hands wide in appeal. "Do you hear him? He denies knowing me. Yet not a year past, he promised me his love and protection."

"I did no such thing!" George said.

The woman held up her hand, silencing him. "I was young and innocent and beautiful, though that beauty would become my curse. I was not born to gentry, but respectable enough. My father was a clergyman who died young, and my mother was forced to take in boarders to feed our family. It was thus that I met Mr. Lockhart. Would to God I had never laid eyes on him!"

"She's lying!" George said, but it was clear to Eleanor that their audience, hanging avidly on the woman's words with open mouths and wide eyes, were less inclined to listen to him than to the magnetic woman speaking.

"I knew little of the world, or perhaps I would have known better than to trust a man's honeyed words. When he said he loved me,

I believed him. When he said he wished to wed me, I trusted him. I gave him everything, and he left me with nothing but his name and a growing child." The young woman put one hand against her stomach, and a single tear trickled down her cheek.

"Boo!" someone called out. Another followed with, "For shame, young man!"

There was a mild stir near the entrance to the taproom, as a slim, sandy-haired young man and a finely dressed woman with dark curls entered, but most of the spectators paid them no notice.

Eleanor caught her breath. *Henry*. But how did he come to be here—and with Countess Lieven? Of all the rotten luck and timing . . .

The young woman whirled back to face George, her lovely face flushed with color. "How dare you deny what passed between us? How dare you deny me, and the child who deserves a father's love and care?"

Conscious of Henry watching them, Eleanor studied the young woman more closely. There was something familiar about her, about the way her lips moved when she spoke, about her brown eyes, though Eleanor would swear she had never heard this voice before.

But then the woman shifted, and Eleanor saw her face more clearly. The woman's dramatic entrance had startled Eleanor, and the golden curls had thrown her off, but she rather suspected it was Sophia beneath the carefully applied makeup and the wig.

For Sophia and Henry to have both found her at the same time was too much of a coincidence. They must have known she would be here—how? With a sinking sensation, Eleanor remembered the letter she had incautiously left in the drawing room, beside Thalia's poems. Had Thalia found it and told them of its contents, even after

Eleanor's cold dismissal of her? Was Owen here, somewhere? Eleanor scanned the taproom, but could not see him.

Terror warred with something warm and soft inside Eleanor—despite her best efforts, her friends had not let her push them away. But she could not quash the fear that George might recognize Sophia or Henry and accuse Eleanor of failing to uphold her part in the bargain and ruin Anne regardless.

The innkeeper, followed by the maid with ink and quill, approached the table. "Miss," the innkeeper said in the kind of firm, soothing voice one might use with a child, "might I offer you a private parlor? You're disturbing my customers."

"*I'm* disturbing your customers?" Sophia's voice rose a full octave. "Your customers are disturbed at *my* behavior and not the caddish manner in which *this man* has treated me?"

Nervous though she was that George might recognize Sophia, Eleanor had to admire her acting. She was flawless as the wronged innocent. Even Eleanor half believed her, though she knew Sophia had never entertained George's advances.

Countess Lieven drew up beside Sophia. "The young woman is right," she said to the innkeeper. "And I, for one, would like to hear her charge in full." She waved the innkeeper away and pinned George with her eyes. "Is what this young woman says true? A gentleman may have his dalliances, but he ought to do the right thing by his children."

George, his color rising again, said through set teeth, "This woman is lying. I have never seen her before in my life."

The countess turned back to Sophia. "And what answer have you for that?"

Sophia straightened, her face taking on a familiar hauteur that Eleanor had seen her assume while on the stage. She reached up and swept off her wig in a practiced fashion. "Your ladyship, to that I will say that Mr. Lockhart pursued me for many weeks, pressing me for an intimacy I was not willing to give him. But the story I told was not a lie. There is such an innocent, and such a child. A former inamorata of Mr. Lockhart's told me as much, when she warned me away from him. Mr. Lockhart had told her himself, boasting of it when he was in his cups." Sophia turned a contemptuous look on George. "Perhaps next time you should believe a woman when she tells you no."

George surged up out of his seat, as though he would choke Sophia in red-faced fury. But Henry, who had joined them while Eleanor was distracted by the interplay between Sophia and George, slipped protectively in front of Sophia.

Thwarted, George turned instead to grasp the pen and ink from the barmaid who still stood, wide-eyed, by the table. He scrawled his name on the document and shoved it back at Eleanor. "You owe me this, you wretched bitch."

Countess Lieven gasped at this. "Mr. Lockhart, you should not speak so to a lady."

Eleanor picked up the pen and looked from the paper to George's snarling face, and then to Sophia and Henry, both watching her gravely. Her eyes went back to George. He did not seem so frightening now, only a man driven to desperation.

And Eleanor was no longer alone.

She set the pen down, the tip still bleeding black ink, and crossed her hands on the table. "No, I don't think I do. You have lied to me about my husband's will and tried to bully me into giving you what Albert gave me freely. I do not owe you anything."

"I think you owe me your friend's happiness," George said. He looked up at Henry. "I hope you're satisfied at securing your sister's ruin."

"His sister? But what has Miss Salisbury done?" Countess Lieven asked. "I saw her, not this half hour past, at the opera with her mother."

Eleanor blinked. But Anne had run away—had she returned? Or was some other wizardry at work this night? Never mind. She'd have the answer soon enough.

Henry said, "Anne is safe, George. Your threats won't work anymore."

Anne is safe. Eleanor released a long breath, tension melting away from her stiff shoulders. She picked up the legal document Mr. Talbot had so carefully drawn up for her and held it to the candle flickering on the table until it caught fire. Then she tipped it, first one way, then the other, as the flame ran along the page, turning those promises to so much ash.

George swore and tried to grab the paper from her, but she held it back, out of his reach. The flame reached her fingers, burning her briefly before she dropped the remnants onto the table.

"Threats?" Countess Lieven echoed. "Mr. Lockhart, I do not know exactly what you have done, but it seems to me that you've behaved rather badly. First the poor girl that you ruined, then your excessive gaming debts, and now threatening the children of my good friend Mrs. Salisbury. I advise you to give up London at once and head to the continent for a year or three. You'll find no welcome here for some time, I guarantee you."

George, with one last, pointed curse, snatched up his hat and shoved his way out of the room.

Countess Lieven watched him go, then turned to Henry with a bemused expression. "Well, you did promise me better drama than that which could be had at the opera, and you fulfilled that promise beautifully. Was that all you needed from me?"

Henry bowed. "Yes, ma'am, that was everything I wished for and more."

"I should like to return to the opera now. Will you take me?"

Henry cast a pained glance at Eleanor, then Sophia. "May I call you a hansom cab instead?"

The countess pinched his cheek. "I suppose that would be acceptable. I do not blame you for hoping for younger and prettier charges to escort."

Henry held out his elbow to Countess Lieven and led her from the room. Eleanor stood from the table, a little unsteady on her feet at the rapid change in her future prospects. George was gone—routed by Sophia and Henry and the countess. And indeed, by her own refusal to cooperate. She would not have to leave London, or her friends. She turned to Sophia, and the taller woman put a hand on her arm.

"Why did you not tell any of us that Mr. Lockhart was threatening you?"

Now that the intensity of the moment was fading, reaction was setting in. Tears prickled the back of her throat. "I didn't want to bother anyone with my problems—I'm used to relying upon myself."

Sophia folded Eleanor in a gentle hug. She smelled of roses and lavender. "My dear Eleanor, simply because circumstances have forced you to support yourself does not mean you must always act alone. Friends support one another." Sophia pulled back to study Eleanor. "At least, I hope I can claim you as such?"

Eleanor smiled at her, if a bit tremulously. "Yes," she confirmed.

"Good. Then I hope you will not ever again offer to give *your entire fortune* over to a worthless profligate of a man without telling anyone of your decision."

"That I think I can safely promise," Eleanor said.

Henry returned to them, with his sister on his arm. When Anne caught sight of Eleanor, she broke free of her brother and ran toward her friend. Her eyes were red-rimmed, but she appeared otherwise healthy and whole.

"Oh, Eleanor," Anne said, flinging herself into Eleanor's arms. "I have been so foolish."

Eleanor returned her embrace, relieved to see Anne safe and secretly gratified that Anne preferred her comfort to Henry's. "As to that, I think we have both been less than wise. But what has happened?" She looked past Anne to see Owen hovering behind Henry. Their eyes met. Eleanor flushed and looked away, unable to reckon, yet, with what his presence might mean for her.

The group settled back at the table George Lockhart had lately abandoned, Eleanor sandwiched between Anne and Sophia, with the gentlemen opposite them. Henry ordered wine for Anne and Eleanor, "to settle their nerves," and beer for himself and Owen. Sophia, grinning at the serving maid, said she would have a beer as well.

Anne's story poured out in disjointed fits and starts. Anne explained how she had agreed to elope with George, thinking it romantic. He had brought her to the inn and had supper ordered for her, but told her to stay in her room while he made arrangements for their travel. That was all she knew, until Owen had come knocking at her door. She had arrived downstairs just in time to hear Sophia's accusations about George. In turn, Owen told about Thalia discovering the letter and going to Henry, and Sophia interjected with her contribution: turning Thalia into Miss Salisbury for the evening so her absence would not be marked.

Henry added, "Countess Lieven was not part of our initial plan, which was simply to distract Mr. Lockhart while Owen looked for Anne, but when I saw her sitting beside my mother, I got the idea that she might be a good witness to shame Mr. Lockhart into doing the right thing."

"I am so glad you are all here," Anne said. "May we please go home now?"

Henry went to call for their carriage to be brought round, saying, as he left, "Eleanor, I hope you don't mind that we've borrowed your coach and coachman!"

Eleanor linked her arm through Anne's and began to follow him to the door, but stopped as she drew even with Owen. "Thank you for helping me and my friend tonight. I am very grateful. Will I see you tomorrow?" There was much she wanted to say to him, but she didn't yet know quite what, or how to say it.

Owen said only, "I believe so," in an oddly formal tone that revealed nothing of what he thought. Then Henry returned, explaining that he'd hired a separate cab for Owen and Sophia, and there wasn't time to say more.

They took Anne home first, and Eleanor snuck Anne up to her room and delivered her to the care of her maid before returning to her carriage. She looked at Henry, waiting to shut the door for her. "When you go to fetch your mother, will you bring Thalia home?"

"You discharged her," Henry said. "She may need to return for her things, but I do not know if she will want to stay."

"I know," Eleanor said. "I reacted poorly to seeing you together. I was hurt and angry."

"Eleanor—" Henry began, but she raised her hand to silence him.

"Please don't apologize again. Let me finish. I owe you an apology myself. I should never have asked you to fake an engagement. Had I understood my late husband's will better, there would have been no need for it in the first place."

"You're releasing me?" Henry asked, elation stealing across his face. Eleanor wondered if she ought to be affronted by his patent relief, but she was too tired just now to feel much of anything.

"George cannot pressure me now," Eleanor said, "and it turns out that my marriage alone is not enough to break the terms of my husband's will." She explained briefly about the stipulations Albert had set.

"I would have married you to save Anne," Henry said, perhaps feeling his earlier enthusiasm might have been insulting.

"I know," Eleanor said. "But I think there's someone else you'd rather be with."

She could see the color flood his face, even in the dim light from the streetlamp.

"You should tell her," Eleanor said.

Henry hummed in response, though Eleanor couldn't tell if he agreed or disagreed.

As she rode in her carriage back to her house—*her* house now, not George's, not ever—she wondered if she would have the courage to take her own advice.

CHAPTER TWENTY-SIX

Thalia

I cannot name the moment when I fell.
Love came upon me by degree, so slow
I might have outraced it, might have quelled
Desire before it bloomed, the faint glow
Of fire snuffed before it kindled red.

—Thalia Aubrey

Countess Lieven returned to the box just as the farce was concluding but said nothing to Mrs. Salisbury or Thalia about her disappearance. She looked pleased, though, rather than vexed, and Thalia took some small comfort from that.

After the show finished, Thalia followed Mrs. Salisbury to the lobby, trying to slouch as she walked to disguise her height. She kept her face turned down, hoping to hide her features as much as possible, but she need not have bothered. While several people greeted Mrs. Salisbury, no one said a word to her daughter trailing behind her. Thalia's heart hurt for Anne—overlooked and snubbed as she so often was by her own mother, she must have been an easy target for someone like Mr. Lockhart.

Mrs. Salisbury flirted gently with an old acquaintance in the lobby, and it was not until the lobby thinned of company that she began to fret that Henry had not yet appeared.

"Drat that boy," she said. "It's so very like him to pursue his own plans at our expense. Where could he have got to?"

Thalia hid a smile. That description was not at all like Henry, who was more likely to inconvenience himself to save someone else trouble.

But just as Mrs. Salisbury was threatening to find a cab herself, Henry rushed through the doors into the lobby, his face flushed but smiling.

Smiling. They had done it, by George. Or rather, no thanks to George Lockhart, but they had done it.

Henry ushered them down the stairs to a waiting carriage, linking his arm through his mother's and settling her solicitously into the vehicle before turning to Thalia.

"Is Anne safe?" she whispered.

"Quite safe. She's sleeping back at the house."

"Thank goodness," Thalia said.

Thalia took her seat across from Mrs. Salisbury, hoping that the darkness would aid her charade a little longer. Henry climbed in and sat beside his mother.

As soon as the carriage had jolted forward, Mrs. Salisbury said, "Is this a prank, Henry? I must tell you, it's in very poor taste."

Henry and Thalia exchanged glances.

"Prank, Mama?" Henry asked.

Mrs. Salisbury waved her hand in Thalia's direction. "You must think me quite stupid, not to recognize my own daughter. I don't know who this young woman is or why you have foisted her on me, but I am most displeased."

"I do not think you stupid, Mama," Henry said, taking his mother's hand in his and pressing it. "It was not you I meant to deceive, but everyone else in the theater. Anne was in a spot of trouble, and we needed a ruse to draw attention away from her until we could get her home safe."

"And is she?"

"Yes, she's at home."

Mrs. Salisbury was silent for a moment before nodding. "Very well then. You are lucky I held my tongue earlier. I had half a mind to expose you both at the opera. You might have told me!"

Thalia shivered at the idea of Mrs. Salisbury shouting at her in front of the entire theater. Thank goodness for small mercies.

"I didn't wish to alarm you."

"Hmm." Mrs. Salisbury eyed Thalia, who was fidgeting with her gloves. "Did anyone at the house see Anne return?"

Henry shook his head. "Aside from her maid, I don't believe so. We have tried to be discreet."

"Then having committed yourselves to this farce, I suggest you see it a bit further. So that no one has cause to wonder at Anne's appearing with me at the opera but not arriving home with me, this person—"

"It's Miss Aubrey, Mama," Henry said.

Mrs. Salisbury continued as if she had not heard his interruption. "This person can accompany me into the house for everyone to see, and then you can return her whence she came."

Thalia choked on a laugh. This was becoming farcical indeed.

They drew up outside the Salisbury house, and Henry helped first Mrs. Salisbury and then Thalia from the carriage. Mrs. Salisbury yawned widely and marched into the house, Henry and Thalia trailing behind her.

Henry gripped Thalia's hand as they crossed the threshold where

261

a footman waited, then climbed the stairs toward the bedchambers. "You've been a godsend. We've asked so much of you already—only a little more and then you can be free of us. I'll take you home as soon as I can."

Home. To Eleanor's town house, as though it were as easy as that. Swallowing against a sudden sharpness, Thalia said, "I'll need to stop by Eleanor's, to retrieve my belongings, but I was hoping you might recommend someplace quiet and clean where I can stay for a day or two until I go back to Oxfordshire."

He hadn't released her hand yet. Was it only her imagination that his grip tightened when she mentioned leaving?

"Eleanor gave me strict instructions to bring you back to her house. I believe she wishes to apologize. In any case, she made it clear you were welcome to stay with her as long as you needed."

Relief bubbled through Thalia. She did not need to find another place to stay tonight. She could still ensure Freddy did the right thing by his publisher, and she could talk to Eleanor.

Outside Anne's room, Thalia pulled off the wig that had been obscuring her own fair curls and ran her fingers through her hair.

"*If it were done when 'tis done, then 'twere well it were done quickly,*" she said.

Henry raised an eyebrow at her.

"*Macbeth,*" Thalia explained.

"More Shakespeare?" Henry complained, though his smile robbed the complaint of any sting. "I suppose I should be grateful this business of ours is much less murderous." He held out his arm to her, and ushered her down a back passage, out into the mews behind the house where the carriage was waiting, yet again.

"Tell me what happened," Thalia said, once they were settled and the carriage was rocking forward. She wondered if they had gotten Anne away with Eleanor's fortune intact, or if Henry had had to promise to wed Eleanor at once. She wished she did not feel so sick at the thought. She had no claim to Henry, after all.

Henry recounted how he had persuaded Countess Lieven to come with him to confront Mr. Lockhart, how Sophia had challenged Mr. Lockhart with his own scandalous behavior, and how Owen had helped find Anne while Mr. Lockhart was thus distracted.

Thalia, as much relieved as amused by his recounting, laughed more than his self-deprecating asides warranted. "I am sure you did more than simply stand about, looking decorative."

"I would not be so certain of that," Henry said. "Sophia and Owen were the true stars of the night, and I shall be forever indebted to them."

"And Eleanor?" Thalia asked. "Is she all right?"

"Truth be told, she seemed rather in shock, but I think she will be well enough," Henry said. "If it's agreeable with you, I will call on you both in the morning, to see how you get on?"

"Of course," Thalia said. Henry still had not answered the question she most wanted to ask, but she didn't know how to raise it without seeming heartless and abominably forward. *Are you still betrothed?*

When they reached Eleanor's town house, Henry escorted Thalia to the front door, wished her a rather formal good evening, and offered her a slight bow. Eleanor was nowhere to be seen, but a footman greeted Thalia and told her Mrs. Lockhart had gone up to bed. Thalia retreated to her bedroom with the lowering sensation that she was losing something, but she did not know what to do to stop its loss.

Breakfast was not, after all, the awkward affair Thalia had anticipated. Though Eleanor was already seated at the table when Thalia came downstairs, reading the newspaper with a distracted air, she rose at once when Thalia arrived.

To Thalia's considerable surprise, Eleanor came around the table and threw her arms around Thalia in a hug.

"Thank you," Eleanor said. "God only knows why you helped me, after everything I said to you—but thank you."

Thalia hugged her back. "You are most welcome. I do care for you, you know—though why you insist on pushing everyone away as you do is beyond me."

Eleanor released Thalia with a sigh. "It hurts less to keep apart from people than to watch them inevitably abandon me."

"Part of caring for people means opening yourself to the possibility that they might not love you back and loving them anyway. My father says that you cannot avoid pain. If you try to live your life to avoid being hurt, then you may find yourself living a life without much joy either." Thalia's heart pinched as she finished speaking, missing home and, absurdly, missing Henry.

"It must be nice," Eleanor said, a bit wistfully, "to have such a family."

"Yes," Thalia said, "though I do not always appreciate them as I ought. But, Eleanor, not all family looks the same. Some families are born; some are made. You have Anne, and Henry, and Owen, and Sophia—and me. We all of us care for you, just as you are."

"Stubborn and prickly?" Eleanor asked. But though she smiled, the look in her eyes seemed a bit guarded, as though even now she was forestalling pain.

"And generous, and loyal, and funny, and independent," Thalia said. "You should know that I do not bestow my friendship out of pity—it must be earned."

Eleanor flushed. "Thank you. If you feel you cannot stay on, I would understand. But if you feel you might be able to forgive me, I would like you to stay."

Had Eleanor been one of her own sisters, Thalia might have punished her a little by pretending to need to think over the offer. But Thalia could see Eleanor's rawness written in the anxious expression on her face, and said simply, "I would love to stay on as your companion."

"I've broken off my engagement with Henry. I thought you should know. We—our engagement was never an earnest one. Henry agreed simply to spare me from Mr. Lockhart's constant pestering. I—I owe you an apology. I should not have spoken to you and Henry as I did yesterday, or held Henry to that betrothal once I saw how he looks at you."

Now it was Thalia's turn to blush.

And then, as if Henry's name were a talisman summoning him, the footman was opening the door to say, "Mr. Salisbury has come calling, ma'am. What shall I tell him?"

Eleanor looked consideringly at Thalia. "Bring him to the breakfast room." When the footman had left, she added, "One should not receive a suitor on an empty stomach."

Henry did not seem surprised to be shown into the breakfast room, though he did apologize for coming so early. "Only, I wanted to make sure you were both all right."

"I am feeling surprisingly well this morning," Eleanor said. "Rather free, in fact, save for a few business items that demand my attention." After pressing Henry to help himself to tea and toast, she left the room.

Thalia, who had risen at Henry's arrival, sat back down, her mouth suddenly dry. She sipped her tea.

Henry took the chair beside her, setting a wrapped package on the table before him. "And you, Miss Aubrey—Thalia? Are you well?"

Thalia set her cup down. "I am. How is Anne?" She was stalling, she knew. But all her carefully fashioned words had deserted her.

"She seems well enough. Her spirits are a bit bruised, not surprisingly, but I think she will rally. Perhaps you could talk with her? Since you've both—" He broke off abruptly.

"Since we've both experienced failed elopements?" Thalia asked. She remembered how she'd felt the morning after realizing James did not love her as she loved him, as though her entire body were a mass of nerve endings, everything exposed and sensitive.

Henry looked appalled. "I did not mean—that is, I did, but I should not have said so."

Perhaps she would have felt less vulnerable back then if she'd known someone who had survived the same experience. Thalia softened her voice. "I would be happy to, if you think it would help."

Henry covered her hand, resting bare on the table, with his. "I do. You're a good woman, Thalia."

The warmth of his hand rippled through her.

Henry was mistaken. She wasn't particularly good: She was

jealous and selfish and more ambitious than it was safe for a woman to be. Any goodness Henry thought he saw in her was only a reflection of his own.

What had she been thinking, when Henry stayed to speak to her alone? That a man who had once fancied himself in love with Thalia's gentle, kindhearted sister Kalli would suddenly discover that he favored Thalia instead?

Ridiculous.

Thalia was not lovable. Desirable, maybe—James had taught her that much. But love went much deeper, and one could not love what one did not know. Outside of her family, whom had Thalia allowed to see her true self? Eleanor had caught glimpses. And Henry—

Thalia was quite sure she had shown too much of her real self to Henry for him to love her.

"I brought you something," Henry said, pushing the package toward Thalia. It was square, about a handspan in height and width, a little more in length. "I have been working on it for some time, but I did not know if I would have an occasion to give it to you. It did not seem fitting when I was—" He broke off, looking adorably confused for a moment, then started again. "Did Eleanor tell you that we are no longer engaged?"

Part of Thalia wanted to deny it, just to listen to Henry's undoubtedly awkward explanation, but she took pity on him. "She did. This morning." Eleanor had said it was a sham engagement—and perhaps it was, on her side. But on Henry's? "Are you—are you much hurt by it?"

"Hurt? No, though perhaps my pride is a bit bruised by how relieved Eleanor was to be rid of me. But then, I am rather relieved myself. Excellent as Eleanor is, I do not believe I would have made her happy, or she me."

Thalia wanted to ask what—or who—would make Henry happy, but she could not bear the pain of the sudden hope surging through her. Instead, she pulled the package to her and began to unwrap the paper. When it fell away, she stared at the gift for a long moment.

It was a small wooden box, open on one side, and fitted out to resemble a room, as if from a doll's house. A tiny window let in light on one side, and a cunningly placed mirror reflected the light to illuminate the space. A miniature desk sat before the window, and a sofa ran along one wall. A tiny rug lay on the floor. The room was the exact replica of the drawing room upstairs, where Thalia had written so many of her poems, where she had talked to Henry about her writing dreams, where she had cried in his arms when she read that terrible letter from Taylor and Hessey. And there, sitting at the desk in a pale blue dress, was a miniature Thalia herself.

The real Thalia looked up at Henry. He was watching her with a burning intensity that made her whole body flush with heat.

"Did you make this?" she asked.

He nodded.

"For me?"

"I certainly did not make it for Eleanor," he said. "Will you ask me why I was relieved when Eleanor released me from our engagement?"

Thalia dropped her hands into her lap and wound her fingers together. Her heart beat hard and fast. "Why were you relieved?"

"Because the most astounding thing had happened to me. As you may know, I have a habit of falling for pretty girls, at least one of whom has rightly turned me down on the grounds that I did not know her well enough, nor she me. That was fair criticism—growing up with my mother, I learned that anything less than my best self wasn't valued. If I was charming, I was worthy of love. If I was not—I was unlovable. As a result, I think I have been rather more shallow than I should have been."

Thalia's heart hurt for the child Henry had been.

Henry continued, rubbing at a spot on the tablecloth with his finger. He didn't look at Thalia. "But this Season, I met a woman who was not simply beautiful, or kind, or funny. She also had a depth to her and an ambition that made me, for the first time in my life, wish that I had a depth that might match hers, an ambition to be more. And because most of our friendship unfolded while I was engaged to someone else, I did not worry about misleading her with my intentions, and was, instead, free to simply be myself. As she is always wonderfully, beautifully—sometimes disastrously—herself, it was impossible not to see her. It was equally and damnably impossible not to love her. The miracle, though, is that I think she saw me too."

Henry loved her. Somehow, he had seen the best and worst of her and found it not something to despise, but to love.

Henry looked up, finally, and the open vulnerability in his face set affection swelling inside Thalia. She took his hand in hers and drew a deep breath. Henry had given her honesty, and she owed him her truth in return.

"Do you remember the night I made you fetch me writing supplies at a dance, and then ruthlessly ignored you?"

Henry laughed a little. "How could I forget? I was bitterly jealous that words alone could transfix you more than I could ever hope to. You never did tell me what the poem was about."

"I couldn't," Thalia said. "It was about you, about thoughts and feelings I had no right to feel when you were engaged to someone else."

"I'm not engaged now," Henry pointed out, hopeful.

"I know," Thalia said.

She took a deep breath. *Courage*, she told herself. Then she began to recite the words that had burned themselves into her mind, into her heart:

> *I cannot name the moment when I fell.*
> *Love came upon me by degree, so slow*
> *I might have outraced it, might have quelled*
> *Desire before it bloomed, the faint glow*
> *Of fire snuffed before it kindled red.*
> *But I saw no danger in friendship,*
> *In warmth and laughter and hearts kindred,*
> *And so was lost before I knew the risk.*

"And yes, I know that last bit doesn't rhyme," she said quickly, before Henry could say anything. "I'm working on it. But I want you to know that I see you too—that I see how hard you work to make sure everyone around you is cared for, and I want to be the one to care for you, to lavish you with imperfect affection."

"I love you, Thalia Aubrey," Henry said. He bent his head toward hers and stopped, a hair's breadth away, looking a question at her.

Thalia said, "I love you too, Henry Salisbury," and Henry took that, rightly, as an invitation to kiss her.

Henry tugged her closer, one hand firm against her back and the other resting gently on the nape of her neck to position her better for kissing. His lips were soft at first, almost tentative, but Thalia pressed up against him, and suddenly the kiss was no longer so soft, but insistent and demanding. Hungry even. Once, she had thought nothing in the world could be more splendid than kissing James Darby, but she was wrong. There might be a thrill in kissing a handsome man who thought you were pretty, but that experience could not hold a candle to kissing a man who saw you, your faults and flaws alongside your graces, and still wanted you. Fire washed through her, chased by something sweet and more tempered, something that would remain when the fire had passed.

Henry scooped Thalia up onto his lap, and Thalia did not demur, as eager as Henry to be as near to each other as possible. Thalia ran her fingers across Henry's chest, dancing over his cravat to his chin, where she rested her hand for a moment, stroking the smooth skin of his cheekbone before following her touch with a rain of featherlight kisses. It astounded her that she could do this—touch Henry however she pleased, as she had longed to for so long. She slid her fingers up into his hair, tugging gently until Henry moaned and recaptured her mouth, and something inside Thalia ignited at the sound and she forgot everything else, losing herself in the kiss.

Some time later—minutes? hours?—Thalia drew back, trying to catch her breath. Henry looked just as dazed as she felt, his hair standing up and his lips rosy and a bit swollen. They stared at each other for a moment, before Henry broke into the widest grin. Thalia thrilled. *She* had brought that look to his face.

"It might be a trifle fast to announce a second engagement on the heels of a broken one," Henry said, "but I would like to court you, if you will let me."

Thalia put her whole heart into the smile she gave back to Henry. "I would very much like to be courted by you, Henry Salisbury—so long as you let me court you too." After all, why should romance always be one-sided? She meant to be a full partner in her marriage, and one ought to begin as one meant to go on.

Henry looked suddenly wary. "What, exactly, would that entail?"

"I'm not sure yet," Thalia said, grinning at him. "But I'm looking forward to figuring it out."

Then she leaned forward and kissed him again.

CHAPTER TWENTY-SEVEN

Eleanor

The world sees but the surface of life; it knows not what little things may influence and guide, and how much female friendship — in general so scorned and scoffed at — may be the invisible means of strengthening in virtue, comforting in sorrow, and, without once interfering with any nearer or dearer tie, may heighten inexpressibly the happiness and well-doing of each.

—Grace Aguilar, *Woman's Friendship*

Well, that was one bit of business satisfactorily concluded, Eleanor thought smugly as she settled herself at her desk. She trusted that Thalia and Henry were both intelligent enough to take advantage of being left alone in the breakfast room.

Then she sobered, tapping her fingers against some papers. In those dark hours the night before when she thought she was about to lose everything, she had recognized what she would most miss from her old life. It was not the trappings of wealth she had mourned, though she did find them pleasant. When faced with the prospect of being well and truly alone, it was the thought of the loss of friendship and camaraderie that had hurt Eleanor most. It was the thought of losing Anne and Henry and Thalia and Sophia—and Owen. Owen most of all. Eleanor was certain she could survive without maids and footmen. She was not so certain her heart could survive being solitary again.

When her friends had found her, Eleanor thought that she might not ask for more from her life. But it seemed that after a night's sleep, she was becoming greedy. Grateful as she was for friendship, she wanted more. She wanted what she saw in Thalia's and Henry's faces when they looked at each other.

She wanted to tell Owen that she loved him. She had realized, sometime during those long hours walking the streets of London alone, that she was prepared to give up everything for Anne, whom she loved as a sister. Why had she been afraid of doing the same for the man she was coming to love?

And though she had not been able to exchange above a dozen words with him the night before, she felt hopeful as she sifted through Albert's papers on her desk. Owen had shown up to help her, unasked, which meant he must feel something for her. Perhaps he could give her a chance, if she could find the right words to explain herself. She meant, in any case, to try—she had let her own pride nearly cost her everything, and she would not make that mistake again.

The minutes of the morning lengthened. After three-quarters of an hour, Thalia appeared in the office, her eyes bright and her cheeks flushed and her hair—it must be confessed—rather disordered.

"Well?" Eleanor asked. "Has he proposed?"

"No—at least, not yet. We thought it might be more seemly to let some time lapse between the end of one engagement and the beginning of another. But, oh, Eleanor, I am so happy it seems ridiculous."

"Not ridiculous," Eleanor said, shaking her head but smiling. "Well-deserved."

"I hope you will find the same happiness," Thalia said. She glanced around the room. "Is Owen not coming in this morning?"

"He said he meant to come," Eleanor said, though a tremor of doubt passed through her. Had he said so? Or had she only imagined he had? "It is not so very late, yet. Your Henry came unfashionably early."

"Abominably so," Thalia agreed cheerfully. "Do you need anything from me? If not, I mean to write my sister and cousin."

"And how will your sister feel," Eleanor wondered aloud, "hearing you plan to accept the man she refused?" Henry had, naturally, thought the story funny and recounted it to Eleanor on one of their early rides in the park.

"I think she'll be happy for us both," Thalia said. "Kalli is too kindhearted to be otherwise, and she always did like Henry." She frowned thoughtfully. "Charis might be harder to convince. Henry has rather mastered the act of the amiable but stupid dandy about town, and Charis won't easily believe that I've fallen for such a man."

"Perhaps you may cure him of that," Eleanor said.

"Oh, I don't know. I find it rather endearing that Henry saves the finest part of who he is for those he loves most. It's infinitely preferable to those whose public faces are the best part of their character."

Eleanor agreed, and Thalia went off to write her letters. Another hour passed, then two. Where was Owen? Eleanor was beginning to worry that perhaps something she had done—not seeking his counsel, perhaps?—had offended him. Or perhaps he had met with an accident?

After a light luncheon with Thalia, where Eleanor picked at some fruit and cheese, Eleanor invited Thalia to accompany her to visit

Anne, to see how she was faring. With any luck, Owen would arrive while she was gone, so she would not look as though she had waited all morning for him to arrive. She meant to be honest with him—not appear desperate.

Anne had not yet come down when Eleanor and Thalia arrived at the Salisbury house, and they were forced to endure an awkward interview with Anne's mother while a maidservant went to fetch her.

"Good day." Mrs. Salisbury inclined her head graciously. "My son tells me that you are no longer betrothed, Mrs. Lockhart? I must say, I am glad. One hopes that Henry's next pick will be someone more suited to his social station. A titled lady, perhaps, from a well-established family." She made no reference to Thalia, or the previous evening.

Eleanor and Thalia exchanged a look, and Eleanor was forced to cover an unseemly burst of laughter with her handkerchief, while Thalia whirled abruptly away to study a painting over the mantle-piece. It was lucky that Henry's opinions were unlikely to be influenced by his mother.

Henry and Anne came into the room a moment or two later, before Eleanor was forced to make further conversation with their mother. Henry made a beeline toward Thalia, so obvious in his intention that when Anne met Eleanor's gaze with raised eyebrows, Eleanor was nearly betrayed into laughter again.

Eleanor hooked her elbow through Anne's and propelled her toward the window embrasure, where they might speak privately. "Are you well?" she asked.

Anne looked pale and drawn, with dark, tired circles beneath her eyes, but she answered readily enough, "I am well. At least, I will be." She took a long, shaky breath. "Mr. Jones told me about the letter Mr. Lockhart wrote you, how he meant to use me to force your hand. I heard what Sophia accused him of too. How could I have believed he loved me?"

Eleanor rubbed her arm reassuringly. "You didn't know. Please don't berate yourself—you have a generous heart, and you did nothing wrong in loving someone who deceived you."

Anne sighed. "I still feel I ought to have known, somehow. You tried to warn me."

"As you tried to warn me about Henry and Thalia," Eleanor said, nodding toward the pair beside the fireplace. "It's not easy to hear what we don't wish to hear."

"Do you mind?" Anne asked. "I think Henry likes her a great deal."

"More than he liked me," Eleanor said. She smiled at her friend. "Henry only agreed to an engagement at my request. I thought it would get Mr. Lockhart to leave me alone, but I believe it only made him more desperate, and for that I owe you an apology."

"If I am not to feel bad for loving Mr. Lockhart, you cannot feel bad for the choices he made," Anne said. "You don't owe me an apology—particularly not when you were willing to give up your entire fortune for my sake." Anne leaned forward to press a kiss on Eleanor's cheek. "I may already have a sister by blood, but you will always be my sister by choice."

Eleanor blinked back sudden tears. This opening of her heart was making her soft—but perhaps that was a good thing. "Always," she said.

Eleanor tried to calm her suddenly racing heart when they arrived back at her town house. She followed Thalia up the stairs, and when Thalia went into the drawing room to write, Eleanor continued down the hallway to the study. She took a long breath and opened the door.

The study was just as she had left it, papers scattered across the desk, the window open a crack to allow the spring breeze to freshen the room.

Owen was not there.

Eleanor went back into the hall to catch a passing footman. "Has Mr. Jones called?" she asked. "Or left word for me?"

"No, ma'am," the footman said, and Eleanor released him to his duties.

She sifted through Albert's papers once more, reading and rereading the same page three times without comprehending, before abandoning her work with a sigh and going to pester Thalia.

At half five, Eleanor went upstairs to dress for dinner. As it was Friday evening, she was unlikely to see Owen before Monday now. Maybe she could write him a letter? But she lacked Thalia's gift for words.

Her maid had just buttoned her into a seafoam-green satin dress when a knock came at the door. "Mr. Jones to see Mrs. Lockhart," said the muffled voice of one of her footmen.

Eleanor looked at her reflection. Her hair was all undone and she had not yet replaced her stockings or slippers. She decided she did not care. She raced downstairs to the study, which was still empty, and then on to the drawing room, where she found Owen, sitting stiff and uncomfortable on the sofa.

His eyes went almost at once to her bare feet and stopped there, arrested. A slight flush built in his cheeks, and Eleanor curled her toes beneath her.

With visible effort, Owen dragged his eyes up to meet hers. "I'm sorry I was so late. I—had an errand at the Stock Exchange."

"I was worried you weren't coming," Eleanor blurted. She winced. She had meant to appear cool and collected, to not scare Owen away by the intensity of her feelings.

But dash it, she did feel. Keeping people at a distance and hiding her emotions had not kept her from feeling pain—on the contrary. Owen himself had encouraged her to take off the mask she wore. So she would. If Owen did not like what lay underneath, better to know at once.

"I told you I would come," Owen said.

"I know. But I—I missed you."

Owen's eyebrows lifted.

Eleanor couldn't have this conversation from across the room. She sat beside Owen on the sofa. If Owen was uncomfortable at their nearness, he didn't move away. "I'm more grateful than I can say for your help and friendship—with Albert's papers, last night with my friend Anne."

She took a deep breath. Her heart seemed to flutter in her chest like a trapped bird. *You can do this*, she told herself. Telling Owen how she felt could not be more frightening than the prospect of giving up everything to George. If she was wrong, if she had misjudged how he might feel—well, she had lived through humiliation before.

Eleanor faced Owen, so close beside her that she could see the shallow rise and fall of his cravat as he breathed, so close she could count his eyelashes, if she wished. "Owen, I—there's something I must tell you. When I kissed you, I said—I let you believe that I did not care for you, that I was more interested in comfort than love. In truth, I was afraid. Most of my life, I have had to rely on myself. I am not very good at trusting other people. But you showed me, last night, that I could depend on you, even when you stood to profit nothing from it."

"It was the right thing to do," Owen said. "Though mostly, I only assisted your betrothed."

She winced a little at the sharpness in his voice. Perhaps she deserved that. "I am no longer engaged to Mr. Salisbury."

Surprise flickered across Owen's face, but he wiped it away almost at once. "I suppose you no longer need his money to secure your future."

"No—it seems I misunderstood the terms of my husband's will." She explained the true terms to Owen.

"Why are you telling me this?" Owen asked quietly.

Eleanor faltered. She'd said something wrong. "I'm trying to tell you that I am falling in love with you."

"I don't know what you want from me, Mrs. Lockhart."

She wanted Owen to love her. She had thought maybe he did. "Is my caring for you so horrible?"

"Yesterday, you were promised to someone else. Today, you want me to believe you love me? Forgive me, but this seems too convenient. You say you have always relied on yourself, and you no longer fear to lose your husband's money, but you are so young. You have not had the time to learn who you are without someone. Is it possible that you fear being alone?"

He didn't believe her. "Doesn't everyone fear being alone? When I faced the prospect of losing everything last night, it was not the loss of my fortune that cut deepest. It was the loss of my friends. So yes, I do fear that." She forced herself to look at Owen, though every instinct of self-preservation was screaming at her not to. "But that fear gave me clarity. I wasn't just afraid of losing my friends—I could not bear the thought of a life without *you*."

Owen sighed and rubbed his chin. "Mrs. Lockhart—Eleanor. Any man would be flattered to learn you cared for him. But even if what you say is true, I told you, I'm not capable of romantic love—not as you deserve. You deserve someone like Mr. Salisbury, someone openly affectionate."

"I do not want someone like Henry, and I am very sure he does not want me. I never loved Henry, not in that way. Our engagement was merely an agreement between friends. But you: I could love you with my whole heart, if you'll let me. You're forthright, and loyal, and smart, and devoted to your family and friends. And you care about me, the real me, not the mask I put on for society. At least, I thought you did. Was I mistaken?" Eleanor set her hand on Owen's.

He pulled his hand back. "Of course I care. Last night, when I realized you were giving up everything, everyone, I was wild with worry. I care too much to hurt you. I don't want to watch you live my mother's life, shackled to a man who cannot love as you need."

"I wish you would let me judge that," Eleanor said. Her heart felt brittle, about to crack. She was losing him, and she didn't know what to say to keep him. "I do not think you're like your father. I have seen you with Sophia, how kind you are, how considerate."

"Is kindness enough? Is consideration enough? Eleanor, you deserve so much more than that."

"Kindness is not the worst foundation for a relationship. You forget that I have lived through just such a marriage. But Owen, I am not talking about marriage—not yet. I am only talking about us, about seeing if our friendship can become something more."

"Eleanor, I'm sorry. I—I can't." Owen shook his head and rose from the sofa. He walked a few paces to the center of the room, then turned back. "You never asked what my errand was to the Stock Exchange. I've found a broker who has agreed to take me on and train me. It's the opportunity I've been waiting for, to build a career that does not depend on my father."

"That's wonderful!" Eleanor said, genuinely thrilled for him. She hesitated, but she had to know. "And Albert's papers?"

"If you're willing, I thought I could take the papers with me, to work on them when I have time. I don't imagine my days will be free for a while. I'll return periodically to report on my progress."

Was this what their friendship was to be reduced to? Occasional visits over business? Eleanor was not sure she could endure that.

Owen walked back to the sofa and thrust out his hand. Eleanor rose mechanically and took it. He shook her hand. "I wish you every happiness, Mrs. Lockhart."

Do you? she wondered.

Owen put on his hat. "If you need to reach me, send a message to my home."

Home. "Do you know," Eleanor said, "I've never truly had a place that I thought of as home. Not even this beautiful house or Albert's estate. Home, for me, has always been people. For these last weeks, home has meant you." She took a deep breath, trying to see past her own hurt to Owen. She had been willing to give up her fortune for the love she bore Anne. What was she willing to give up for Owen? He wanted her to be happy, he claimed—did she want *him* to be happy? Yes, of course she did. And if that happiness was outside her?

"I'll always be grateful to you and Sophia, for giving me that sense of home. I do love you, and I'm not ashamed of it, but if my love isn't what will make you happy, then I wish you to find what will. I hope we can stay friends so that you will tell me when you find whatever—or whoever—that is." Eleanor swallowed against the sharpness of tears. She could not hold on to her dignity much longer.

But Owen, despite the clear dismissal, did not seem to be in a hurry to move. He stared at her intently, a faint furrow between his thick eyebrows. "Do you mean it?"

She stared back, not sure which part of her speech he meant.

"That you love me enough to let me go out of your life."

Eleanor shrugged, a little helplessly. "Yes."

"Then you must indeed love me—not some fantasy of a future."

"I told you I did."

"And if you love me—" Owen's brow furrow deepened, and he dropped his gaze to the floor. He spoke under his breath, as though he were working through a complex mathematical proposition, meant more for himself than for her. "If you love *me*, all of me, that includes my flaws too. Including my tendency to work too much. Including my fear that I may not be enough for you."

Eleanor said nothing, unwilling to interrupt his careful thought process. But her heart began to beat with a painful, sudden hope.

"And if you are willing to give so much, perhaps I can give

something too." Owen looked up, rather dazed by whatever conclusion he had reached. He crossed the room again, taking Eleanor's hands in his. Eleanor's heart hammered.

Owen continued, raising their joined hands between them and kissing her knuckles. "I cannot promise I will be the kind of lover you need, but if you are willing to take a risk on me, I am willing to try to learn."

Eleanor pulled her hands free so she could wrap her arms around Owen's waist until the softness of his stomach was pressed against her chest. She tilted her head back to look up at him. "I cannot imagine a risk I want to take more."

Owen's arms tightened around her. Eleanor raised herself on her tiptoes and pressed a kiss against his clean-shaven chin, then his cheek, moving closer to his mouth. She had almost reached her target when Owen pulled away.

"I nearly forgot! I've had this in my pocket for weeks now, meaning to give it to you, but the moment has never seemed quite right." Owen fetched a small velvet box from his coat pocket and held it out to Eleanor.

She opened it carefully. There, nestled against the black velvet, was the pair of topaz sunburst earrings that she'd first admired in his father's shop. Speechless, she looked up, one hand going to touch her mother's pendant, still clasped around her throat. "Owen, I—"

"I meant it only as a gift, because you seemed so struck by them, but I want to give them to you now as a promise. To us, to our future, to learning together."

"To us," Eleanor murmured, as Owen helped her put on the earrings.

He bent to kiss each starred ear, his breath against her throat sending delicious chills down her body. When he had finished, Eleanor caught his chin in her hand and finished what she had started earlier. She kissed him.

And Owen, who had never been slow, caught her up in his arms, carried her back to the sofa, and kissed her most thoroughly.

Epilogue

London, early October 1818

Thalia was going to be late for her own party, and it wasn't even her fault—it was Urania's. Her family had descended on London (staying with her aunt Harmonia, thank goodness, not with Eleanor), and nine-year-old Urania had been underfoot all afternoon "helping" with the party preparations. Urania had just now managed to spill a glass of punch across the new frock Thalia had been wearing in anticipation of the party. Standing in the privacy of her room, Thalia dabbed ruefully at the pink stain down the front of her pale yellow gown. Hopefully Eleanor's maid could get the stain out, but it was too late to do anything about it now. With a sigh, Thalia shucked off the spoiled garment, put on a blue satin dress with a lace overlay, and went downstairs and out into the small garden behind Eleanor's town house.

In truth, not even a stained dress could ruin tonight.

As Thalia emerged from the house into the warm evening, a dozen faces turned toward her—nearly all the people she loved in the world. Kalli and Adam, Aunt Harmonia and Uncle John, her siblings— though Edward seemed to be missing? No, there he was, hiding under the table bearing an assortment of food and drink. Squirreling away sweets, most likely. Her parents had come with Thalia's new baby sister. Kalli had taken possession of the baby, showing the sleeping girl off to anyone and everyone.

Charis and her husband, Mark Leveson, were there too, having returned from India only a week earlier. Time away had not cured Charis of her ebullience—and she seemed to have cornered Henry about something that was making him look slightly hunted. Eleanor and Mark, standing nearby, both appeared amused by whatever it was.

At Thalia's appearance, Henry broke away from Charis. He whispered to Thalia, "Your cousin is terrifying."

Thalia laughed, asking, "What has Charis done this time?"

"She was telling me about snakes," Henry said. "Particularly something called a king cobra, that can be more than twice as long as a human and can spit poison. She said she tried to bring one home with her."

A thrill of alarm raced through her. "She has not done so?"

"No. Her husband said he persuaded her not to."

It was nice to know that some things about Charis—namely, her fascination for anything in the natural world—had not changed despite her time abroad.

Thalia led Henry around the party, introducing him formally to those family members he had not yet met. Her mother studied Henry with a long look that made Henry blush and Thalia squirm, though it was a rather open secret in their family that he was courting her.

Urania, seemingly unrepentant after spilling her drink on Thalia, took a long sip of another glass of the pink concoction and asked Henry, "Are you going to marry my sister?"

"Which one?" Henry asked, earning him a poke and a mock glare from Thalia. Henry laughed, then crouched down until he was on Urania's level. "I hope so. Should you object?"

Urania thought about this for a moment. "I suppose not. Thalia has liked many a stupider man," she said with an air of worldly wisdom that made Henry laugh again.

"Urania!" Thalia said. She could only suppose that someone—Aunt Harmonia?—had been speaking incautiously around the child.

"Have you, though?" Henry asked, as she led him back to Charis and Mark.

"Have I what?"

"Liked many stupider men? Rather gratifying to know that I'm not at the bottom of that list."

Thalia, refusing to indulge his vanity, said, "As I plan to like no one but you from here on, I do not see what it signifies."

"That is not an answer," Henry said.

Thalia smiled enigmatically. At least, she hoped it was enigmatically, and then she hugged Charis so she did not have to respond further. Thalia had a delightful chat with Charis while Mark and Henry caught up. Charis was full of stories from her trip, and it was comforting, somehow, to fall briefly into old patterns and old relationships even as so much of her life was changing.

Eleanor, who had disappeared into the house for a bit, reemerged with Owen and Sophia, with Henry's sister Anne close behind them. When everyone had found a place in the garden, Eleanor said, "Welcome, friends! We are so glad you can join us. As most of you know, we are gathered tonight to celebrate the arrival of Thalia Aubrey's first book of poems!" She held up a slim, maroon volume reading *Poems* in gold lettering on the spine.

It still thrilled Thalia to see her book, only this week released into bookshops. Freddy had, despite his grumblings, eventually gone to see Taylor and Hessey and admitted his wrongdoing. While they were, understandably, displeased, it turned out that they did still want the poems—*her* poems. They had requested some edits, which Thalia was happy to comply with, and here it was: a book with her words. The reception had been mixed. Some of Freddy's poet friends had blamed her for the rumors of plagiarism that preceded Freddy's return to Oxford, and their reviews dripped with that irritation. Freddy had not, it seemed, seen fit to inform his friends that Thalia was the victim of *his* behavior, not he the victim of her false rumors. Thalia tried not to let her anger at Freddy's pusillanimous behavior spoil the triumph of her debut—though she did let Henry pen a delightfully outraged letter to the editor in rebuttal of one of those "reviews."

Another reviewer, wholly unconnected to her or her brother, found the verses "sweetly moving." For now, it was enough.

Around Thalia, her family cheered, clapping and calling out. Beside her, Henry squeezed her hand.

Eleanor cleared her throat. "I hope you do not mind if I add an additional celebration to this. We have just this day received word,

Owen and I, that Owen's essay based on my late husband's work is to be printed in the *Gentleman's Mathematical Companion*."

A second round of cheering, no less loud and no less heartfelt, despite the fact that fully half of those present had only met Eleanor that day. Truly, Thalia loved her family.

When Eleanor finished, Thalia moved forward to hug her friend and to shake hands with Owen. "I am so pleased for both of you! A fitting partnership, indeed."

Thalia did not have Eleanor's attention long, as others were waiting to congratulate her. Thalia turned away to find Anne Salisbury waiting for her. After her failed elopement that spring, Anne had come to Thalia for advice in dealing with the aftermath, and they'd had several conversations about unworthy gentlemen and recovering one's faith in oneself and one's dignity. Such talks, allowing for mutual vulnerability, had had the natural consequences, and Anne had lost her reserve around Thalia. This Season Thalia had gained two more sister-friends in Eleanor and in Anne. It felt like an impossibly rich gift, in a season overflowing with good things.

Anne said, "Your poems are delightful, Thalia."

"I'm glad you liked them! Perhaps for my next volume, we can work together—my poems, with your drawings. Henry tells me you are a very capable artist."

Anne's cheeks turned pink. "Oh! I don't—"

"You should not believe everything I say," Henry said, snaking his arms around Thalia. "I take it all back. Anne's work is merely adequate."

Anne glowered at him. "*You* are merely adequate." She looked at Thalia. "Are you certain you wish to marry Henry, Thalia? He does not deserve you."

"Quite certain," Thalia said, folding her arms over Henry's.

"May we all find better love than we deserve," Henry said, whirling Thalia behind a flowering bush to steal a kiss.

"My family can see us," Thalia said, but she laughed and did not resist.

"Let them," said Henry, and kissed her again.

Eleanor nodded at Sophia. Owen's sister took up a central position in the garden and then, when the others had quieted and turned toward her, began to sing. Eleanor recognized the tune, "Una Voce Poco Fa," from Rossini's new opera, but she had never heard it as Sophia sang it: a triumph of love and joy, her voice cascading effortlessly through the tune.

Eleanor observed Thalia's family watching her friend, and a strange wistfulness settled over her, making her feel almost shy. Thalia's parents stood nestled together, her mother leaning against her father. Thalia's sister bounced a baby as her betrothed curled protectively over them both. Thalia's cousin listened to Sophia with rapt attention, while her husband nodded in time to the music. What must it have been like to grow up surrounded by so many people, by so much love?

Eleanor could feel Owen's eyes on her, but she didn't turn to him. Much as she loved him, she didn't want to expose this particular weakness to him just now. Thalia brought with her a whole community as dowry. What did Eleanor bring besides money?

Sophia transitioned into a second song, and Thalia's sister Kalli circled the garden to approach Eleanor.

Eleanor eyed her with some trepidation. She had met Kalli Aubrey a handful of times and liked her, but while they were technically about the same age, there was something about the confidence with which Kalli carried herself and handled an infant that made Eleanor feel young and inexperienced.

"Would you like to hold her?" Kalli asked, holding the baby toward her like an offering.

"I—" Eleanor looked around, wondering if anyone else could see what a very bad idea this was. But Owen only smiled at her and no one else seemed to be attending.

Kalli's own smile faltered. "That is, you needn't if you don't want to, but you looked a little sad, and I've found that holding a baby can help. They're rather like puppies that way."

Eleanor had had a puppy once that she loved, before she'd been sent to boarding school. Somehow, she found herself holding out her arms and then letting Kalli show her how to hold the baby. "What's her name?" Eleanor asked.

"Cleta," Kalli said. At Eleanor's raised eyebrows, she said, "My mother named her after one of the graces, in keeping with the rest of us."

The baby, who had wakened with the transfer from her sister's arms to a stranger's, didn't seem alarmed, but blinked gray-blue eyes at Eleanor. Something inside Eleanor turned warm and soft. "She's beautiful."

Thalia's next-youngest sister rushed past, the younger boy chasing her and shouting something. Kalli frowned after them before running to catch the boy.

Eleanor looked down at the baby again, then around at the

delightful chaos of Thalia's family. Eleanor had not had much of a family, but what if, perhaps, she could create her own? That did not seem as frightening a prospect as it once had.

Actually, it seemed rather nice. Hopeful, even.

Owen leaned toward her and tickled the baby's cheek. The little girl cooed at him. Owen folded his arms around Eleanor, holding both her and the baby, and pressed a kiss to the top of Eleanor's head. Eleanor relaxed into his embrace with a sigh. This was the feeling she'd sought all those years without being able to name what she wanted, or how to find it. This *sense of belonging*, as though she belonged to herself, but to Owen too, and he to her, and together they could face anything.

And not just Owen, Eleanor thought, watching Thalia approach to fuss over her new sister, Henry following faithfully behind her. Eleanor's proposition to Henry, however unlikely, had led her to a family she had never expected to have: Anne and Henry, and Thalia, Owen and Sophia.

Love came in many forms, and her life—all their lives—were richer for it.

AUTHOR'S NOTE

As much as I love the research part of writing historical fiction, I make it a rule never to let historical accuracy get in the way of a good story. Thus, while most of the details of time and place are as accurate to the period as I can get them, sometimes I have taken liberties for the sake of the story I'm trying to tell, as the following examples explain.

The poet John Keats likely needs no introduction, but his inclusion in the story may need some explanation. His book *Endymion* was published in the spring of 1818 (sources are not clear on the date: The Poetry Foundation's biography of Keats suggests late April; Andrew Milton, in his biography, says May 19) and was subject to savage reviews. I have moved the release date up by a couple of weeks, and relocated Keats from Teignmouth, Devon, where he spent much of the time from March to May in 1818, back to London (where he spent the winter). Still, Keats and the other authors present at the Lambs' salon would have been very much part of the London literary scene in the spring of 1818, and I hope readers will forgive a little fudging of the historical timeline for Thalia's sake. Many of Keats's lines are taken from his letters (*John Keats Selected Letters*, Oxford World's Classics, 2009—see 22 November 1817; 21, 27 December 1817; 3 February 1818). Dr. Jill Treftz helpfully read through his scenes and offered insight into the world of the Romantic poets.

Samuel Coleridge lived in Highgate (then just north of London) from 1816 until his death in 1834. Much of his conversation with Thalia comes, as he notes, from his *Biographia Literaria* (1817). The "illness" Coleridge speaks of was an opium addiction, which plagued him for most of his adult life.

It's unlikely that young women of Eleanor's and Thalia's social class would have found themselves at a ball hosted by high-class prostitutes, though such a ball was not unthinkable: According to an 1826 publication, *The Spy of London*, a courtesan known as Lady Hawke hosted a ball, also known as the Cyprian's Ball, at the Argyll Rooms in 1818, attended largely by gentlemen and their prospective mistresses. Scholars and Regency writers often use the term *demimonde* to describe this class of prostitutes, as I have done in the novel, though the term itself was not widely used until later in the nineteenth century. Members of the demimonde were introduced to sex work for a variety of reasons: Some women chose it; others may have been forced into it by family pressure or economic need. Whatever the case, many women chose to pursue work within the demimonde, where they sought the patronage and protection of wealthy men, as a more profitable alternative to other forms of labor available to women at the time (see Nina Kushner's *Erotic Exchanges*, Cornell University Press, 2013, which describes the emergence of this class in eighteenth-century Paris).

Modern authors can never hope to perfectly capture the past—my only hope is that this imperfect rendition nonetheless helps transport readers to a different time and era.

ACKNOWLEDGMENTS

Every book feels like a small miracle—that it exists, that a community helped love it into existence.

My heartfelt thanks to everyone involved with the publication: my agent, Josh Adams; my editor, Janine O'Malley, whose generous readings always amaze me; the fabulous team at Farrar, Straus & Giroux and Macmillan Children's Publishing Group—including Asia Harden, Chandra Wohleber, Lelia Mander, Elizabeth Clark, Meg Sayre, and Morgan Rath.

Thank you to my sisters in writing, for unflagging insight and enthusiasm: Helen Chuang Boswell-Taylor, Erin Shakespear Bishop, Tasha Seegmiller, and Elaine Vickers. I'm also grateful to friends who offered early reads, excitement for the project, support, and/or advice: Cindy Baldwin, Joana Barker, Shannon Cooley, Julianne Donaldson, Sarah Eden, Samantha Hastings, Amanda Rawson Hill, Melanie Jacobson, and Lydia Suen.

I'm especially indebted to Karin Bean and Cristie Charles, who were (and continue to be) the kind of friends every prickly, awkward teenage girl needs. If Anne and Eleanor's (and indeed, Thalia and Eleanor's) friendship feels in any way real, it's largely because of them.

Thanks to Dr. Jill Treftz, for geeking out over Jane Austen with me in grad school, and being my expert in all things nineteenth-century poetry. Thanks also to the sensitivity readers who helped me think more carefully about representation in this book.

Thanks to the readers, book bloggers, and bookstagrammers who have expressed early excitement for this story—stories don't truly exist until they find people to love them.

Finally—and most important—thanks to my family (both immediate and extended) for being the anchor that keeps me centered (or tries to, anyway). I love you more than all the love stories put together.